THE CHLOE FAMILY CHRONICLES

THE *Secret Dreams*

OF DOLLY SPENCER

KAY D. RIZZO

D1519359

Pacific Press® Publishing Association
Nampa, Idaho
Oshawa, Ontario, Canada

Edited by Eric Stoffle
Art direction & design: Michelle C. Petz
Cover illustration: Marcus M. Mashburn

Copyright © 1999 by
Pacific Press® Publishing Association
Printed in the United States of America
All Rights Reserved

Rizzo, Kay D., 1943-
      The secret dreams of Dolly Spencer / Kay D. Rizzo.
         p.   cm.
      ISBN 0-8163-1689-9 (pbk)
      I. Title. II. Series: Rizzo, Kay D., 1943- Chloe family chronicles.
PS3568.I836S44   1999
813'.54—dc21   98-50934
                                                                   CIP

99 00 01 02 03 • 5 4 3 2 1

Table of Contents

Prologue

On that early spring morning, in the darkest hours before dawn, the Erie-Lackawanna local's lonely whistle sliced through the early morning fog. Patches of scrub oak trees grew close to the railway. The train crossed a trestle and slowed for the sleeping town of Shinglehouse, Pennsylvania.

A shabbily-dressed figure slid open the door on a green New York Central Railroad boxcar—number 557. He paused for an instant as if questioning the wisdom of jumping. Then without warning, he leapt from the moving train into a patch of black-berry briers. He yelped in pain, but the train's whistle drowned his cry.

George Randolf Claiborne Jr., seventeen-year-old son and heir to a vast oil fortune, touched his cheek to find blood oozing from one of the scratches. He ran his fingers over his neck and discovered more blood. Painfully, he struggled to his feet.

As he straightened, he sensed the intrusive stare of someone watching him. Instantly, he froze. His father's words echoed through his head. "Always face down your enemy." The 5 feet 8 inch wiry boy swung a slow, fearful glance over his shoulder to find himself staring into the face of a curious Jersey cow. With one swipe, the heifer licked the boy's chin, nose, and forehead. George heaved a sigh of relief then laughed.

Once he'd freed himself from the briers, he hobbled up a gentle slope beyond the tracks to a grove of pine trees. The pine needles brushed across his face like trailing ice-encrusted fingers as he made his way to the center of the grove. Reaching a place hidden from view, he stopped to get his breath then turned to check behind him. He brushed aside a branch to get a clear view of the valley below.

Through breaks in the fog, he could see an unpainted clap-board house and a matching barn, along with several smaller buildings in varying stages of disrepair. A light seeped through the cracks in the barn's siding. A second light shone through what George imagined to be the kitchen window of the farmhouse. *Some farmer's wife*, he mused, *probably fixing the family's breakfast while her husband does the morning chores.* His stomach growled at the thought of food. He fingered the silver medallion in his trouser pocket. What he'd give for a plate of Cook Edith's flapjacks, slathered with her homemade currant jelly.

It had been twenty-four hours since he ate the last of his stash. Both his knapsack and his stomach were empty. He'd even collected and gratefully eaten crumbs of corn bread that had fallen to the floor of the filthy boxcar. At one point, he'd stolen wormy apples from an orchard growing next to a siding where the train on which he traveled had been forced to wait while an express train passed, heading toward New York City. He had wished, for a moment, at least, that he was on the train going home instead of away from his safe, familiar world.

George sat down on the pine-needle carpet. Folding his legs in front of him, he rested his elbows on his knees and his chin in his hands. He must determine his next move. Should he skirt the farm and continue toward the oil fields on the far side of the county—his ultimate destination? Or? His stomach growled again.

No, he thought, *I'm too hungry.*

The wooded slope dropped down behind the rear of the farmhouse. *Perhaps I can beg a meal off the farm wife,* he thought. Pine needles rustled under his feet as he stood and made his way carefully down the hillside. At the edge of the trees, he paused and glanced about the clearing. A child-size pair of long johns hung limp on a line behind the house, along with two well-worn dishtowels. A stone walkway led away from the kitchen door to a chicken pen and house.

The kitchen door to the farmhouse opened, sending George for shelter behind the trunk of a fallen elm. A dog bounded from the house, barking and leaping in the morning fog. A tall, young woman stepped out onto the small wooden porch and bent down to set a large pan on the porch floor. A tumble of strawberry-blond curls tumbled forward, covering her face. She straightened, smoothed back her tousled hair into a knot at the back of her neck, and reinserted a bone hairpin. "Wiggles!" Without hesitation, the dog bounded up the porch steps and began wolfing down the contents of the pan.

Shivers of fear trailed up and down the boy's spine as he watched the black-and-white spotted dog gobble the scraps. George was wary of dogs. Once, after visiting a cousin who had a terrier, he asked his parents for a dog, but his father refused. He said animals were a bother. His mother agreed, adding that they were also unsanitary. She reminded George of his delicate health. To George, it seemed his parents believed that everything in life was either too dangerous, too unsanitary, or too much of a bother.

Dangerous, he thought. *I hopped a moving train and jumped from one without injury. Unsanitary? I ate food off the floor of the boxcar. And a bother? Hunger is a bother.* He'd never been so hungry in his life. George reminded himself that he'd made it this far. He'd show them. His dream would come true. He told himself that he'd prove himself a man or die trying.

He'd listened to the stories of his father's youthful adventures prospecting for oil in western Pennsylvania, racing against wildcatters like John D. and the other famous oil magnates of the industry. He'd weathered blizzards, searing heat, and life-threatening fevers, all for the fortune he now possessed. The boy yearned to live the life his father described, not for the money but for the adventure. But having always been considered too fragile for such a life, he found his days filled with violin lessons, math, and reading assignments.

Tired of having his every move monitored by his live-in tutor or the prep school's headmaster, George longed to break free, to live the real-life adventures he read about in the tales by James Fenimore Cooper and heard about from his father's days as a boy. He decided to go West to Pennsylvania where his father acquired all his wealth. He planned to change his name. He'd work in his father's oil fields as a lineman or a rigger. He knew the dangers in the fields, the chance that a line would snap and decapitate the worker. He knew the threat of sudden explosions and raging fires. He'd show them. He'd measure up, maybe even exceed his father.

It had been simple to slip out of the French doors to the garden and disappear into the woods behind the family estate before Stuart, his Latin tutor, realized he'd gone. Days earlier, he had hidden a pack of clothes and a cache of food in the tall ornamental grass near the iron gate at the back of the property. The only snag came when he thought he'd left behind his grandfather's silver medallion, the one his own father had carried as a young man and passed on to his son.

The growl of his empty stomach reminded George of his immediate problem—food. He ran across the clearing to the western edge of the house then inched toward the dog and the pan of food. The boy's mouth watered as he watched the dog slobber over the food scraps. George drew closer. He thought that if he could get close enough, he could grab the metal pan and run for the woods. Hopefully, the dog wouldn't follow him.

Suddenly the dog lifted its head and spotted the boy. It let out a threatening snarl, and George flattened himself against the side of the house.

"Never let an animal sense your fear." His father's voice sounded in his head. He inched forward several feet before the dog raised its head a second time. Then, as if George crossed an invisible line set in the dog's mind, the mutt squared off, its snarling body between its breakfast and George. For some reason, the dog looked much more fierce than it had from a distance.

George hunched over, his hands hanging loose before him. "Come on, doggy; be a nice doggy and share. You can't eat all of that now, can you?"

The dog growled and snapped. George leapt back and considered running away while he still possessed the seat of his pants. But the growl from his stomach encouraged him to try one more time to steal the dog's food. Under the dog's watchful gaze, George inched forward once more.

"Nice doggy, nice doggy." George held out his hand as if to pet the animal, and the dog's tail wagged despite its agitated bark. Warily, George inched close enough to scratch the dog's head. The dog lifted his head and licked George's hand. George eyed the scraps in the pan—hominy grits. His stomach gurgled at the thought of grits covered with melted butter.

Inching closer, he grasped the rim of the metal pan. Slowly, he pulled the pan toward him. The dog, delighted to have found a new friend, bounced about his feet, begging for attention. "Good doggy. What a good, good doggy you are!"

Without warning, the screen door flew open. "Wiggles, what is all the noise ab—? What? Wiggles, stop barking! Who in the world are you?"

George stared up into the face of the red-haired woman wielding a broom in one hand and a dustpan in the other. His eyes widened.

"I-I-I . . ." He followed her gaze to the metal pan clutched in his hand. "I'm sorry, ma'am. I-I-I . . ." He dropped the pan onto the ground and turned to run toward the woods.

"Hey, boy! Come back here. Are you hungry?" The word *hungry* brought George to a stop. "Would you like something to eat? I have biscuits and gravy left over from breakfast."

George turned toward the young woman, whose height more than filled the doorway. He swallowed the fear lumped in his throat and nodded. "I am a mite hungry, ma'am."

"Good. Then get yourself in here before Wiggles decides to sneak back into the house. Pa hates that."

George hesitated.

"Come on. My offer is only good for the next half hour." She laughed and set the broom and dustpan next to the doorway. "What's your name? I'm Dolly, and I promise not to bite, unless you try to steal my breakfast like you did Wiggles's."

"Er, sorry, ma'am, er, Dolly."

Dolly looked beyond George's shoulder and called out a Hello to a man carrying a pail of fresh milk from the barn. "Got company, Worley. Worley, meet . . . What did you say your name is?"

"Geo—John, John Smith."

"Oh," the woman nodded her head. "Like Captain John Smith, I presume?"

"Uh, yeah, that's it. John Smith."

"Nice to meet you, Captain John Smith." Worley reached for George's hand. "Mind if I call you Cap for short?"

"Fine." George mumbled and glanced away.

"Well, come on in, Cap and brother dear. I made plenty of biscuits this morning and at least a gallon of gravy. Sorry about the grits. I burned them, I'm afraid. I gave them to Wiggles.

"Hey, Sis, you know my favorite. I'd rather have biscuits and gravy anyday over grits. That's fodder for cattle." Worley pushed past his sister into the changing room. "Gotta get changed out of these smelly overalls before my sister will let me into the house."

The lightly flavorful biscuits, drowning in hot white-flour gravy, warmed the young boy right down to the cockles of his heart. He smiled to himself as he recalled the quaint cliché Cook Edith always used. Once he'd asked her, "Exactly, what are cockles?"

She'd laughed. "Your cockles are your heart's pleasure pockets." She patted her generous girth. "My cockles are especially warmed by those European chocolates your parents give me at Christmas."

Barely stopping between mouthfuls to answer the questions Dolly fired his way, George realized that for the first time in a week his stomach felt full, his cockles satisfied, and he felt ready to sleep.

"Have you been on the rails long?" Dolly picked up the heavy crystal pitcher of milk and refilled George's glass.

George looked up at the talkative redhead. "I beg your pardon?"

"On the railroad. You did hop a freight train, right?"

"Oh yeah. It's a rough life, but you get used to it after a while."

Dolly smiled and nodded. "I imagine. Would you like another biscuit or two? How about a slice of apple pie? I made it fresh yesterday."

George rubbed his protruding stomach. "I would love to, but I'm afraid I'll pop. I'm so full."

"So where are you heading, Cap?" Worley asked. "California?"

"Naw, I heard there were good jobs going begging here in the oil fields. Thought I'd try walking the lines."

The young woman smiled. "That's what my father does for a living, that and herbal doctoring on the side."

The boy's eyes brightened. "So, did I hear right? Are there jobs in the fields?"

Dolly shrugged. "Pa would know. Why don't you hang around the farm until he gets home this evening?"

At the far end of the table, Worley pushed his chair from the dark oak trestle table. "Guess I'd better get on home to Sofia and the kids. Pa already gone to work?"

"Yes, there was an emergency on the line. I agreed to see the kids off to school before I left for the newspaper office. Which reminds me, those scamps are still asleep." She skidded her chair from the table. "Excuse me, I have to wake my younger brothers and sisters."

She hurried toward the open staircase in the front corner of the great room and glanced over her shoulder before climbing the stairs. "Make yourself at home, John. If you'd like to catch a little shut-eye, help yourself to the hay mound in the barn. That's where I head when I want to escape my raucous family."

"Th-th-thank you. That's awfully nice of you, Dolly. I'd like that."

When Dolly arrived at her desk at *the Shinglehouse Sentinal* office, she read the headlines coming over the office teletypewriter from New York City. She nodded and grinned. "So that's who you are, my dear Captain John Smith, the boy who loves my crumbly biscuits and lumpy gravy. George Randolf Claiborne Jr., runaway heir to the Claiborne fortune. *Hmm* . . . now, what do I do?"

CHAPTER ONE

Runaway Home

MISSING CLAIBORNE HEIR RETURNS HOME. George Randolf Claiborne Jr., heir to the railroad millions, returned home Monday, September 1, 1916. Missing from his parents' Manhattan apartment since July four, the seventeen-year-old boy walked into the Shinglehouse, Pennsylvania, train station and asked the agent to send a telegraph to his parents to assure them of his safety. When local reporters interviewed him, the young man said, "All my life I heard stories about my grandfather making it on his own at twelve-years-old. I wanted to see if I could do it too. And I did!" In the accompanying photograph, a confident young man stood poised and smiling, one hand behind him and the other raised in triumph.

I brushed my fingers across my lips and smiled. With pride, I reread the lead article in Friday's edition of the *Shinglehouse Sentinal.* What a surprise it had been to the entire Spencer family to discover that the skinny waif of a boy on the back steps of the Spencer's farmhouse would prove to be the missing Claiborne heir. After convincing George to notify his frantic parents of his whereabouts and after Pa, Joseph Riley Spencer, wrote to George's parents inviting them to let George stay at the Spencer farm for the rest of the summer, they reluctantly consented.

Throughout the summer, George worked in the oil fields with Pa, walking the line and repairing frayed cables and strained connectors. The frail fifteen-year-old built muscles where none existed before coming to Pennsylvania. An easy smile replaced his frightened, defiant gaze. He walked with firm, sure steps. The night before he left he handed me a silver medallion. "This is a family heirloom. I want you to have it to remember me by."

I remembered the silver medallion, with the likeness of Queen Victoria embossed on its face. Gently, I placed it back in his hands and cupped them with mine. "No, Georgie, it's a family heirloom. I can't take it. Besides, I don't need a coin to always remember you. You, I can't forget." I placed a kiss on his cheek.

That evening, before he was to return home to New York City the next day, he told me the story of the medallion. We were sitting on the porch, looking at the stars.

"I've never seen so many stars in my life," he said. "Dolly, you believed in me when no one else did. I'll always love you for that." By the look in his eyes, I knew he had more than a slight crush on me.

It figures. I laughed to myself. *I'm good at attracting homeless cats and runaway children.* I was proud of the young man standing before me. What a change had taken place in two months. He'd become strong, confident, ready to return home for his last year of secondary school, and he eagerly looked forward to college.

And, thanks to George, I got my first exclusive story and proved myself as a reporter. I sighed with pleasure at the memory of the editor-in-chief's string of compliments on the story about George Claiborne Jr., delivered in front of the entire newspaper staff. Of course, the *Sentinal* only employed five people.

He concluded his accolades with, "With your permission, I am sending this story to my friend, Matt Collingsworth. He publishes the daily *Tribune* in New York City. This is a piece he will want to see."

I reddened to a fiery hue—the curse of all redheads—and mumbled my permission. The glow from Mr. Ames's compliments lasted the entire afternoon. Later, in the dark room as I developed a roll of film for Ted, the paper's photographer, I could still feel the heat coming from my face. Even as the hands of the clock struck six, I could still hear the editor's words echoing in my ears.

To be honest, I remembered *every* word that fell from the lips of Charles (Bud) Ames, dashingly handsome owner (maybe not dashingly handsome, more like comfortably handsome) of the *Shinglehouse Sentinal*, which served the tri-county area of northwest Pennsylvania.

That night, after George and I finished talking, I wrote a letter to my favorite sister.

September 2, 1916

Chloe Mae Chamberlain
140 Nob Hill Way
San Francisco, California
Dearest Chloe,

The greatest thing finally happened (well, maybe the second greatest thing—first might be having Mr. Ames declare his love for me). I got my first exclusive story, thanks to George. Bud, as I call Mr. Ames in my thinking, asked permission to send the story and the photo to a friend of his in NYC. Imagine that! My story! Isn't God good? I can't believe it. If the editor of that paper publishes the article, it will be under the name of D. M. Spencer. Bud says that a big-time paper would never print an article written by a woman.

Bud says I have great possibilities as a writer and as a photographer. He says that it's too bad I'm a woman. Then he laughs and says, "But, personally, I like you that way."
Love,
Dolly

Falling in love with Bud Ames had been easy, especially since he was the only eligible man in the county to exceed my height of 5 feet 11 inches, if only by an inch. My heart fluttered the first time I gazed into his twinkling, deep blue eyes. I had always heard descriptions of eyes that twinkled, but I'd never actually seen "twinkling" eyes until I met Bud Ames. One glance and my right hand had flown nervously to my hair, where, sure enough, a couple of pesky curls had worked their way loose from the tight chignon at the back of my head.

Taking after my father both in hair color and height, I'd towered over the boys in both elementary school and high school since fourth grade. As a tall redhead, I could never blend into the crowd, no matter how badly I tried.

While in high school, I oiled my tangle of red curls into a bun. But before each day ended, the springy curls would be flying in the breeze. I also hunched when around other young people, trying to make myself shorter and somehow invisible. Teachers told me I was intelligent, that I should consider college. *College?*

What a laugh my father had over the idea of me going to college. "What does she need college for? Cooking meals? Having babies? My wife could do that with only four years of schooling." My father, with his old-fashioned ideas, didn't know that women today were pursuing all kinds of careers they never dared consider in my mother's day.

Charles Ames had hired me as a photographer's assistant a week after I graduated from high school, and it took a lot of convincing on my part to get the job.

"You're a woman, Miss Spencer, not to mention young. What? Seventeen?" I nodded Yes. He continued, "The camera equipment is heavy. That's why our photographer needs an assistant in the first place. Certainly you don't expect—"

"I expect I can lift, carry, or haul as much, if not more, than my male counterpart, Sir. I'm a country girl. I grew up haying in the fields next to my brothers. And I can outbale the best of them."

"I don't know . . ." Charles Ames leaned forward at his

desk and smiled.

"Give me a chance, Sir, just a chance. I'll do whatever odd jobs you need done around here. I need the job."

"Why? Certainly a pretty woman like you would rather be stitching bluebells on linen for her hope chest."

His words touched a sore nerve. I lifted my chin in defiance. "You and my father! Marrying me off to the highest bidder? Sir, there are no acceptable bidders."

He started to speak, but I interrupted. "Please don't insult either of our intelligences. I am anything but a delicate house plant."

Charles Ames arched one eyebrow and cast me a grin that set my heart to fluttering faster than ever. "Then shame on the foolish boys of Shinglehouse who identify exquisite beauty in flowers or women."

I opened my mouth to reply then clamped it shut before I said something really stupid. Before I recovered, he spoke.

"Miss Spencer, one thing you do have is spunk. I'll give you that. All right, against my better judgment, I'll hire you on a trial basis—one month. If in that month I believe the task is too much for you or I hear you complain about the work, I'll have to let you go."

The month passed, and I was hired as a photographer's assistant. By the end of six months I added junior reporter to my status. While there was no extra pay in the title, I felt good about it. My father sputtered about his "old-maid" daughter working at the paper, but in time he grew accustomed to the idea. The first time he saw my name in print—it was only a report on the county fair—his attitude changed drastically. At every opportunity, he bragged about his "career woman" daughter.

In the three years I'd been working at the *Sentinal*, I found Charles Ames to be a kind, easygoing employer. And he had a delightful sense of humor that complimented mine perfectly. We saw humor in the most prosaic of situations. And puns, he and I could banter puns back and forth like tennis balls at Wimbledon.

Members of the office staff soon recognized the spark between us. Mrs. Rogers, the receptionist and homemaker columnist, never missed the opportunity to point this out to me. Ted, the photographer, didn't talk much, but he did cast a you-can't-fool-me look my direction whenever he'd find Bud and me studying a strip of negatives in the darkroom.

Horton, the pressman, and Max, the full-time reporter, teased me at every opportunity. And Mabel, the middle-aged, single lady in charge of classifieds and advertising, sniffed her nose away from me whenever I walked by her desk. I think she harbored the same crush as I did.

As for me, I let God do most of the worrying about Bud Ames and me. While it was true that I sometimes got impatient with God's progress, I had no doubts that He would bring Bud and me together in His own good time. I'd given my heart to Jesus Christ at the age of ten, and I had never regretted it. I believed then, and now, that my life and my future was securely in His hands.

When I wrote to my sister Chloe of my belief, she wrote back, cautioning me not to run ahead of God.

> Sister dear, remember, the heart is deceitful above all things. Only God knows our true desires. I deal with young women every day who fell unwisely for the wrong men and lived to regret it. Be careful. Don't give your affections away cheaply. I love you so much, and I'd hate to see you bear any unnecessary pain . . .

I treasured the bond between us, but her words irked me, as her words seldom did. She had delivered me at birth, and we shared the red hair, although hers was a deeper, more coppery red than mine. Compared to her hair, mine looked faded. Our special bond grew despite the 3,000 miles between us. That's why her opinion was so important to me. I would never want to disappoint her. Yet, with Chloe so far away and Bud Ames so near . . .

The evening of the giant toy-factory fire, I worked late developing Ted's photographs while he continued photographing the burning building. Bud and I were in the darkroom trying to choose the front-page shot. "Wait a minute. Here's another plate I developed earlier. Look at this one."

I stepped back from the developing tank while he moved closer. I grew heady when I inhaled the aroma of his shaving lotion. I closed my eyes and held onto the metal table to steady myself. I could feel color suffusing my face and neck. I blew a stray curl from the side of my face.

Gently, Bud brushed the curl behind my ear. "Your hair is like spun copper. I always wondered. . . ."—his voice grew husky— "How you keep from getting those beautiful curls of yours into the developing solution is beyond me." He chuckled softly then cleared his throat.

Stepping away from me, he pointed to one of the photographs drying on the wire. "This one. Let's go with the old man watching the burning building, unless, of course, Ted comes back with something better." With that, he turned and left the room.

As I began relaxing my tightly coiled nerves, an incredible joy flooded through me. I wanted to sing, shout, and dance in circles all at once. I knew. I just knew Bud felt the same about me as I did about him. I clasped my hands to my chest to quiet my thundering heart. "Oh, dear heavenly Father, can this finally be happening? You promised that if I took delight in You, you'd fulfill the desires of my heart. Thank You, dear Father, thank You."

That evening I wrote to my sister. First, I told her about the fire at the toy factory. Then I mentioned the precious moment in the darkroom.

I can't describe the feelings that arose within me when he touched my cheek. He's so tender and compassionate. Isn't God good? I know, be careful, right? He was nothing but a perfect gentleman, sister dear. Always a perfect gentleman . . .

I chewed on the cap of my fountain pen for a moment while I relived my precious moment with Bud. *So this is what true love is like,* I thought. No wonder the great poets of the world wrote about it so glowingly. I thought about my favorite poet, Elizabeth Barrett Browning, and her burning love for her husband, Robert. Was it true, I thought? Had Bud and I discovered that same palpable, overwhelming love as the famous Elizabeth and Robert Browning?

I gazed about the bedroom that had once been Chloe Mae and Hattie's room. I had cajoled Pa into some blue wallpaper with tiny white flowers, and I'd painted an old desk the folks had stored in the barn for several years. I ran my fingers over the desk's smooth white top. A heavy, carved oak bedstead, a straight-backed chair, a dark oak dresser with a mounted mirror, and a homemade clothing credenza completed the room's ensemble. I thought a moment. Ensemble, *is that the right word?*

I shrugged and returned to my letter.

So you see, all is well here—more than well, in fact. I honestly believed I would never find a man who could love the gawky, freckle-faced woman I face in the mirror every day. Be happy for me, Chloe. Please be happy for me.

After folding the letter and placing it in the previously addressed envelope, I dropped it into my purse to mail during my lunch break the next day.

Now, I thought, *what shall I wear tomorrow?* I wandered over to the rough-hewn armoire my father built several years ago for his daughters and analyzed the slim number of choices I had. I wanted to wear something feminine and soft, but what? My eyes fell on a soft, lavender, silk-flowered bodice Chloe Mae had given me for my birthday a few months earlier. *Yes, that's it.* When I first saw the blouse, I wondered where I'd ever wear such a delicate thing. Now I knew. Had God planned for this moment even as Chloe made her purchase in far away San Francisco?

The next morning as I piled my stubborn curls atop my head and pinned them into place, I felt almost pretty. I dabbed my nose with rice paper purchased at Green's Drug Store, then pinched my cheeks to heighten my color.

I was sitting at my office desk writing up the week's obituaries when Bud, er, Mr. Ames, arrived at work the next morning. "Good morning, all. A lovely fall day, is it not? Mrs. Rogers, the Holt boy and the Tremper girl announced their engagement last night. Better get on over there and get the story. Ah, Miss Spencer, I have a friend coming to visit on Friday next. Could you drop by Annie's Boarding House during your lunch break and make a two-week reservation for me?"

"Yes, Sir, I'd be glad to." I beamed. It meant I wouldn't be able to mail Chloe's letter until after work, but that was fine with me. I would work around whatever inconveniences necessary to be helpful to Bud.

On the Friday Bud's friend was scheduled to arrive for the visit, I received a letter from Matthew Brewster Collinsworth Jr., editor-in-chief of the *Tribune*. Bud handed it to me just before he left to meet his friend at the train station. "See," he said, "I told you you were talented. Do I know talent when I see it? Hmm, you look especially lovely today, Miss Spencer." I'd been thinking the same thing about him—not lovely, of course, but decidedly handsome, like he'd taken special care when he dressed that morning.

When Bud placed the letter in my hand, his hand lingered an instant longer than necessary, or so I thought. I opened the letter. A twenty-dollar bill fluttered to the floor. Surprised, I bent to pick it up only to bump heads with Bud as he also tried to retrieve it for me. We laughed as he carefully placed the cash in my hand.

"That's no way to take care of good money." He winked, squeezing my hand before pulling away from me.

"No, I guess not. Thank you." I blushed and glanced at the letter in my hand.

"Well, I gotta go meet the morning train. I'm taking a long lunch. I won't be back until late afternoon. Mabel, Mr. Larson at the mercantile told me he wanted to buy more ad space for his big holiday sale. Better check it out. Max, we need a short piece on

21

the grange meeting last night. They elected new officers. And Dorothy, er, Miss Spencer, please process the plates for tomorrow's front-page photo when Ted gets back from his shoot. See y'all." And he breezed out of the building.

"So, tell us," Mrs. Rogers sidled up to me. "What does the letter say?"

I took a deep break and began reading aloud. "Dear D. M. Spencer, Enclosed please find a twenty dollar bill for the publication in the Manhattan *Tribune* of your article regarding the return of George Randolf Claiborne to his family. Five dollars of the twenty was for the use of the photograph.

"You are very talented, Mr. Spencer. I would be pleased to see more of your work. I told old Bud to send me your work any time." Sincerely, Matthew Brewster Collinsworth Jr.

I took a deep breath and stared at the scrawling signature. "I don't believe it."

"Believe it, cookie"—Mrs. Rogers gave me a squeeze about my waist—"you are a very good author. And Ted has taught you well on the camera too. If you were a man, you'd go far."

I laughed. "You sound like my father. What does being a man have to do with it?"

"In a small town like Shinglehouse, not much, but a big city like Manhattan . . ." She shook her head sadly.

Max got up from his desk and wandered over to where I stood. "So, you made it in the big time, kid."

I tried to slump down to his height of 5 feet 8 inches because I knew my height disturbed him. I also knew that this development would unsettle him as well.

"The news business isn't a place for women, at least not the big time. First of all, it's a cutthroat business."

"Well, one article will not a career make." I laughed nervously. "It's just a fluke. I was in the right place at the right time." I needed Max's goodwill in order to maintain peace. I knew that he could be very difficult to work with if he took a disliking to me.

I sailed through my tasks in record time. After lunch Mabel

sent me over to the mercantile to pick up the information for the store's upcoming sale. At three, Ted returned with plates to process. We were headed toward the darkroom when the front door swung and a grinning Bud stepped into the newspaper office. "Everybody, gather round. I have an announcement to make. Come, come, come. Ted, forget the plates for right now. Horton, leave the press for a couple of minutes."

The smiling editor-in-chief took a deep breath. "I want you all to meet someone who is very special to me." A strikingly beautiful, raven-haired woman, barely five feet tall, stepped out from behind him. Her dove gray taffeta gown rustled as she slipped a matching doe-skin gloved hand possessively about his waist.

"This is Meredith Armstead, half-owner of the *Sentinal* and soon-to-be my wife."

My breath caught in my throat as the faces of my co-workers swam before my eyes. When Bud began introducing the newspaper staff, the room began to spin. I closed my eyes and clutched the glass photographic plates with my two hands.

". . . and this is Dorothy Spencer, our assistant photographer and junior reporter. She's quite the little trooper."

I rolled my eyes at the "little trooper" comment. I was anything but little compared to the delicate porcelain doll extending her gloved hand to me. I glanced at my hands to discover smudges of printer's ink I'd managed to get beneath my nails when I helped Horton repair the press earlier in the day. I looked up and shrugged, withdrawing my hand.

"Sorry, I, uh, well, this is partly your newspaper, right?"

"Ah yes, and I am so eager to learn everything I can about the newspaper business. Budsy has talked about you incessantly. If we were not so in love, I would have been jealous, I fear."

"Oh, no problem there," I assured her. "Mr. Ames has been nothing but a perfect gentleman."

Meredith lifted her delicate little hand and caressed Bud's cheek. "So you *have* been a good boy, just like you said." She giggled then placed her hand on my forearm. "Dorothy, I hope you and I will become fast friends once I come to Shinglehouse to live. It will be quite an adjustment living in a quaint little town like Shinglehouse after spending most of my twenty-two years in Albany."

I nodded graciously. "I am sure you will be quite happy here, Miss Armstead."

Mrs. Rogers moved sympathetically close to my side. "Our Miss Spencer is everything Mr. Ames says and so much more. She's an absolute delight."

Bud cleared his throat and urged his fiancée toward Ted. "Meet Ted, our photographer—extraordinaire."

Meredith reached out and caressed Ted's upper arm. "So you're the man who manages all that heavy equipment."

He laughed nervously. "Not exactly. Dorothy's my assistant. She carries most of the stuff for me."

"My . . ." Meredith's hand fluttered to her chest, and her left brow arched delicately. "A woman of many talents, I see. We city girls would never be able to do such a thing. Is it the milk you drink?"

"It runs in the family, I think." I laced my voice with syrup. " 'Good stock always shows,' my father always says."

After I spoke I regretted my words. I heard Mrs. Rogers gasp, and I heard Bud clear his throat. From over by the layout desk came a snicker. Mabel had already buried herself in the advertisement section of tomorrow's paper, but she'd been listening. Obviously, her reaction to little Miss Meredith Armstead resembled mine. I hoped we wouldn't become best buddies fighting a battle of hearts in the weeks to come.

Horton pushed his visor from his forehead and scratched his head. "When's the wedding, boss?"

Again Meredith wrapped herself around Bud. He glanced down lovingly. "We'll be having a holiday wedding. Of course, you're all invited to attend, though the ceremony will be held at Meredith's parents' estate in Albany."

Bud gave Meredith a squeeze around the waist. "Well, we had

better let you folk get back to work if we want to meet tonight's deadline. If there are no problems, Meredith and I will be leaving. We need to pick up a few things for a picnic in Honeoye Park this evening."

"A picnic in November?" Mrs. Rogers exclaimed. "Isn't it a little chilly for a picnic?"

Meredith fluttered her eyelashes delicately and blushed. "Budsy and I first dated on a cold November day last year in Boston along the Charles River. Budsy fed the pigeons while I supposedly studied for an English literature test. It was magic, huh, Budsy?"

"Budsy" gazed lovingly into his fiancée's misty brown eyes. "Magic."

"Got your buggy all shined up for the lady?" Horton asked.

"As shiny as a new penny."

I remembered the first time I saw Bud's black-and-burgundy Packard roll into town. I'd never seen a motorcar more beautiful. And now she, Meredith Armstead, would be riding next to him in the front seat.

I seethed inside until quitting time then rushed home. I needed to be alone. I reached my bedroom without too many curious glances. Pa wasn't home yet, and the little ones were doing their chores.

Slamming the bedroom door behind me, I threw myself onto the bed and buried my face in one of the down pillows. Tears flowed uncontrolled until I began hiccuping. I couldn't stop. I arose from the bed, walked over to the wash basin, and splashed water on my face. Using the last of the water in the porcelain pitcher, I poured it into a cup and drank it.

"Lord, You let me down! You built me up only to let me down. How could You? You said You wanted to give me the desires of my heart. And just as it seemed to be happening, wham, You take him away from me. I don't understand." I threw a small hand-embroidered pillow across the room. It bounced off the wall next to the window. Ory, my sister closest in age to me, always threw things when she became frustrated. I remember cups and plates shattering against the wall, and I also remembered Ma making her pay for the broken china as well. I had rarely thrown anything when I became angry, especially not something breakable. I was too practical for that.

For the first time in years, I missed my mother. She wasn't the kind of mother to cuddle or hold you when you were hurting, but I needed someone. Mama died at the age of forty-two, giving birth to her sixteenth baby. Four of the babies didn't make it out of infancy. While she never talked about the children she lost, I would often catch her staring out the kitchen window at the family burial plot on the hillside where they lay sleeping in Jesus. Her loss seemed to separate her from those of us who were living, as if she feared that by loving us too much she might lose us as well.

Sometimes I think I hatched, like an ugly duckling. Perhaps I'd drawn closer to Chloe Mae for that reason too. I could always pour out my heart to her in a letter, and she'd answer, even if it took a month for her to reply. My other sisters and my brothers' wives were busy living their own lives. While my older sister Hattie lived less than a mile from us, she had her own brood to care for. Besides, she was always aching somewhere or sick with something. Pa said she had "tired blood."

Overwhelmed with self-pity, I hugged my pillow. I felt like a lovesick schoolgirl, but I couldn't help it. I'd held in my emotions long enough. Alone in my room, I saturated my bed pillow with tears then grabbed a fresh pillow and began again. Within my head I argued with this childish imitation of the real Dorothy Mae Spencer, the mature and responsible woman. But the injured child in me won out. If only Chloe Mae were here right now . . . If only Bud loved me instead of Meredith Armstead . . . If only I didn't have to go back to the newspaper tomorrow and the day after that . . . If only I could run away, far, far away . . . If only . . . If only . . .

I wept myself to sleep only to awaken the next morning to discover nothing had changed, except that I had developed a throbbing headache. I still had to be to work at the newspaper by eight. Bud still loved Meredith and would marry her in another month. And I had nowhere to run or to hide.

CHAPTER TWO

The Long Winter

After Meredith's surprise appearance that chilly November afternoon, the atmosphere at the paper changed. Gone was the easy banter between Mr. Ames and me. (Yes, I forced myself to think of Bud as Mr. Ames once more). An undercurrent of tension developed between the co-workers. And most of all, gone were my dreams. Going to work each morning turned from a joy into a chore.

As the Christmas holidays approached, I grew more and more restless. What would it be like working with the soon-to-be Mrs. Ames and having to watch them exchange coy glances? Would she take as active a role in the paper as she implied? I could only imagine what that would change.

When I tried to talk with Pa about my concerns, he suggested I give up the nonsense of being a reporter and let him find me a husband from my own station in life. Lest I give a bad picture of Pa, he was only repeating what his father had said, much like every other father in Allegheny County, in fact. Poor Pa tried to straddle the traditions of the past and the enlightenment of the Twentieth Century.

"And what station is that?" I asked.

"A good solid farmer or a store owner or, or—"

I lifted an eyebrow and folded my arms across my chest. "And do you have someone in mind?"

"Well, no one immediately comes to mind, but if you give me your say so, I'll make a trip down Coudersport way. Jenny Oberon wasn't doing well the last time I saw her. Consumption. Her husband, Joshua, will need a wife and mother for those five young-uns of his."

I stared in disbelief at him. "The wife's not even dead yet?"

"Well, no, but . . ." He shrugged. "It's only a matter of weeks."

I threw my hands into the air. "I don't believe you, Pa. I guess I should be grateful. At least this Joshua isn't a forty-year-old tenant farmer like you tried to foist on Chloe Mae."

My father reddened and cleared his throat. "That was a bad move on my part, I admit. But I've done real well with the rest of your sisters, you must admit."

"I really don't want to discuss this. You should know that I wrote to Chloe Mae to ask her if I can visit her in California for a while."

"What? I don't want you to go to California. I need you here to help with the younger children."

"I'd leave home if you married me off." I clicked my tongue and grinned. "Pa, you need to take some of your own advice and find yourself a sweet little widow to wed."

Pa's brow darkened. "How can you suggest such a thing? Your mother hasn't been gone more than—"

"Six years, Pa. Kendrick is six now, remember?"

"Your ma was a special woman, Dolly girl. She's not that easy to replace."

"I didn't say replace her. I think you should start a fresh and totally different relationship with a new woman."

Pa grimaced. "That's easier said than done."

I laughed aloud. "Well, well, well . . . The gander seems to have trouble swallowing the feed he's been expecting the goose to eat." I waltzed up the stairs to my room, closed the door, and laughed aloud. It felt good to laugh again. My laughter didn't come easily of late.

Over the years, I've discovered that situations anticipated are never as bad in reality as they were in the mind. However, after the happily married Ameses returned to Shinglehouse, conditions at the paper grew much worse than I anticipated, at least, for me. While I'd long since dealt with my disappointment over Mr. Ames's marriage, the little bride had not. Her caustic remarks draped in fine satin and aimed at me never failed to hit their mark.

Not accustomed to being the object of another woman's jealousy, I tried to tell myself I was imagining things. But when Ted, a middle-aged father of six daughters, who never caught on to even the most obvious of innuendoes, asked me how I managed to keep from snapping back at Meredith—boss or no boss, I knew I'd not misread the woman's attempts.

Whatever article I wrote, Meredith found something to change or a mistake to point out in front of the office staff but never in front of her husband. When I took photographs for the paper, she noted the ways I could have improved the shot, again in front of the staff. Meredith positively gushed over the work of the other members of the staff. She won their hearts and loyalty before the end of the month of January.

I also sensed a change in Mr. Ames's behavior toward me that went beyond the proper decorum between a married man and a single woman and even beyond an employer and an employee. He, too, began dissecting my work more stringently than ever before.

The atmosphere of censure became oppressive to me. I dragged myself to work in the morning and home again at the end of the day. Of course, I wrote to Chloe Mae about my dilemma. My sister said, "Of course you're welcome to stay with Cy and me as long as you like. We'd love to have you. CeeCee says it would be fun to have a 'big' sister."

In the meantime, Chloe advised me to ignore Meredith's comments whenever possible and when not, answer her honestly, sprinkled with grace. "A soft answer turneth away wrath, every time." Not so easy to do, I mused. I continued reading.

"Perhaps it is time for you to move on to a new challenge. Have you considered college? Cy and I would be happy to sponsor you should you choose to continue your education." I blinked at the thought. "If you are serious about your writing, college deserves your serious consideration. There are several fine women's colleges along the Eastern seaboard. Pray about it and let us know."

College? *Hmm . . .* I remembered the advice of Mr. Briggs, my high school English teacher. Just last week when I ran into him at the post office, Mr. Briggs complimented me on a recent article then mentioned college again. "Miss Spencer, a good college education would take you far beyond the *Shinglehouse Sentinal*, you know. And you definitely have the talents for greater things."

Talents, I don't know about my talents, I thought, *but a change of scenery would be nice.* I began to organize my thoughts regarding California until Pa received an unexpected telegram from Cy: "Moving east to NYC. See you in the spring. Love, Cy and Chloe."

Moving east? I couldn't believe my eyes. My heart skipped a beat. This development changed everything. More and more I considered enrolling in a small business college near home until the day Meredith mentioned college to me. "Have you considered attending college?"

I pressed a reluctant smile into place. "I've considered it."

"You should, Dorothy. I attended Wellesley College. Wellesley is a great place to meet a Harvard man, you know. That's where I met Budsy, at a Harvard fraternity party."

I frowned. I couldn't understand why the woman was suddenly concerned with my future. "Well . . . thank you. It's surely something to think about."

"Don't wait. You're already older than the average student there. Tell you what, I'll write a letter to my major professor, Dr. Edna Grimes, and recommend you to the program."

"How very nice of you. Thank you." *A smooth way to remove me from close proximity to her husband,* I thought. I chuckled at the idea of me, nature's original ugly duckling, being a home-wrecker, with my too-wide mouth and a set of eyes that threatened to swallow up the rest of my face. And freckles, why I had freckles gone berserk! Speaking of my body, I wondered if I would ever develop the soft curves men preferred. My angular body gave new dimensions to traditional geometry. Worst of all was my towering height. No, I was hardly a picture of grace and beauty. Meredith had no cause to worry. At least, not from me.

Long ago I had decided to use my wits as my "shield and buckler" against a society that judged women mainly by their appearance. With the idea of marriage becoming less and less an option, college would be the logical step for me. The idea haunted me day and night. Whenever the Lord and I discussed the possibility of furthering my education, He kept saying "Wait. Wait on Me."

All my pondering changed on the weekend that Pa, the little ones, and I visited Chloe and her family in New York City. It had been so long since we'd seen one another. The first night of our visit, after the rest of the family retired for the night, my sister and I sat in her book-lined library, eating chocolate bonbons, drinking mint tea, and talking.

She told me about her California clinic for the women of the streets and how difficult it had been for her to leave her friends to come east. "I've lived in San Francisco for more than ten years now."

"CeeCee and Rusty seem to be adjusting well to the move," I volunteered. "They are lovely children. You should be proud."

"I am. CeeCee is at a difficult stage. I think she resents me at times. But when I think of myself at her age and the strong feelings I had against Ma, I consider myself lucky. And now, what about you, my dear? How are you doing?"

"I've done better." I told her about my disappointment with Mr. Ames and how God had been helping me heal during the last few months. She listened as I told her of my difficulties with Meredith and about the woman's surprising suggestion.

"Meredith's major professor assured her that if I was as gifted a writer as reported, Wellesley would be happy to accept me into their program."

"Dolly, it's up to you. If you'd like to attend a college here in the city, you know that you're welcome to stay with us. On the other hand, Wellesley has an excellent reputation. Maybe it would be good for you to be on your own for a while." My sister took a sip of mint tea from an exquisite teacup, probably imported from China itself. "Either way, the treat is on Cy and me. The minute you mentioned college, Cy insisted I tell you that we'd be happy to finance it."

"But I can't let you—"

"Yes, you can and will. Pa, as much as he's modernized his thinking, has not come that far. And the last time I noticed, you aren't exactly burdened with money."

I laughed. I had saved enough to pay for the train ticket to Boston and that was all.

"Look, honey, Cy and I believe you are a good investment, that you should be able to develop the talents God has given you. One of Cy's talents is making money. So, why shouldn't he use his talent to help you improve yours?"

I laughed aloud and reached for another bonbon. "You make it sound so logical."

"It is. God has blessed us in abundance and expects us to pass it on to others. That's our responsibility before our Creator. Please let us carry it out?"

I started giggling before she finished her argument. "Chloe Mae, you are the only person I know that could make me feel guilty if I turned down your offer."

She cast me a devilish grin. "We wouldn't want you to carry any unnecessary guilt, now would we? Have you sent in your application?"

"No."

Chloe laughed and unwound her feet from beneath her and stretched. "We can take care of that tomorrow. My first husband's parents live in Boston. I'll call dear Julia. She's been eager for us to return their visit."

"I-I-I, this is moving too fast."

"You can always change your mind, darling. School doesn't start until the fall." She peered out the lace-covered windows. "Do you realize it's morning? We've been talking all night!"

"Oh, my goodness. I need to let you get some sleep."

"I have a better idea. Let's take a walk in Central Park." She leapt to her feet.

"Now?"

"Sure. Why not? Oh, wait until Julia McCall gets her hands on you, sister dear. She's going to add some much-needed spice to your life." Chloe grabbed my hand and pulled me to my feet. "Grab a jacket from the hall closet and any one of those foolish little bonnets from the shelf." Before I could protest, she was already out of the library and into the foyer. She threw open the double-leaded glass oak doors. Brilliant early morning sunlight streamed in onto the marble floor. "I just love the city in the morning. The light is beautiful."

"You sound like an artist." From her abundant supply of clothing in the hall closet, I chose a beige knitted wool clutch sweater to wear and modest brown crepe bonnet.

Chloe laughed and stuffed her curls under the rim of a light blue bonnet bedecked with a flashy array of rather flouncy silk roses. "I see beauty better than I create it."

During our visit to the city, Pa and I called upon the Claibornes. While George and I talked in the library, Pa and George's parents visited in the parlor. George told me about his growing desire to join the army. "I believe it's only a matter of time before America gets into Europe's fight. I want to be a part of it."

"George, I thought you got all that adventure-seeking stuff out of your system. What about college?"

"When I get back, I'll have time for that. Right now, my

country needs me."

"I don't understand." I frowned, thinking about Chloe Mae's stepson Jamie's decision to do the same.

"You can't understand, you're a girl. It's different for men."

"That's a weak argument."

He shrugged. "Weak, but true."

I leaned forward in the well-worn burgundy leather armchair. "Please pray about it before you enlist. You do remember our talks about God and the way He directs in our lives if we let Him?"

"I remember. And I assure you, I've thought and prayed about little else these last few months."

Before we left, Mr. and Mrs. Claiborne thanked us repeatedly for opening our home to their son. "If we can ever return the favor, please don't hesitate to let us know." We assured them we would, as if such a situation would ever present itself.

The next morning we waved farewell to Chloe Mae and her family at Grand Central Station as we boarded the train for the long ride to Shinglehouse, Pennsylvania. I slept most of the way, thanks to the rhythmic clickity-clack of the train rolling west.

Even with all the sleeping I did on the train ride home, I still hadn't caught up from my weekend in New York City. I dragged myself to work on Monday morning. As I entered the newspaper office, I sensed an excitement in the air.

I paused at Mrs. Rogers's desk and asked, "What's happening around here this morning?"

"You haven't heard?" Her eyes looked swollen and red.

"Heard what?"

"Look." She handed me a strip off the teletypewriter. I glanced down at the headline:

"PRESIDENT WILSON CALLS FOR DECLARATION OF WAR. Washington, April 2, 1917, at 8:30 p.m. President Woodrow Wilson appeared . . ." My breath caught in my throat as I stared at the thin strip of teletype in my hand. "Wilson asked Congress to declare war on the German Empire and promised full cooperation with the enemies of the Kaiser. The president declared 'the world must be made safe for democracy.' Wilson's message was met by thunderous applause."

Mrs. Rogers broke into my benumbed brain. "Mr. Ames wants to see you in his office immediately."

I barely heard the woman's voice. "This is terrible. Jamie! George!" I whispered.

"I know. My boy, Edgar, said he'd sign up the minute America declared war on the Kaiser."

"Why?" I crumbled the paper in my hand. I glanced about the empty room. Even Mabel wasn't at her desk. "Why do otherwise normal young men feel the urge to risk their lives in an argument between a bunch of dyspeptic old men?"

"I don't know. Men are like that."

I shook my head as I hung my woolen coat on the coat hooks behind the front door then made my way to Mr. Ames's office. He hadn't called me into his office since before the wedding. I couldn't imagine what he wanted from me now. I knocked then waited until I heard him call for me to enter.

I stepped into the oak-finished office. Meredith sat in one corner sniffling into a lace handkerchief while Mr. Ames stood at the window, his face in profile.

"Yes, Sir?"

"Sit down, please, Miss Spencer." He gestured toward the straight-back wooden chairs in front of his desk.

I chose the one on the left, farthest from Meredith.

"You've heard the news?" he began.

"About the war? Yes, Sir."

"I have an assignment for you today. I'd like to interview townspeople as to their reaction to Wilson's announcement. We'll run it in tomorrow's paper. Horton will run a special war edition."

I started to rise. "Wait," he called, "there's more. I have enlisted in the army. My wife, being pregnant with our first child, will return to live with her family in Albany while I'm gone. My uncle from Massachusetts will take over the publishing of the paper. He'll cut it back to a bare-bones staff." He paused to run his fingers through his sandy brown hair. "Only Horton will be staying on past the end of May. And he'll only stay until my uncle can learn to set type."

I tried to speak but couldn't. In all my calculations for the future, this was one situation I hadn't considered.

"Your work has always been exceptional, Dorothy. If you were a man, I'd recommend you to work for my friend Matt. But, under the circumstances . . ." He turned toward his desk and picked up a business-size envelope. "I did send Matt your last series of articles, the one on living Civil War legends. I think he wants to buy the rights. Here."

I took the envelope from my employer's hands. "I-I-I, thank you, Sir." I turned toward the sobbing Meredith. My heart ached for her. "Mrs. Ames? I'm sorry."

She nodded and sniffed.

"Well . . ." I swallowed. "If you'll excuse me, I'll get busy on the assignment."

Mr. Ames stared at his wife. "Horton will need the piece by three to set the type in time."

"Yes, Sir." I turned and left the office.

When I reached my desk, I remembered the envelope crumpled in my hand. As I removed the letter from the envelope, a bank check tumbled out onto my desktop. I picked it up and examined it. "Fifty dollars?" I started in surprise. The letter thanked Mr. Ames for sending the series of articles and me for allowing him to publish them. Mr. Collingsworth closed his letter with "keep them coming."

Keep them coming? Hardly possible with Mr. Ames's latest announcement. *Oh well* . . . I studied the check in my hand. *This will help with my tuition bill.*

By closing the door at the newspaper, God left no doubt in my mind about the direction I should follow. During the next few months, my sister Hattie and I convinced my father to hire Maddie Sweet, a light-hearted, middle-aged widow with no children of her own. She would keep house and help care for our three youngest siblings. That would ease Hattie's burdens since she was taking care of Pa's three as well as her own brood each afternoon until I could get home from the paper.

Before Pa even met Maddie, he decided he wouldn't like her. I think it was her darling set of dimples when she smiled, which was most of the time, that won him over.

Along with my letter of acceptance from the college, I received an invitation from Mr. and Mrs. James McCall of Boston inviting me to stay at their home while I attended the college. She said she'd be delighted to have a young person around the house once again. "Having you present will allow James E. and me to travel more. I dislike leaving the estate totally in the hands of the staff."

As my plans took shape, I walked down to Foote's grocery to call my sister in New York. Foote's had the only telephone available in town. On my trip to Boston, I'd planned to spend a few days in New York City. I managed to catch Cy between trips to Washington, D.C. I learned that Chloe Mae and the children had gone up to the Cape for the summer. Cy assured me they were eager to see me once I reached Massachusetts.

As I prepared to leave for Boston, Pa spoke more and more of his dream to search for gold in Alaska. We'd grown close over the last few months. Each evening we'd have long talks in the parlor and arguments over anything from politics and the war to the plight of women in America. Yet between us there was an aura of mutual respect and admiration.

While he pretended otherwise, Pa seemed proud that one of his surviving twelve children would be attending college, even if it was one of us girls. It was one of his own unfulfilled dreams, that and Alaska. From his talk I knew that if it weren't for the need to care for nine-year-old Martha, eight-year-old Sylvia, and six-year-old Kendrick, he would pack up and head north the moment I left home.

The night before I left for Boston, I put the younger children to bed for the last time and came down the kitchen stairs to find Maddie finishing up the supper dishes. She'd moved into Hattie's old room earlier that afternoon.

"It took an extra story tonight to get the girls to settle down." I strode across the room to the wet sink and pumped myself a fresh glass of water.

"Those children are so precious. They're going to miss you, Dolly."

"I'll miss them too." I took a second gulp of water from the wooden ladle. "Where's my father?"

"He headed for the barn as soon as you went upstairs."

I smiled. I knew exactly where I'd find him—up in the loft room with his herbs. That's where he always went when he didn't want to face the day's events. Chloe Mae used to do the same, so she said. Grabbing my blue-and-white woolen shawl from the back of the rocker, I wrapped it about my shoulders and headed for the door.

"Mr. Spencer isn't happy I'm here, is he?"

I turned to face Maddie's serious face. "Don't worry. He'll get used to the idea. Just remember, Pa's a lot like Wiggles, more bluster than bite."

Maddie nodded, but the wariness in her eyes remained. I hurried outside and followed the moonlit path to the barn. A light glowed from the window at the top of the barn. Before climbing the ladder to Pa's retreat, I patted and talked to each of the milking cows. We'd been friends throughout my childhood.

I climbed the wooden ladder to the hayloft and strode to the far end of the barn. As I reached the door, I heard Wiggles growl. "Stop growling, you dumb dog. It's just me. Pa, may I come in?"

"It's unlatched."

I stepped inside the room nestled high in the eaves of the barn. The mysterious old trunk my mother brought west with her to Pennsylvania sat beneath the window. Only the bravest of children ever had the courage to peek inside. Certainly not me. A long oiled oak table lined with herb jars shone in the pool of kerosene lamplight. On the far side of the room was the wooden cradle that had held each of us children. A scrap quilt lay thrown across the foot of the cradle.

Pa sat in the small rocker Ma had used when nursing her babies. In his lap was the family Bible. The light shining on his face gave him a haggard look, far beyond his years. Tears welled up in my eyes. My heart ached for him. Long ago, after one of Chloe Mae's visits, I decided that leaving was always more difficult for the one staying that it was for the one going.

"Oh, Papa . . ." I glided to his side. "I'm going to miss you so much." I fell to the floor beside his feet and rested my head on his knees.

"Precious Dolly. You're such a good girl. I couldn't ask for a more obedient child." He stroked the side of my head. "It is time for you to leave. More than time. I admit my heart would be more at ease if you were marrying some young buck, but it seems that God is leading you on a different pathway." He paused to clear his throat. "I'm proud of you for having the courage to follow it. You are an exceptional woman, my dear. Your mama would be proud."

I sniffed my tears into my shawl. "I love you, Pa."

"I know. I love you too." He continued stroking my head as one would a small child. "Of all my children, I think I have enjoyed getting to know you the most. I love them all, but you have become very special to me." He pressed a twenty-dollar gold piece in my hand.

I looked at the coin then glanced up at him. "I thought there was always something special between you and Chloe Mae."

"There was, and is, but we've lost so many years being apart from one another. Maybe that's what I dread the most tonight, knowing how different things will become between us."

"No, don't say that. We'll always—"

"Honey"—he took my face in his hands—"it's all right. This is the way it should be. Life is about change, growing. And because I love you, I would never want you to miss out on life's unexpected surprises."

"Then, you're not giving up on me?"

"Giving up on you? Of course not."

"But the gold piece is for brides in the family. Do you think I won't find someone to love?"

He laughed. "Any man who doesn't snatch you up doesn't have

the sense of a fruit fly. Those Harvard men are bound to have more smarts than our country locals."

"Papa," I scolded, "I'm not going to Boston to find a husband, you know."

His eyes twinkled as he gazed at me. Lifting a hand, he caressed my cheek. "I know, I know."

My frown deepened. "I don't want you to be disappointed in me." I wrapped his fingers around the gold piece and looked deeply into his eyes. He understood that I wanted him to hang onto it.

"I will never be disappointed in you, child. You are an absolute joy to me."

The next morning I waved goodbye to Pa until the train rounded the bend at the edge of town. Hours later, I could still see him standing there on the wooden platform, holding my little brother's hand and waving with the other. Most of my older brothers and sisters and those I'd worked with at the paper had come to see me off to college. What started as a simple decision turned into a major event. Half the town showed up to wish me well. Two of my grade-school friends carried a wide banner that read "We love you, Dolly." In the front row, I spied Professor Briggs.

Now that I think about it, not many of Shinglehouse's youth ever chose college. Most of them graduated high school, married, then went to work raising families. Good country stock, the backbone of the nation, as Pa would say. I waved until the platform and my family disappeared from view. As the eastbound train gathered speed, I watched as we passed the family homestead. Tenant farm or not, it was the only home I knew.

Tears fell as I spotted two large sheets spread out on the roof of the barn. On them, someone had painted the message, "Study hard and come home soon, Dolly."

By the time my train pulled into Grand Central Station where I would transfer to a Boston-bound train, I'd made a momentous decision in my life. From that moment on, I would no longer be called Dolly. My name was Dorothy, and Dorothy I would be.

The train eased into the busy New York depot. When it came to a complete stop, I gathered my purse, a stack of books I'd brought along to read while traveling, and my valise. I twisted and groaned. I had a major backache, and the trip was little more than half over. The stiff horsehair seats were designed to keep the passenger sitting ramrod stiff.

I considered finding a shop in the station that would carry something for pain. Even a refreshing cup of chamomile tea sounded good—and I'm not too fond of chamomile tea. As I disembarked from the train, Cedric, Chloe Mae's butler, met me with a giant picnic basket filled with Cook Elsie's most tastiest dishes. "Mr. Chamberlain sends his apology for not being here to meet your train. He's in Washington today. He hopes this little repast will make up, in part, for his absence."

I stared at the monstrous basket in the butler's arms. "I-I-I'm sure it will." I had no idea how I was to carry the oversize basket, along with my portmanteau, to the next train.

"Miss, if you will allow me?" Cedric handed the basket to the Chamberlain family's driver and reached for my portmanteau. "Is there anything else?"

"Er, uh, no. I'm sure a porter will transfer my trunk."

"Exactly, Miss. If you will allow me?" The butler took my arm and escorted me along the platform until we reached the correct train. At the steps, he handed the porter a new ticket. "Miss Spencer will be enjoying new accommodations."

"Very well, Sir." The porter bowed and directed Cedric to the correct car.

I tried to ask the butler about the change, but he just smiled. "Right this way, Miss. While the trip to Boston is not overly long, Mr. Chamberlain wanted you to arrive there rested and relaxed, so he arranged for a private compartment for your comfort."

"A private comp—But I can't—"

"Here we are, Miss." Cedric opened the door to the neat little compartment. The soft green of the walls and the overstuffed upholstered benches looked inviting and relaxing, more so than the seats in the coach. He placed my portmanteau on a high shelf on the left and instructed the driver to place the basket of food on the seat below. "If there is anything else I can do for you, Miss?"

"Oh no, you've done more than enough. Thank you so much. All of this was totally unexpected." I tried out the bench and found it to be as comfortable as it looked.

"Well, Mr. Chamberlain felt terrible that he couldn't be here for you. But when the president calls . . ."

I slid my gray leather gloves off my hands. "The president of the company for which he works?"

"No, Miss, the president of the United States."

Stunned, I dropped one of my gloves. Cedric immediately picked it up and handed it to me. Tipping his head toward me, he added, "Should you need anything while traveling, pull this cord and someone will serve you almost immediately." With that, he and the driver bowed and left.

Hunger and curiosity sent me pawing through the basket of food like a child unwrapping gifts on Christmas morning. *I—I'm supposed to eat all of this?* Along with a blue-and-white-checked tablecloth and matching napkin, a table-setting of china and silver, a piece of crystal stemware, I found a crock of creamy potato salad, several other salads of undetermined content, sandwiches enough to feed an infantry, an eight-inch chocolate cake, a pack of sliced carrots and celery, a thermos bottle of milk, plus enough cookies and candies to keep me fat and sassy for a very long time.

Seeing the food set my salivary glands in action. I ate until I grew concerned that the wide velvet belt on my linen traveling gown would burst. Cy certainly knows how to spoil a girl, I thought, as I licked a dollop of chocolate frosting from my fingertips.

When I could eat no more, I closed the lid to the basket, removed my bonnet, kicked off my shoes, and leaned back against the soft cushions. *What a wonderful way to begin my new life,* I thought, as the train rolled past the Massachusetts' graceful Berkshire Mountains. When I prayed to my heavenly Father, I felt like a little kid asking her dad, "What's next, Papa?"

CHAPTER THREE

The Boston Affair

Julia McCall proved to be everything Chloe Mae said she'd be. Past sixty—but by how much, it was difficult to say—the woman had a lovely English complexion and carried herself with the grace of an empress. White satin edged the neckline of her black silk suit and matching swooping black hat. But, it was the force of her personality and not her clothing that struck me, even from a distance.

When she and her husband met me at the train station in Boston, I felt I'd been swept away by a Midwestern tornado. By the time the shiny black Packard eased between the gray stone lions at the McCall mansion, I was exhausted, not by the long trip from Pennsylvania to New York and to Boston but by the woman's incessant energy. I glanced at her patient husband, his bushy eyebrows and his handlebar mustache carefully trimmed. I wondered how he survived the dizzying force of his wife's whirlwind.

Lawrence, the McCall's butler, met us at the front steps to the manor, though Mrs. McCall led the way into the house. The woman tossed her hat and gloves into the waiting arms of a maid who was about my age. Her curly light brown hair piled high on her head and a cap pinned atop, the girl looked quite smart in the navy blue and white crisply pressed uniform. Her rosy-cheeked, fresh complexion glowed with health. By the twinkle in her eyes, I suspected she could be jolly good fun when not on duty. I promised myself that I would make it a point to get acquainted with her in the days to come.

I followed Mrs. McCall up the shiny oak staircase, glancing into the oak-paneled library as I passed the second-floor landing. Leather-bound books lined the walls. Stacks of books sat idly beside the heavily draped, narrow, floor-to-ceiling windows. Richly furnished in the fashion prevalent in the second half of the last century, the room was cluttered with curios, postcards, mementos, stuffed birds, and dried flowers. Dried palm plants filled the gloomy corners. And what the palms didn't fill, tables did—tables and photographs. A massive, gold-overlaid, silver-backed mirror hung above the marble mantle. Paintings of several women, who I assumed were McCall ancestors, hung about the room wherever space allowed.

Braid and fringe looped the draperies and trimmed the lamps and the mammoth drab-green furniture. The oppressive atmosphere caused me to shudder. I'd never seen so many cushions of every size strewn about a room. From Mrs. McCall's clothing style I would have expected a tastefully decorated home, perhaps like Chloe's Mae's townhouse in New York City. But, to be fair, Chloe had all but started over with her move East. "James E.'s and my room is on this floor." She waved her hand in the vague direction of her bed chamber.

When we reached the third floor, Mrs. McCall led me into the last room on the left, one with a view of the front entrance. I stepped into the room, preparing myself for the same overdressed style I'd seen in the drawing room below. To my surprise, the walls were covered with light-blue corn flowers printed on an ivory silk paper. An ivory satin spread covered the massive four poster bed. Ivory lace draped across the wide set of windows. The armoire, bedstead, dresser, and ladies' secretary were all mahogany. The dark blue velvet upholstery on the platform rocker and on the seat of the desk chair accented the room beautifully. I clasped my hands together with pleasure. I loved it. I absolutely loved it.

"I hope this will be to your liking. My granddaughter, Ashley, helped me redecorate in here. I started at the top of the house and am working my way down to the living quarters. Perhaps you are gifted in interior design?"

My hostess looked at me hopefully. "I-I-I-I'm afraid not, Mrs. McCall, but I certainly can write about it afterward."

"Oh, well, none-the-matter, we'll have a great time together. Too bad you have to bother with school while you're here. We could have so much fun."

I nodded and smiled, and I thanked all the powers of the universe that I would be busy taking a make-up Latin class during the summer months. Having had but one year of Latin in high school, I needed Latin II to qualify for the fall term.

"Now, first off, Dolly, please stop calling me Mrs. McCall. It makes me feel absolutely ancient! Call me Julia."

I dipped my head and smiled. "I will, if you will call me Dorothy. Dorothy is my real name. Somehow, Dolly doesn't suit me any longer."

Julia laughed and grasped my hands in hers. "It's a deal, my child. No Mrs. McCalls or Dollys in this house."

I enrolled in my class the next morning. When I arrived home from the college at noon, Julia clapped her hands with delight. "Superb. That will give us the rest of the week to do a little shopping."

Shopping, I thought, *I don't think that's a good idea at all. This woman's expense account far surpasses mine. Chloe and Cy may be footing my college tuition, and the McCalls may be housing and feeding me, but clothing . . . I'm on my own.*

Before I could voice my objections, the woman took me by the arm, pulling me close to her side as we walked into the parlor. "How do you feel about women's issues, my dear?"

I blinked. My mind spun around to this entirely new topic.

"Do you think women should have the same rights as men?"

I looked down at the surprising woman next to me. "I've always thought—"

"Good. There's a protest meeting Thursday afternoon in downtown Peabody that we can't miss attending." The woman looked up at me, her eyes twinkling. "Oh, this will be so much fun. I can't wait."

Again, words failed me. *What has Chloe Mae gotten me into?*

"Oh yes, I almost forgot, we're expecting a few friends over for dinner tonight. You, of course, must attend. And yes, we'll have one delectably unattached young man there for your enjoyment."

"Mrs. McCall, er, Julia, I don't feel comfortable with this. I could smuggle a sandwich up to my—"

"Nonsense! I won't hear of it. Now, you do have something to wear that will be appropriate for such a dinner party, do you not?"

Mentally I rifled through the upstairs armoire until I remembered a pale pink silk dress Chloe Mae had sent to me on my last birthday. While I had nowhere to wear it, I loved putting it on and prancing before a mirror. The drape neckline accented my long neck, which I wasn't sure I liked. But the long, loose cut of the gossamer fabric swept about my calves and ankles like the corners of several scarves. Nowhere did it bind, press, or inhibit movement. It made me feel like I was wearing a luxurious sleeping gown instead of a party dress.

"Well, my dear? Shall we go upstairs and see what we can find?" Her eagerness had nothing to do with charity. The woman was anticipating a party before the party, like teenage girls preparing for a first date. In a small way, Julia was right. Her little dinner party would be my first date, but she didn't need to know that.

"Thank you so much, but I think I have just the right dress. But may I use your ironing room? I'm sure it's terribly wrinkled from traveling in the trunk."

"Nonsense, give it to my girl to do. You use your time getting ready. She can handle the dress." The woman turned toward the kitchen, calling over her shoulder as she went, "In the cupboard at the end of the tub, there are several kinds of French bubble bath that my granddaughter uses when she visits. Help yourself."

I grabbed the balustrade to support myself. I shuddered like the passenger train did when it had been sidetracked for a freight train racing by. *Does that woman ever slow down?* I wondered. *Will I still be alive enough to find out?*

I hurried up the stairs and laid out the dress I wished to wear, slipped out of my scratchy woolen garments and into a softer cotton robe, then headed for the bathroom.

I had never taken a bubble bath, but I had heard Chloe Mae's daughter, CeeCee, talk about them, especially something called lemon verbena. The pipes clanged and protested when I started hot water running in the massive iron tub. I thought about Thursday bath nights at home in Pennsylvania. I'd heat the water on the kitchen stove then pour it into the round washtub sitting in the middle of the kitchen floor. From the littlest to the oldest, we'd be scrubbed clean. My ears would ring from the scrubbing they received. As soon as each child was dried, we'd be kissed and sent to bed.

I opened the door to the cupboard and found dozens of brightly labeled bottles with titles that sounded like the menu of an ice-cream shop. Strawberry cream, vanilla haze, peach perfection, apple delight . . . I toyed with the peach perfection until I spotted a bottle labeled lemon verbena.

Within a few minutes, I slipped beneath the thick layer of lemon-scented bubbles. I closed my eyes and whispered, "Father, if heaven is like this . . . ah . . . eternity's too short for a pleasure like this . . ." My bath water grew cold, and my skin shriveled before I lifted myself out of the heavenly bliss I'd discovered.

The dress looked lovelier than I remembered. I whirled about in front of the mirror while Julia's girl, Agnes, *oohed* and *aahed* over it. While the smooth lines did make me look tall, they also flattered whatever nuance of a figure I had.

Agnes helped me pile my unruly curls atop my head and pin them into a semblance of order.

"Wait!" Agnes ran over to the armoire and threw open the doors. Standing on her tiptoes, she removed a rose print hatbox from the shelf. "If I remember right, Miss Ashley left a few things here after her last visit."

"I can't use Julia's granddaughter's belongings without permission," I protested.

Agnes opened the box and held up a multilayered satin bow with a pink cameo nestled in the center. The bow was sewn to an ivory comb. "Perfect. I'll tell Madam. She said to do whatever it took to help you get ready for the dinner party. Besides, by now Ashley's forgotten she has such a comb, what with all the gewgaws she possesses."

While I wasn't sure about the maid's assessment, I allowed her to fasten the comb in my hair. I had to admit, the bow did compliment the dress and my hair beautifully.

She dusted my nose with rice paper, sprinkled lemon verbena perfume (Again, thanks to the absent Ashley) behind my ears and on my wrists. "Perfect! If I must say so myself. You look like a fairy-tale princess."

I looked at the stranger in the mirror. "You are a magician, Agnes. An absolute magician."

Agnes smiled and hugged herself. "Franklin Bowles will be bowled over." She giggled at her pun.

"Who?"

"Your escort tonight. Mr. Bowles is a lawyer in the prosecuting attorney's office. Mr. McCall says that Franklin Bowles is an up-and-coming young man in Massachusetts politics." She leaned forward and whispered, "He's a widower, you know. No young children."

"Is that good?"

"Very. A new wife of his wouldn't be saddled with another woman's children."

I thought of my father. Some things never change. You can

put on a layer of silk and satin, but the game's the same. I laughed.

Agnes looked askance. "What is it, Miss Dorothy, that makes you laugh?"

"It's a long story." I pointed to my stockinged toes. "Should I go as the barefoot princess?"

"Oh no, Miss, that would not do."

I laughed again. "I was teasing, Agnes. I expected you to laugh."

Agnes let out a polite little laugh.

"I have shoes, but should I wear my white pair or, perhaps, a beige?"

"White, definitely white, as it is past Memorial Day. Ideally, a pair of matching pink would be best, but you'll have to make do with white."

"And gloves?"

"The matching satin ones would look best, I think."

Again I had to thank Chloe for supplying me with an outfit I thought I'd never have cause to wear, gloves included. Would I ever be able to pay her and Cy back for all their love and generosity? And now I would be beholden to Mr. and Mrs. McCall as well.

All my life I'd heard Pa expound on the importance of never being beholden to anyone. Was I making a mistake going to college on other people's generosity? Was it God's leading, or was it my own desires that guided my judgment? Sometimes I wasn't sure.

"Miss Dorothy?" I snapped out of my thoughts at the sound of Agnes calling my name. "Sorry, daydreaming, I guess."

Agnes tucked a stray curl under an ivory comb. "I understand. Sometimes I get to gabbing and forget myself."

"Oh no, Agnes, it wasn't you. I think I might still be weary from my journey."

The maid nodded as she scooped up my cast-off petticoats. "I understand. It took me two weeks to feel normal again after my crossing from England."

"You're from England?"

"Yes, Miss Dorothy. Bristol." The woman beamed.

"How exciting! Why did you leave to come to America, if I may ask?" I swung around on the vanity seat to face her.

"As you said before, it's a long story. And if I'm not mistaken, I think I hear the first of Mrs. McCall's guests arriving."

Terror filled my heart. My hands flew to my face. "Oh no, not already. What if I commit some social faux pas? What if I use the wrong tableware?" Then a new thought struck, "What if I fall down the stairs?"

Agnes laughed. "Don't worry. You are so lovely that whatever faux pas you might commit will be overlooked. As to the tableware, always follow the lead of your hostess. As to the stairs, hang onto the railing with all your might."

I stared at her in horror. She laughed. "That was a joke. You were supposed to laugh."

"Oh." I chuckled. "You got me that time."

Outside my window, I heard the sounds of two more motorcars arriving. "Maybe I should hurry down to help Julia greet her guests."

"Oh no. You're the guest-of-honor. You will make a grand entrance after the last guest arrives."

"Guest-of-honor? Julia didn't mention anything about guest-of-honor." I clutched the bodice of my gown.

"Mrs. McCall has several intimate little gatherings planned in your honor. You are a godsend to her and Mr. McCall. When her grandson, Jamie, enlisted in the army, she fell apart for a while. But anticipating your arrival brought her new life." The maid took my arm and led me into the hallways.

I wasn't sure I wanted the burden of that responsibility. I knew Chloe Mae had been heartbroken when her stepson enlisted. That was what prompted her unscheduled retreat to Cape Cod, according to Cy. *War certainly has a way of wreaking havoc with family and loved ones,* I thought.

Below us I heard the voices of Julia and James E. welcoming their guests. Agnes peered around the balustrade, then straightened. "They're all here. It's time for your grand entrance."

She eased me to the top of the winding staircase. "Go ahead," she whispered. "There are only seventeen steps."

I swallowed hard. "Please, God, don't let me stumble and fall. Don't let me twist my ankle. Don't let me slip on the carpeting. Don't let . . ." As I carefully descended the staircase, a smile pasted on my face; I recited everything I could imagine happening to embarrass my hostess and me.

"Ah, here she is, the lovely Miss Dorothy Spencer, my daughter by marriage." Julia, the perfect Back Bay hostess, turned to her husband. "Just what would be the correct relationship between us and Chloe Mae's siblings?"

He started to reply, but she interrupted. "Isn't she a vision of loveliness?" She extended her hand to mine, and I descended the last two steps without holding on for dear life onto the railing. "Come, my dear, let me introduce you to our oldest and most dearest friends, Judge Harold Meyers, his wife, Blanche."

The white-haired judge took my hand and gave a polite bow. "Charmed." His wife cooed a similar greeting. Next I met Dr. John Landes and his wife, Harriet; then, Mr. Charles Bond and his wife, Celia. I knew I'd never remember all their names throughout the entire evening.

Last, I met the graying and distinguished Franklin Bowles. He was a man lost in the ageless years of his thirties, who needed to look up to converse with me. I slouched as much as possible but was still two or three inches taller than Mr. Bowles. Behind his neatly trimmed beard and mustache, a sardonic smile lurked. I wasn't sure if he was laughing at me or the strange dinner party custom insisting that for every woman there must be a man present.

Julia led the way into the parlor where silver platters of hors d'oeuvres awaited us. James E. walked over to the Victrola and chose a piano concerto. The judge joined him. Even from a distance I could tell that I liked Judge Meyers. He had a kindly twinkle in his eyes. While I'm sure he could be firm with offenders of the law, I sensed he was also a fair man as well. Picking up what little

I could of their conversation regarding the war effort, I wished I could join their circle, but alas, I would probably find myself chatting with the female guests.

The ladies seated themselves on the violet satin brocade sofa and matching love seat. I could hear them discussing the "delicious spread" on the tea crackers. I glanced around the parlor and had to admit that the violet-and-cream motif was easy on the eyes. A large rosewood grand piano filled half the room. A fireplace of highly polished hand-carved rosewood and marble divided the seating area from the piano and the bank of lace-covered windows. Gold tasseled ties held back pale jade-green and velvet draperies. Yes, despite the clutter of expensive china and crystal in the room, I felt comfortable here.

Just as I took a step toward an empty straight-backed chair near where the women gathered, Franklin caught my arm, drawing me back toward the large double doors. Obviously, Franklin took his responsibility seriously, me being his responsibility. When the other men wandered over to join in the discussion between the judge and James E., Franklin ignored them.

"Julia tells me that you are a writer. What do you write? Children's books?"

I smiled. How many times had I heard that question? As if children's books were the only acceptable books for women to write. I had an overwhelming urge to say, "No, I write gothic romance novels." Anything to wipe that condescending smile off his face.

"I'm a news reporter."

He studied my face for a moment then broke into a grin. "Ah, ladies' column, recipes and the like, I presume."

I tipped my head to one side and arched an eyebrow. "No, personality pieces. I'm always looking for good subjects."

"Really? How interesting." The man preened before me as if I should recognize a good subject when I see one.

Somewhere I'd heard that if one person could get another talking about himself, that person would go away thinking he had a great evening. "And you? Tell me about yourself."

Franklin needed no additional prompting. He began with his adventures in early childhood. He'd barely entered his wild adolescent years when Lawrence, the butler, rang the dinner bell.

Ah, saved by the bell, I thought, allowing Franklin Bowles, the attorney, to escort me to the dinner table. The conversation flowed as smooth as the vanilla ice cream that would complete the meal. That is, until Judge Meyers baited Julia.

"So, Julia, have you been cavorting with those blue stockings anymore?" The judge grinned and twirled one tip of his mustache.

"Harold, a Boston blue blood does not *cavort* with anyone. Since my blood is bluer than yours, I have the last word. As to the poor unfortunates dragged before your court for perfectly legal assembly, I am amazed that a great legal mind like yours is insensitive to the injustice of it."

I glanced from the judge to my hostess then back again. The judge chuckled at the blank look on my face. "It seems that our fine hostess has recently done jail time, arrested for loitering and unlawful assembly."

"Now, wait one moment, Harold," Julia interrupted. "You make it sound worse than it really was. If your goons of policemen would have only listened to reason—"

James E. lifted his water glass. "Here's to my spunky sweetheart."

Julia clicked her tongue in disgust. "James E., and you, too, Harold Meyers, one more word about this from either of you and you will not get a piece of the cook's famous strawberry-rhubarb pie. With freshly made vanilla ice cream on top, I might add." To me, she said in a stage whisper, "I'll tell you what really happened later."

I laughed and dotted my lips with my linen napkin.

"Ah, you're hitting my weak spot, Julia." Judge Meyers patted his abundant stomach. Turning to his host, he asked, "So, what have you heard from the European front?"

"Reports are sketchy." Mr. McCall sat back from the table to allow Lawrence to remove the dinner plate and used silver. "For the most part, the first U.S. troops haven't landed in England yet."

The talk of war and what it would mean to America continued throughout much of the rest of the evening. I was relieved when the guests said their Goodbyes, especially Mr. Franklin Bowles. As neatly appearing and congenial as he'd been all evening, there was something about the man that irritated me. Obviously, the feeling wasn't mutual. When he asked if he could call on me the next day, I hesitated. "I'm sorry, but I'm here in Boston to study, not socialize."

He leaned forward until his lips were brushing the loose tendrils of curls on the side of my face. "But even students need to eat. How about dinner tomorrow night?"

I stepped back, accidentally bumping into an asparagus fern sitting on a marble-topped plant stand in the foyer. Franklin caught the porcelain pot before it crashed to the floor.

"Oh, thank you. I wouldn't want to inconvenience a busy attorney like yourself." My fingers fluttered against the bodice of my dress.

"Nothing is so pressing that I can't leave the office a trifle early. It will be a pleasure."

"That is so nice of you, but I must study tomorrow for a quiz. Latin has never come easily for me, I'm afraid."

"Latin? At Yale, I was a straight A student in Latin, my dear. Greek, however, remained Greek to me, I'm afraid."

I gave a polite laugh. He rubbed his hands together. "Then it's all settled. I will tutor you. How does four o'clock tomorrow afternoon sound? We can conjugate verbs over tea and scones."

"Four o'clock will be fine," I whimpered in defeat.

"Jolly good." He lifted my hand to his lips and kissed my gloved fingertips.

I'd barely arrived back at the McCalls' residence from class the next day when Franklin Bowles drove into the estate's circular driveway.

I paused at the massive mahogany double doors and shook my head. "Right on time," I mumbled under my breath. "Just what I might expect."

Lawrence opened the doors before I could use the brass doorknocker. "Welcome home, Miss Dorothy." The butler gazed past me. "Is that Mr. Bowles?"

Franklin Bowles leapt from his sporty Pierce-Arrow convertible like a teenage boy at a track meet. As he bounded toward me, I controlled the urge to run.

"Mr. Bowles," Lawrence bowed ever so slightly. "What a surprise. Is Madam expecting you?"

"No, I am not calling on Mrs. McCall. I'm here to take Miss Spencer to high tea." He grinned at me affectionately.

This man is unbearable, I told myself. *Either he's the most pitiable of males when it comes to females or the females in Boston are hook-nosed biddies. No man had ever shown such enthusiasm at the prospect of seeing me.*

I remembered my totally inappropriate attire. I was dressed for school, not "high tea," whatever that might be. "Oh, dear, Mr. Bowles. I am hardly dressed for such an event. Perhaps we can reschedule our tutoring session?"

"Nonsense, Miss Dorothy," Lawrence interjected, "Madam would be put off should you cancel your assignation. She has made it clear to the staff that this is your home now with accompanying rights and privileges, one of which is to entertain your own guests. Please, Mr. Bowles, may I take your hat and cane?"

"Superb, Lawrence. Shall we?" Franklin held out his arm for me. Reluctantly, I allowed him to escort me into the house. Once inside, I excused myself and hurried up the stairs to my room. I applied rice paper to my nose and chin, touched up my hair, straightened my shoulders, and marched back down the stairs to my waiting guest.

I found him relaxing in the sunroom and charming Julia's cook out of English shortbread and tea. Orange-mint, my favorite.

"Ah, there you are, looking as lovely as ever." He rose to his feet.

"Thank you, Mr. Bowles . . ." I restrained myself from sarcasm. I wondered why this man could bring out the nastiest disposition in me. ". . . but I've only been gone five minutes."

He chuckled and escorted me to a natural bamboo rattan love seat then sat down beside me. "Well, where shall we begin? Conjugating love?"

I shot a glare at him. He laughed. "The verb, my dear, the verb." I reddened and fumbled with the pages of my Latin II textbook.

By the time Julia returned from her afternoon adventures, our teapot was cold, the cookies were eaten, and Franklin and I were laughing over one of his college antics while attending Yale. "Coming back to Boston to practice law was a slap in the face for all my Harvard friends. I might as well have called them out for an old-fashioned duel."

He glanced past my shoulder and shot to his feet. "Ah, Mrs. McCall, I do hope I am not trespassing on your good humor by being here unannounced."

Julia slapped her elbow-length gray leather gloves against his shoulder. "Of course not, Franklin. Dorothy is always free to invite her friends here. This is her home away from home." She patted my shoulder affectionately. I sighed with relief. Julia glanced at the tea service and empty cookie plate. "I'm glad to see that the staff is taking good care of you in my absence. I must tell Lawrence to freshen your tea."

"No, thank you, that won't be necessary. I think we're finished studying for the day." Franklin looked at me for confirmation. I nodded and smiled.

When Julia saw the easy camaraderie between us, she smiled. "Tonight James E. and I are attending a concert by the Charles River. The cook is packing a special lunch for us to eat al fresco. And, of course, we would like your company, Dorothy." Before I could reply, she turned to Franklin. "What about you, Mr. Bowles? Will you make it a foursome?"

"I don't mind if I do."

"Good. The concert begins at seven. The Boston Symphony

is really very good, you know." Julia added.

Franklin took his watch from his vest pocket and snapped open the lid. "Goodness, I'd better leave now if I intend to make it home and back again, what with the late afternoon traffic in Boston. My humble flat is on the north side of the city. Public Defenders live a bit more simply than do Boston's aristocracy."

"*Pshaw!*" Julia flung a hand in the attorney's direction. "My husband has the most outrageous talent for making money, that's all. And I have an equally outrageous talent for spending it." The woman giggled like a little girl, as did both Franklin and myself.

Julia's contagious laughter did that to people wherever she went, so I was soon to discover. She could say the most incredible statement, then laugh and people would not only forgive her lack of reserve but join in her hilarity.

CHAPTER FOUR

Picnic in the Park

Brightly colored blankets dotted the manicured lawns at the Boston Commons. Diners, picnic baskets, and pastel-printed sun umbrellas added to the festive array. When we finished gorging ourselves on what Julia called a "light repast," she insisted we, meaning Franklin and I, stroll along the river to walk off the spice cake with the carmel frosting.

"From shirtsleeve to shirtsleeve in three generations," Franklin said. He strolled beside me alongside the Charles River, nodding amiably to other couples as we passed. My self-consciousness diminished as I grew accustomed to my arm resting in his.

"That's the maxim for many wealthy families both here in Boston and in New York City. Papa makes the money so junior doesn't need to slave as he did only to have sonny, who's never worked an honest day in his life, squander the fortune, thus forcing his grandchildren to work for everything they get." Franklin chuckled. "With the recent recession, some hard-pressed families, too proud to admit their financial situations, rationed their food in private so they could afford to give the lavish dinners and balls, to which they were accustomed."

"That seems so foolish." The evening breeze blew several stray curls past my cheek. I brushed them aside.

"Appearances are still everything: The upper floors of great houses are often nearly empty, the contents sold to put food on the table, while one story down, the sumptuous decor and ten-course meals are enjoyed by guests."

We passed two small boys playing marbles on the slate sidewalk. "When I was a kid I envied all the blue blood brats that attended the same prep school. I attended both the prep school and college on a scholarship, thanks to a grizzled old sea captain who took a liking to me."

I chuckled aloud. I'd assumed Franklin Bowles to be a member of the wealthy and spoiled upper class. I was surprised to discover that I was wrong. "I'm attending Wellesley, thanks to my wealthy sister and her husband."

"Really?" Franklin stopped walking and looked into my eyes. "And I thought you were born with the proverbial silver spoon in your mouth."

I laughed. "Oh no. I've never been around wealth. I grew up in an unpainted Pennsylvania farmhouse. My father is an herbalist and works for the oil company. Pa still walks the oil lines every day."

"Then how did you meet the McCalls?"

"My sister Chloe was married to their eldest son, who died in a mining accident in Colorado. When she remarried, the two families remained close. And when I chose to attend college, she made arrangements for me to live with her in-laws. I've only been here a few days and, I must confess, I am overwhelmed."

Franklin threw back his head and laughed. "I never would have guessed. Last night, I thought I was the only one terribly out of place at the McCall's dinner party."

"Oh no. When I had to walk down that flight of stairs, I was certain I'd fall flat on my face at everyone's feet."

"And I was sure I'd spill soup in my lap or drop an hors

d'oeuvre on the carpet."

We took turns listing off our worst fears from the night before until we were both laughing aloud. When others were casting side-long glances at us because of our hilarity, I remembered my place. "I give, you win. So how did you come to know the McCalls?"

"A few weeks ago, Mrs. McCall and her two granddaughters got arrested for taking part in a suffragette rally, and I helped un-ravel things for them. When Mrs. McCall discovered I was both single and an orphan in the city, she took pity on me." Turning abruptly to me, he asked, "Did she know about your arrival then?"

I shook my head. "No, I don't think so. I believe she needed an extra male at her table, and you were the freshest one she knew."

"Fresh? Am I fresh?" He lifted one eyebrow and grinned.

I blushed at the implication. "I didn't mean that the way it sounded. I meant a new face on the scene. She wanted to be the first of her friends to invite you, an eligible young bachelor, to her party. From what she said, many of the appropriate specimens are too long-in-the-tooth for a fair flower like me." I patted my curls and fluttered my eyelashes.

"Mr. Bowles. Miss Spencer." Franklin and I glanced up to see Judge Meyers strolling toward us, his wife at his side. "My, my, what a surprise meeting you two here."

Instantly, I felt the need to defend myself. "The McCalls in-vited us along for a picnic before tonight's concert. They're here somewhere. Have you seen them?" I glanced about frantically try-ing to locate my host or my hostess.

Franklin pointed toward the white gazebo bandstand where the musicians were tuning their instruments. "There they are, your honor. Dear Mrs. McCall took pity on a homesick and lonely bachelor two evenings in a row."

"Julia is a kindhearted soul," the judge admitted.

Mrs. Meyers snuggled against her husband's arm. "Come, Harold, let's go find the McCalls and leave these two youngsters alone, shall we?"

I blushed at the woman's inference, though I realized she interpreted what she saw, nothing more. I glanced out of the corner of my eye at Franklin. He appeared to be watching the rowboats on the river as they jockeyed for position around the wooden dock.

The attorney at my side cleared his throat and continued studying a distant object on the river. "Sorry. I hope I haven't put you in a compromising position. We did meet only yesterday."

"Yes, I suppose we shouldn't have strayed quite so far from the McCalls. I wouldn't want anyone to misinterpret our, er, companionable stroll as anything more." I coughed lightly into a linen handkerchief I'd been clutching in my free hand.

His eyes grew serious. "Discretion is the better part of valor, I believe."

"Shakespeare?" I asked.

"Yes . . ." Franklin swallowed a chuckle. "The words of the Bard's greatest fool, actually."

I laughed nervously. "Which only goes to show that even a fool can occasionally be wise."

This time Franklin didn't try to bury his laughter. "Miss Spencer, you are a delight. The women with whom I've been acquainted wouldn't have had an iota of an idea about what I was talking."

"Why Mr. Bowles"—I batted my eyelashes and fluttered my gloved fingers delicately against my throat—"I do believe you are flirting with me."

He laughed at my affectations. "You are one refreshing young woman, Miss Spencer."

Suddenly shouts erupted near the bandstand. We whirled about in time to see a mob storming the gazebo. On the steps of the bandstand stood a small group of women all wearing saffron yellow outfits and carrying sticks with placards protesting everything from women's right to vote to the war to outlawing alcohol consumption. The signs read WOMEN UNITED FOR EQUAL RIGHTS! WE LOSE OUR SONS TO A WAR FOR WHICH WE CANNOT VOTE! LIQUOR IS AS EVIL AS THE KAISER HIMSELF! I chuckled at the sign a particularly attractive young woman carried, LIPS THAT

TOUCH LIQUOR WILL NEVER TOUCH MINE!

"Mrs. McCall told me about—" I started toward the action.

"Miss Dorothy," Franklin called, but I continued walking toward the commotion.

Behind the cluster of women on the gazebo steps, frightened musicians clutched their instruments to their bodies and cowered. A percussion player, abandoning his snare drums, dropped over the side of the railing and disappeared to safety. A cellist, grasping his instrument by the neck, looked poised, ready to bean the first person to come near where he stood.

One of the protesters stood regally above the rest. Along with a saffron yellow silk suit, she wore an outrageous orange ostrich-feathered concoction in the tower of ebony curls piled atop her head. As ridiculous as the feathered hat might have been on the head of a shorter woman, the suffragette carried it off with aplomb and grace. The sign in one of her hands read "Women Need the Right to Vote!" Her other hand gripped a megaphone.

"We are here tonight . . ." she began. The mob of angry men shouted above the sound of the megaphone and rushed the steps. I couldn't understand the rest of what she tried to say. By now, a curious crowd had gathered between me and the unfolding event. Frantic policemen blew their whistles as they tried to break through the crowd. I could hear wailing police sirens in the distance.

Always the reporter, I craned my neck to better observe the disturbance. I felt Franklin's hands grasp each of my elbows. "Miss Dorothy, this is not a safe situation. I need to get you safely to the McCalls' vehicle."

Reluctantly, I let him guide me through the pressing crowd. The explosive shouts of the mob frightened me. I'd never felt the negative power of such fury before. Occasionally, I could decipher a word or two coming from the megaphone, words like "Voting, birthright, mothers, sisters, daughters!"

The curious concert goers pressed in closer to get a better view. The mass of people around me tightened. I felt like a discarded rag doll being bumped, shoved, and brushed against. An unfamiliar fear rose inside of my throat. I had the wildest urge to scream and claw my way free.

A man in front of me shoved aside a well-dressed matron who stood in his way. She lurched forward but managed to catch her balance before she fell. Disgusted with the ill-mannered lout, I pushed against his shoulder and shouted in his ear, "How dare you shove that lady!"

The man turned and glared. "Don't tell me who I can push and who I can't!" His hand slammed against my shoulder, and I stumbled back. Franklin, seeing the man's action, reached past me and laid one hand on the stranger's shoulder. "Don't shove the lady!"

When the man doubled up his fist to retaliate against Franklin, I shouted in the man's face, "I would be careful if I were you, sir. You are about to slug Mr. Franklin Bowles, Boston's prosecuting attorney!"

The man's fist froze midair. His eyes widened. "Prosecuting attorney? Excuse me, sir, madam." He tipped his hat and slipped through the crowd with only a quick glance over his shoulder as he fled.

I'd barely recovered from my laughter when a burly policeman yanked me away from Franklin's grasp. "Mr. Bowles! Help," I gasped. Within seconds, Franklin's hands securely grasped my upper arms once again.

"We've got to get out of here," he shouted in my ears above the din of the crowd."

I nodded.

"Veer toward your left."

I nodded again, fighting the upstream current of the frenzied crowd. The mass of people swept me toward the bandstand. I was suddenly propelled forward. My straw sailor hat flew off my head and disappeared under someone's feet. My hair tumbled down around my shoulders. My foot hit against something, an injured woman.

"Stop! Stop!" I screamed, somehow catching my balance. No

one but Franklin heard me. He grabbed a hold of me and held onto the back of my middy blouse. "Help!" I screamed again. "We must help her!" When he saw the injured woman, Franklin tried to push against the surging crowd. The excited people plowed around us like stampeding cattle.

"I'll try to hold them off while you help her to her feet," Franklin shouted.

I nodded. As I reached for the woman, a shove in the middle of my back sent me tumbling over the top of her. My knee crashed down on one of her wrists. My chest thudded against the grassy sod. *Oh dear! I'm going to be trampled to death,* I thought. *What a terrible way to die.*

A man kicked at the woman's head. Without thinking, I grabbed his foot. He sprawled over the top of the woman and to one side of me. Now there were three of us down. Trying to scramble to his feet, the man pulled to the ground another couple. The woman's parasol shot forward like a dueling sword and pinned one of the men's coat jacket to the ground. Startled cries filled the air. I watched helplessly as several other people fell around me.

Where was Franklin? I started to lift my head to see if I could find him but thought better of it as the herd thundered by. I protected my head as best I could and clung to the injured young woman. She groaned. "It's all right." I assured her. "You'll be all right."

Police whistles blasted around me, people screamed, others cried out in pain. While all this occurred in less than a minute, it seemed to me like hours.

When a familiar voice called to me, I lifted my head but couldn't see Franklin. Where was he? Then rough hands lifted me to my feet. "Are you all right, lady?" A policeman asked.

"I am, but I'm not sure about her." I pointed to the woman on the ground beneath me. I dusted off my navy-blue serge skirt and straightened the sailor bow on the front of my blouse. By the time Franklin broke through the crowd, I was somewhat presentable, except for a few smudges here and there and my horribly tangled hair.

When Judge Meyers's voice boomed out over the megaphone, the shouting died down. "Gentlemen! Ladies! Calm down. Enough is enough. This is neither the time nor the place to decide the Suffrage issue. This is America, a democracy, and issues can't be solved by rioting." He paused to let his words sink in. "Go home and let the state and national lawmakers decide this issue."

Ambulance attendants arrived with a stretcher for the fallen woman. I held the injured woman's hand while the medic splinted her arm and bandaged her head. Behind us, the city policemen were loading the rioters into horse-drawn paddy wagons.

"What's your name?" I asked.

"Marta," the woman said quietly through swollen lips.

"Is there anyone I can contact for you, to let them know where you are?"

The woman shook her head. "No, I don't want to get my family into any trouble."

I eyed the woman's torn saffron yellow cotton dress and for the first time realized she was part of the demonstration. Again, through puffy bruised lips, she said, "I was late arriving at the park. My sister is going to be so angry with me."

"For being late?" I asked.

"No, for being here at all. My sister says I'll only cause her trouble, and she'll lose her job because of me."

Franklin and I followed behind the medics as they loaded Marta onto the horse-drawn ambulance. We waited to be certain she would be all right. Then Franklin touched my elbow. "We need to find Mr. and Mrs. McCall."

I glanced toward the gazebo and shook my head. "Where do we start looking?" I tried to catch my hair back at the nape of my neck, but in the tumble, I'd lost two of my favorite tortoise shell combs and all of my hairpins. "The Packard," I said. "Sooner or later, they'll return to the Packard."

We made our way across the lawn strewn with broken umbrellas, torn blankets, wicker baskets, and food. Dispirited concert goers moved through the rubble looking for their belongings.

Dogs had already moved in on the food scraps. We sidestepped a feisty black-and-white male terrier standing guard over a brown female mongrel gorging herself on someone's abandoned chocolate cake.

We reached the parking area and discovered that the Packard was gone. Our hosts were no where to be found. Frantic, I asked a policeman standing near the parked automobiles if he'd seen the McCalls. He shrugged and suggested we check both the hospital and the police station. "Several people were injured or arrested."

"Have you seen Judge Meyers and his wife?" I asked. "The McCalls could be with the judge and his wife."

"The captain gave the Meyers a police escort out of the Commons about five minutes ago," the officer assured me.

I turned to Franklin. "I can't believe they just abandoned me here!"

Franklin shook his head. "You're right, that doesn't make sense. They wouldn't just leave you here without a chaperon, would they?"

I clicked my tongue. "I am of legal age, you know."

"All of twenty-one? My, my!" He laughed. "I suppose that I shouldn't tease. You did travel from Pennsylvania by yourself. That takes a pretty modern-thinking woman, I must admit."

"That's neither here nor there right now. What should we do?"

"I think we should do what the policeman suggested." He took my elbow and guided me to his jaunty Pierce-Arrow. "And if worse comes to worse, I'll drive you home, right to the McCall's Italian marble-inlaid entryway. Do you think the staff will be scandalized?"

"Call me a prude or a blue-stocking, but a ruined reputation's no laughing matter for a woman."

"You're right. And I'm sorry. The hospital is less than a mile away. And I do have the top down on the Pierce-Arrow. That should be public enough."

He helped me into the passenger seat of his car, cranked the engine, then hopped into the driver's seat. Shouting over the roar of the motor, he said, "Hold on to your hat. Oops! Sorry. Obviously it's too late for that."

For the first time, I realized that he, too, had lost his hat in the uproar. I laughed and pulled my hair back from my face. "I haven't been in public with my hair down since I was thirteen."

Franklin maneuvered his car out of the Common area onto the busy street. "More's the pity."

"You really are scandalous, Mr. Bowles. A lady doesn't—"

He grinned and laughed. "I know, something else a lady doesn't 'do in public.' "

Within a short time, he eased the Pierce-Arrow to a stop in front of the hospital. "Stay here. I'll be right back."

I nodded. While he was gone, I tried in vain to wad the bulk of my hair at the nape of my neck.

Franklin wasn't gone more than five minutes. He came out of the building shaking his head. "They're not here. I checked the patient list myself."

"What a relief. I imagined them seriously injured. I saw Julia run toward the gazebo just before the confusion started."

He restarted the engine and hopped into the car. "Guess it's to the police station."

"That would be a waste of your time, Franklin. Might as well take me home."

"Nonsense! The police station is on the way to the McCall's place. We might as well stop since we're in the area." His suggestion made sense. When we arrived at the station, the police were unloading prisoners from the last of the four paddy wagons. We'd barely stepped inside the station house when I heard Julia's voice above the others.

"This is ludicrous. I demand to see Judge Meyers!"

I stood on my tiptoes to peer over the heads of the bustling throng, but I couldn't spot her. "I know I heard Julia's voice!"

"You have to know the technique for city living survival, Miss Dorothy." Franklin took my hand and elbowed his way through the crowd.

"Julia," I shouted and waved when we got within shouting

range. "What happened to you?"

Julia sat on a long wooden bench with several other women. Handcuffs bound her wrists to those of her fellow prisoners. Blood oozed from her bandaged head. Her left eye was blackening. A bruise covered her patrician cheekbone. She lifted a manacled arm to wave. The woman beside her snarled at her.

"Oh, be still!" Julia scolded. "I don't like you anymore than you like me!" She redirected her attention to me. "Dorothy! Am I glad to see you! You, too, Mr. Bowles. I'm mad as a March hare!"

I dabbed at the oozing blood with a handkerchief I'd stuffed into my pocket that morning. "But are you all right? You look, uh, er . . ."

Franklin saved me. "You look to be in quite a pickle, Mrs. McCall. What happened?"

Julia glared. "Happened? Happened? I was shoved, knocked down, dragged, shackled, and held here against my will. These, these, cretins (she pointed to a uniformed police officer) have the sense of a gnat."

"Where's Mr. McCall?" I asked.

"James E. is trying to spring me from this, this travesty of justice. Did you see? Did you see?"

"See what, Mrs. McCall." Franklin leaned forward.

"I'll tell you what!" The police escorted Judge Meyers and his wife from the park while I was dragged, handcuffed, to a paddy wagon. Do you call that justice, sir? Do you?"

Franklin reddened and straightened his collar. "No, ma'am. No, ma'am, I don't."

Julia lifted her chin and snorted delicately. "Well, what are you going to do about it? You *are* a prosecuting attorney for the city of Boston, are you not?"

"Yes, er, of course, but . . ." Franklin glanced toward me for help. I shrugged my shoulders and rolled my eyes toward the ceiling.

"Then do something! Don't just stand there like a bump on a log!"

Franklin's eyebrows shot upward to meet his hairline. His mustache twitched with humor as he bowed slightly. "Madam, far be it from me to be, what was it, a bump on a log? I will see if I can facilitate things for you."

"Wait!" The woman ordered. "Here comes James E. and a police officer. Maybe he's been able to talk some sense into these buffoonish police officers!"

"Mrs. McCall," Franklin reminded her, "the policemen are only trying to do their job."

"Their job? Lambasting women over the head and dragging them off to jail while the real troublemakers, who just happen to be male, go free? That's their job?" Her eyes flashed indignantly.

James E. arrived in time to deflect Julia's ire. "I think we have everything straightened out, my dear. Oh . . ." He smiled at Franklin and me. "Glad to see that you two got out unscathed." He returned his attention to his wife. "Now, my dear, Officer Keanan here will remove those cuffs. Then, after you sign a few papers, you'll be free to go."

"Sign a few papers? What papers!"

James E. cast a tentative smile at his wife. "Papers that assure the magistrate that you didn't intend to hit Officer McRafferty with your umbrella."

The woman bowed her neck like a provoked peacock. "But I—"

"Otherwise," he interrupted, "you will be booked for assaulting an officer." Julia slowly settled back against the prisoners' bench. "Which, as you know, would guarantee you time in the pokey."

Julia's eyes widened with a look of incredible innocence. "Why, of course, dear. You know I would never—"

Her husband knitted his brow. "Let's not belabor the issue right now, my dear. Officer Keanan here has taken care of everything."

"Yes, dear. Whatever you think is best."

James E. coughed while Franklin and I thrust surprised glances at the suddenly docile Julia. When the policeman removed the manacles from Julia's wrists, James E. helped her to her feet. She swayed and touched her forehead. Franklin rushed to take the woman's other arm. "Here, let me help you, Mrs. McCall. Perhaps you should see your own doctor about that head wound."

James E. nodded. "I agree. We'll stop at Dr. Michaels on the way home." To Franklin, he added, "Once we get her in the car, would be you so kind as to take Dorothy home for us?"

"Of course. It would be a pleasure," Franklin assured him.

I followed behind as the two men escorted Julia from the police station. We'd passed through the double doors when a police officer called her name. "Mrs. McCall, er, here's your parasol." He handed her a closed umbrella, the flowery yellow fabric hanging in shreds from the center post and the post broken in the middle.

"Begging your pardon, ma'am" —Franklin's smile widened— "but that must have been one solid hit you accidentally bestowed on one of Boston's finest."

A quirky grin lifted one corner of Julia's bruised mouth. "Really, counselor, what are you suggesting?"

Franklin glanced over her shoulder at me. "Absolutely nothing, Mrs. McCall. It's definitely an area I would rather not know about at this time."

James E. opened the rear door of the Packard, and Julia gingerly climbed into the back seat. "Imagine, Harold Meyers allowing me to be arrested!"

Her husband retrieved a small tapestry pillow from the floor of the car and stuffed it behind Julia's head. "In all fairness, Julia, Harold probably had no idea that you were arrested."

"No idea? Of course he knew! He had to know that I was on the steps beside him." She closed her eyes. "I hope Dr. Michaels can give me a powder for this pounding headache."

At the McCall estate, the stoic-faced Lawrence greeted us at the door. Franklin left without going inside.

"And Mr. and Mrs. McCall? Will they be returning shortly?" the butler asked.

"I'm not sure. They stopped at Dr. Michaels on the way home from the concert." I didn't know how much to tell the McCall's staff.

"Will I be needing to make additional preparations for their arrival?"

What a sly way to ask what is wrong, I thought. "You might ask Agnes to turn down Mrs. McCall's bed and, perhaps, she'll also appreciate a cup of hot chamomile tea. It's been a grueling evening."

"Miss Agnes left early tonight. She received word that her sister had been seriously injured at a protest rally downtown." He volunteered more information than I expected. *Is this his way of coaxing additional information out of me?* I thought.

"Oh, that's too bad. I certainly hope Agnes's sister is all right."

"I believe so, Miss, at least, that's what the messenger reported to Miss Agnes."

"Good. Mrs. McCall depends heavily on Agnes around here." I placed my soiled-gloved hand on the shiny mahogany stair railing. "Is there someone else who can step in for Agnes tonight? Mrs. McCall will definitely need assistance preparing for bed."

Lawrence's face muscles didn't twitch nor did his eyes reflect the questions that must have been going through his mind. "I will arrange for one of the kitchen girls to help her. Is there anything you will be needing, Miss?"

I started up the stairs. "No, I'm going to take a long, steaming-hot bath." I sighed at the mere thought. My body ached all over.

"A pot of hot tea and a plate of the cook's freshly baked scones will be waiting for you in your room."

"Why, thank you, Lawrence. How very thoughtful of you."

The butler's face broke into a controlled smile. "A pleasure, Miss." He tipped his head respectfully.

I ran up the stairs to my third-floor bedroom, stopped in the bathroom on my way to my bedroom, and started my bath water running. I chose the pink bottle marked Strawberry Cream, opened it, and sprinkled the perfumed pellets into the tub. Then I ran down the hallway to my room and closed the door behind me. I shed my torn and soiled skirt just inside the door and kicked off my black patent leather Mary Jane shoes. I didn't care where they landed. All I could think about was the luscious bath waiting for me.

After wrestling with the buttons, my middy blouse fell to the floor beside the dresser. In the dresser mirror, I caught a reflection of the bruises welting up on my arms, as well as one on my chin. I untied the waist of my petticoat and let it fall where I stood. Crossing the red-and-blue Persian area rug, I sat on the edge of the bed and removed my gray stockings. Now, I could see as well as feel the numerous bruises on my legs. Dorothy Mae, you look like a bruised peach that fell from the tree limb!

Slipping into my navy blue cotton plissé robe, I dashed down the hallway to the bathroom and slipped beneath the mountain of bubbles. "What a strange day," I mumbled to myself as the steamy hot water soothed my bruises and frayed nerves. "First, Franklin Bowles then the riot. Definitely not one's average daily experience." The aches and pains in my limbs eased. I felt coddled and spoiled, and incredibly blessed. "I know you were there for me, Father. Thank You. How Your heart must hurt seeing all that hatred and anger coming from Your children. Will we ever learn to love one another as Your Son prayed we would do?"

Leaning back against the slope of the tub, I closed my eyes, and the next thing I knew, I awakened to shriveled fingers and toes. The bubbles had melted, and the water had grown tepid.

Hearing Julia's voice coming up the stairwell, I leapt from the tub and dried myself off as the staff and her husband helped her to her bedroom. By the time I dressed and went to see if I could help, James E. met me at the foot of the stairs. He assured me that Julia was already asleep, thanks to Dr. Michaels's medication. "She'll be fine by morning."

I cupped my hand over my grin when he confided, "Don't tell her I said this, but she really should avoid fighting such battles at her age."

CHAPTER FIVE

Personal Involvement

The morning after the skirmish in the park, I awakened to aches and pains in parts of my body whose smooth working order I had always taken for granted. I struggled into my undergarments and then into my cotton stockings. I groaned when I bent down to tie my shoes. *If I ache as much as this,* I reasoned, *I can only imagine how Julia must feel this morning.*

My dreams had been troubled throughout the night. Several times I'd awakened, trapped in the bedding that had become wrapped about my sweating body. Each time, I found it difficult to return to sleep. At one point, I turned on the lamp beside my bed, opened my Bible, and read aloud my favorite text, Psalm 91. The assuring words helped settle my troubled mind so that I could sleep.

The colors of dawn were fast spreading across the eastern sky when I awakened and decided to give up on any further sleep. I groaned from a catch in my shoulder when I reached for my Bible resting on the nightstand beside the bed. I opened God's Word as I had every morning for the past ten years since my baptism.

As a ten-year-old, I decided that not only did I wish to be baptized, but I also wanted to discover everything I could about the God I served. That involved studying about Him in His Word.

You see, over the years, I had watched my older sisters and their future husbands. These men were ardent while courting my sisters. They'd spend hour after hour swinging together on the porch swing, "talking," or as my sisters would explain, "getting acquainted." What I liked about my sisters' courtships was that these suitors would get me aside and bribe me with candy to tell them all my sisters' likes and dislikes. I would have told them without the candy, but they didn't know that.

So when I chose to give my life to Jesus, I decided I would do the same thing—no, not bribe anyone with candy to learn about my new Friend—I would do everything I could to learn all about Him from His Word. At first, I found the words difficult to understand, but my brother-in-law, Stanford, helped me find parts of the Bible that were easier for me, books like Philippians, Acts, Psalms, John, and Luke. Slowly I graduated into the tougher stuff like Romans, Isaiah, and Galatians. I still found Lamentations and the Chronicles enjoyable. Yet, whenever I couldn't understand something or the picture I was getting of God didn't seem right, I would return to Psalms and to the book of John for a clearer picture of Jesus, the God I'd come to love.

I also liked discussing theology with Hattie's husband. He was a preacher, and he had studied Greek in Bible college. Since I always liked words and playing with them in my mind, speaking them aloud and "rolling" them around in my mouth, I enjoyed discovering their etymology, or source. My brother-in-law preacher always laughed and said I should study to become a preacher. Imagine, me a preacher? A female news reporter, maybe, but hardly a preacher. I thought about Franklin. I wish I could talk with him about spiritual matters, but whenever I tried, he had a way of changing the subject, almost without my being aware of the change.

I opened my Bible to where I'd stopped reading the evening before. I read about the time Jesus was swarmed by the angry mob at the temple in Nazareth. Imagine having invisible angels surround and lift Jesus out of the mob. I shuddered at the memory of the crowd in the park. "I could have used a little invisibility myself yesterday, Lord." As I read the story, I realized I would never see the incident in Jesus' life in the same way again after experiencing the blinding fury of mob mentality at work.

I placed the Bible on the nightstand and attempted to kneel to pray despite the bruises on my knees. My calves and thighs screamed their protests. I chose, instead, to sit on the edge of the unmade bed for my morning prayer session.

At the end of my prayer, I painfully crossed the room to the armoire and chose a cool, lightweight chambric and lace blouse and an appropriately lightweight skirt to wear to my classes that day.

When I attempted to slip the tiny fabric-covered buttons into the row of loops down the back of my blouse, my fingers refused to work. I grimaced then tugged at the servant's cord beside my bed.

I'd dressed myself since I was a toddler. I couldn't believe, after living in the luxury of the McCall mansion for less than a week, I would need to call one of Julia's chambermaids to help me dress. I could imagine what my father would say about the events of the last twenty-four hours of my life.

Within a few minutes I heard the gentle knock at my door. "Come in," I called. The door opened, and Agnes's questioning face peered around the corner of the door.

"You called, Miss Dorothy?"

"Yes. I seem to be having trouble with the buttons on my bodice this morning. Could you please help me?"

"I'd be glad to, Miss Dorothy." The trim little maid rushed to me. She eyed the bruise on my cheek as she began buttoning the long row of buttons extending down my back. "Ooh, that's a bad one, eh?"

I emitted a derisive laugh. "That's nothing compared to the assortment of bruises on the rest of my body."

"Too bad. Too bad. And after just arriving to our fair city. Really, Boston isn't usually a violent place, Miss Dorothy. Honest."

I laughed out loud. "Compared to what? The slums of Calcutta? Is Mrs. McCall awake yet?"

"Oh yes. She's been up since dawn, just like always." You should have seen Madam's eye this morning. Lawrence put a prime steak on it last night, but it still looks mighty fierce."

Agnes buttoned the bottom loop then reached for my skirt. "Let me help you into this too, Miss."

Remembering Agnes's reason for leaving the house last night, I asked, "How is your sister doing?"

The maid looked surprised at my question. "How did you know about my sister?"

"Lawrence mentioned that you'd left because your sister had taken ill. Forgive me for inquiring, but I'm naturally nosey. I'm a reporter."

Agnes hedged. "Uh, well, yes, but she's doing better now, thank you."

"Was she hurt at the park as well? Mr. Bowles and I met an injured young woman whose name is Marta. Is she your sister?"

The maid shook her head. "My sister was one of the women injured yesterday but not the one you mentioned. Her name is Anna. However, I suspect I know who Marta is." Agnes's eyes glistened with tears as she fastened the last of the buttons at the back of my skirt. "She and my sister are friends. They met at the suffragette meetings a few weeks back. Both have been widowed since coming to America from Ireland, and they each have two wee ones to support."

"Oh, those poor dears."

Agnes touched my forearm. "Please don't tell anyone about Anna's involvement in the protest rally, especially the McCalls. I need this job, especially now with Anna in the hospital and Mama needing to stay home with the babies."

I smoothed the skirt over my hips and checked my stocking

seams in the mirror. "I'm sure Mrs. McCall would understand."

Fear flooded Agnes's face. "I can't take the chance, Miss. Some employers have let their girls go once it was discovered they were involved with the women's movement."

"But Mrs. McCall might be able to help you."

"No, I dare not risk it. Please . . ."

I shrugged. "All right, but I don't think you need to worry about Julia's loyalties, especially after yesterday." I stood before the mirror above the solid oak dresser. "Can you do anything with my hair? I'm afraid I can't lift my arms high enough to take control of this mess."

"I'm sure I can help, but, begging your pardon, you'll need to sit down for me to reach you." She pulled a straight-back chair from across the room. Agnes took the brush from my hand as I sat down on the chair's tapestry-covered seat. She drew the brush partway down the back of my hair. She hit a snarl. I winced. "What would you like me to do with your hair this morning?"

"Ouch! I feel like chopping it all off!"

"Oh no, Miss. That would be a shame. Why, you have such thick, lovely hair. Your crowning glory, as my father used to call a woman's hair."

"I suppose, if you like a washed-out reddish blond dishmop. Now, my sister and my father have beautiful hair. Coppery red. In the sunlight, their hair looks aflame with color."

"But yours, Miss Dorothy, is the shade of a field of ripening rye."

I smiled at her analogy. Since I'd never seen a field of ripening rye, I let it go. "Keep it simple. Pull it back into a wad at the nape of my neck and pin it securely in place."

"Would you like a few wispy curls loosened around your face?"

"No, please. That will happen naturally within a very short time." I glanced at the maid's soft brown hair, every strand neatly in place. "You are so lucky to have such straight hair."

The woman laughed. "I guess one always wants what one doesn't have. As a child, I used to wish I had curls like yours."

We both laughed. "You know, I've been thinking. I may be able to help your sister out a little until she can go back to work."

"Oh, Miss, I couldn't allow that."

"No, it would help me too. I write news stories. If I could interview your sister, Anna, and some of her friends, I could sell the articles to a New York paper."

"I-I-I don't know . . ."

"The editor pays well. He's never turned down anything I've sent to him. It would help us both."

Agnes frowned as she stuck the hairpins into the massive wad of hair at the nape of my neck. "I'll talk to my sister and see what she says about it."

"Good! That's terrific. I'll get the lead article written and off to him today with a proposal for follow-up pieces."

"I guess it would be all right." Agnes gathered up my cast-off chemise and draped it over her arm. "I'll take this down to the washroom. The cook said to tell you that your breakfast is ready in the solarium whenever you are."

The article flowed. My firsthand account of being trapped in the angry mob came alive beneath my pen. Later that afternoon, Julia enthusiastically agreed to be the subject of one of the follow-up pieces. She also promised me an interview with Judge Meyers and his wife. "He owes me that much!" she declared, lightly touching the edge of her blackened eye. "For all the indignities I endured."

I struggled to contain my smile.

"How about interviewing your young man?"

"My young man?" I looked startled.

"Yes, Mr. Bowles. You, too, looked like you were getting along charmingly." She smiled then winked.

"Um, Mr. Bowles and I did well under the circumstances."

She rang for the butler. "Of course you did. I didn't expect otherwise. Lawrence, please bring me my notepaper and pen. I must invite the Meyerses for dinner next Tuesday."

The man bowed slightly and left the room. "I presume you will also want to interview Agnes's sister and some of her friends as well? And would it help if I invited Crystal Eastmen? She was the tall woman at the rally, the one wearing the orange plumed hat."

"You know her?"

"Of course. We did time together, remember?" An impudent whisper of a smile lifted the corners of Julia's mouth. "Crystal is a member of the National American Woman Suffrage Association as well as the Women's Christian Temperance Union. She'll have stories enough to curl your hair, er . . ." She glanced at the flyaway curls framing my face. "You know what I mean."

Except for attending my classes at the college, I spent the next few days gathering information for my articles. An affirmative reply came from Mr. Collingsworth, the editor of the *Tribune,* by the middle of the next week, along with payment for the first piece. Excited, I ran to find Agnes.

"Look! Look! For your sister. Isn't it fabulous?" I waved the money before her eyes.

"I can't let you give her that much money, Miss Dorothy."

I stared in surprise. "But that was our agreement."

"Yes, but I had no idea it would be that much money."

No matter how much I argued, Agnes held firm. Finally, we agreed to split the proceeds fifty-fifty. For the next several days, payments arrived for the articles until all twelve pieces had been printed. With the last payment, a letter arrived that surprised even me.

Dear Mr. D. M. Spencer:

Your series of articles on the women's movement in Boston was brilliant. My readers appreciated the way you captured the emotions of the individuals involved without becoming maudlin or judgmental—a sign of a good reporter.

Should you ever be interested in moving to New York City, please look me up. I'm losing all my best reporters to the Paris front. I may have a job for you, if you can prove to me that you will never be drafted into this abominable war!
Sincerely,
Matthew B. Collingsworth Jr.

I chuckled to myself at the last sentence. *Yes,* I thought, *I can prove to you that I won't be drafted, but not in the way you imagine.* I giggled out loud. When Bud Ames, my editor-in-chief in Shinglehouse, submitted my material using only my initials with my last name, D. M. sounded more professional than "Dolly Mae." *Oh, well,* I thought, *it's not as if I'm trying to deceive the man. My writing is my own whether I wear a corset or not. And whether Mr. Collingsworth knows me as Dorothy or Dolly or D. M. Spencer doesn't affect the quality of my writing or its content.*

To be certain I wasn't doing anything illegal, I showed the letter to James E. that evening after dinner. He read it and laughed. "My, my, wouldn't he be surprised."

"Are you sure I'm not breaking some law somewhere?" I bit my lower lip. "Should I offer to give the money back?"

"Heavens, no! You've done nothing wrong. You have the right to call yourself whatever you like. If you wish, you could say your name is John D. Rockefeller. Of course, that moniker might be more of a problem than it's worth."

Julia sat across the parlor in a large dark blue upholstered winged-back chair, her feet resting on a needlepoint-covered mahogany ladies footstool. She agreed with her husband. "I think it's simply marvelous that you're proving yourself in the man's world of journalism. If this Collingsworth made a false assumption regarding your gender, all the better."

"I just want to be certain that I won't be in trouble when the man discovers his error."

"Oh, pooh! I hope I'm present when he does." Julia sniffed and tilted her nose upward. "The more I learn about the conditions under which so many women exist, the more certain I am that these gender walls must come down. And the only way that can happen is for women to get the right to vote."

James E. cast a sidelong glance at his wife then handed the letter back to me. "I wouldn't worry about the legality of this situation. You're not breaking the law. But then, if you're really concerned, why not ask Franklin Bowles. He could set your mind at ease."

Julia brightened at the mention of the young prosecuting attorney. I blushed. "I'll trust your judgment, Mr. McCall."

I hadn't seen Franklin Bowles since the evening in the park. I did, however, receive a note from him the day after the riot inquiring of my condition, and I replied immediately assuring him that, except for a few bruises, I was perfectly fine.

A few weeks later, when Julia asked him to another of her dinner parties, his R.S.V.P. read, "I'll have to decline. Please forgive me. My court appointments are running heavily throughout the next few weeks. I hope you'll invite me again come October."

With my college classes starting, I placed Franklin on a back shelf of my mind. I threw myself into my education. My younger classmates seemed frivolous and empty-headed, and at times I felt decades older than they. But try as I might, I couldn't get excited about studying ancient history, Philosophy of the Ages, and calculus.

I did appreciate my classical literature class, probably because the teacher, Miss Chase, took a personal interest in me when she discovered I'd been published. She introduced me to individuals living in the area who had known several of America's great writers, writers like Louisa Mae Alcott, James Russell Lowell, and Walt Whitman.

As a result, I wrote a series of articles on the personal anecdotes these people shared with me. I sold the pieces to Matthew Collingsworth. And again in the return letter, Mr. Collingsworth assured me that I'd have a job if I ever moved to New York City.

With many of my classes not being what I'd expected, I thought a lot about taking the editor up on his offer. When I talked with Chloe Mae about my quandary, she assured me that I should do what I thought best. And should I decide to return to college, she and Cy would honor their financial commitment.

The McCalls' lives changed due to the war. Julia held and attended fewer dinner parties. She and James E. went less often to the opera and the ballet. Due to the riot in the park, Judge Meyers's sensibilities for women's issues had been aroused. His support did wonders for boosting both attendance and morale of the members of the local suffragette's chapter.

As the reports of the war trickled across the Atlantic, the women's movement took on a new direction. Along with listening to speakers decrying the unfair laws to women and the problem of alcohol abuse in America, we cut and rolled bandages for the "boys at the front." Mothers, daughters, sisters, cousins, sweethearts, we each had loved ones who had enlisted into what the newspapers were calling "the Great War." I felt useless. I should be doing something more than rolling strips of cotton from bed sheets.

I thought of Chloe Mae's concern for the safety of her stepson, Jamie. I wondered where Bud Ames might be, and, of course, where was George—dear, sweet George? Had he proved himself to be the hero he'd always dreamed of becoming? I tried to picture those I knew and loved, crawling in the mud at the bottom of a foxhole or shivering in the chill of a European rainstorm.

Life went on. The leaves changed from green to gold and crimson then fell from the trees. Franklin visited the McCalls' home, at least once a week, supposedly to talk with James E. After a short time conversing with the McCalls, he often suggested he and I take a short walk through the park. On these occasions, we talked about our families. He talked about his court cases, and I talked about my classes. I looked forward to his weekly visits. Being so far from my friends and family in Pennsylvania, it was nice finding a new friend.

One Sunday afternoon, I shared with him my concerns about staying in school. I'd been doing a lot of thinking about whether or not to stay in college. With the war, it felt as if everyone else was doing their part for the boys overseas. All I was doing was studying about sirens' songs and Oedipus and his personality problems.

I let Franklin read the letters from Matthew Collingsworth Jr. When he finished, I admitted, "Sometimes going to New York and working for a big city paper tempts me."

He looked at me in disbelief. "You don't think this big city editor would actually hire a woman on his reporting staff, do you?"

I bristled. "My gender doesn't have anything to do with my ability to write."

"Marching for the right to vote is one thing, but women in the workplace? That would be a little awkward, don't you think?"

I clicked my tongue in irritation. "No, why should it?"

"Well . . ." Franklin paused a moment, and by the scowl on his face, I knew he was weighing his words carefully. "Men working together have a tendency to use strong language, stronger than ladies' sensibilities are accustomed to . . ."

"Are you saying that cursing goes with hard work? That one must swear to get the job done?" I fought to control my tone-of-voice. "I used to work in the hay field, baling hay, beside my brother Ori. I could match him bale for bale, but I don't ever remember feeling the need to curse or to swear while doing it." I pursed my lips and tilted my chin. "As a matter-of-fact, I don't think he did, either, at least he had enough self-control to abstain from cussing in front of his sister."

Franklin tugged uncomfortably at his shirt collar. "Look, I don't make society's rules, I just identify them."

"Well, some rules should be changed. Last week Judge Meyers spoke to the women's meeting regarding the artificial barriers men have created to keep women from gaining equality. He intends to change things, beginning with passing laws on prohibition."

"What does drinking alcohol have to do with women's rights in society?"

I planted my hands squarely on my hips and turned to him. "I'm surprised you should ask. If husbands didn't spend their paychecks on alcohol at the local bar, they'd be able to better provide for their family. The law says a wife and children are possessions of the man, to treat as he'd like. That's one law women would change if they gained the right to vote. Of course, New York State has already done so." I warmed up to my subject. "As well as the right for a woman to own property. And don't forget, in some states, we can't even check into an inn without written permission from either our father or our husbands. Grown women being treated like children!"

"OK, I've heard all the arguments before."

"Don't you think it unseemly that a wife's adultery can mitigate her murder, while a man's adultery is expected and tolerated?"

"Miss Dorothy, you shock my sensibilities!" Franklin teased. "You should know by now that I am in favor of women having the right to vote. What's right for the goose should also be right for the gander, so to speak." He paused a moment then added, "And I do know Judge Meyer's position on the proposed Volstead Act. There's some big money backing prohibition. The bill to change the amendment will probably pass."

"Really? I didn't think the bill actually stood a chance."

"I predict that we're in for several revolutionary changes in American society, some of which will affect both women and men for generations to come."

Like a light suddenly shining in a dark attic, ideas for potential articles burst inside my brain. "May I quote you?"

He looked at me in surprise then grinned. "Always the reporter, aren't you? That's one of the things I love about you. Sure, quote me whenever you like."

I shrugged and gave him a coy smile.

We kept our relationship friendly but cool. Whenever the subject came up, I encouraged him to see others socially. As a result, I noticed his name mentioned in the local paper, attending one charity function or another with different Back Bay beauties on his arm. I told myself that it didn't bother me, but it did, a little.

When Julia planned a special party for her visiting granddaughter, Ashley, and for Chloe's daughter, CeeCee, she invited Franklin to attend, along with several other young male friends of the girls. With so many eligible men overseas, her list was much shorter than it usually was at the height of the social season.

I felt so old whenever I was around Ashley and CeeCee, although there was only a three-year difference in our ages. And while the girls were polite and considerate, I knew they felt the same way. I was their aunt, not their peer.

The day before the party, Chloe Mae picked me up after my classes and took me shopping for a new dress. I protested, but my words fell on deaf ears. "You and Cy have done more than enough for me. You don't need to buy my clothes as well."

"Nonsense. You grew up 3,000 miles from me. I missed the fun of doing the 'sister' thing. Let me enjoy myself now, all right?"

"But shouldn't you be doing this with CeeCee?"

Chloe laughed. "Seventeen-year-old daughters scorn clothes-shopping with their mothers. Too old-fashioned, so it seems."

I laughed. I couldn't believe it. In my eyes, Chloe was the most glamorous female I'd ever known. As a small child, I would dress in my mother's best church dress and play "California." I'd pretend to be Chloe Mae.

We hopped from store to store in the better shopping sections of Boston. But whatever outfits I tried on either clashed with my hair, looked old-maidish, or made me look like an overgrown schoolgirl. I was ready to quit.

"No, no. One more shop, then we'll stop for a spot of tea and some cookies. But we won't quit."

I groaned at the thought of trying on dresses right up to the hour Julia's first guest would arrive. But when Chloe Mae found a dress that floated from my shoulders into layers of wispy light blue and lavender chiffon, I no longer wanted to protest. The bottom layer, a slip, really, was made of the softest, smoothest silk I'd ever touched. I swung around in front of a three-way mirror. The uneven hems of the layers swished about my ankles.

"Straighten your shoulders, honey. Walk tall and proud."

Chloe Mae turned to the saleswoman. "My sister will need a pair of white silk hose and a pair of white kidskin pumps as well. What size, sweetie?"

Walk tall? That was the last thing I wanted to do. I studied my reflection in the mirror for a moment. I loved it. I almost looked pretty.

Behind me, I heard my sister say "No, No!" to the clerk. "She needs a pair with a heel on it. Something very French."

"Not heels!" I argued. "I'm already taller than Mr. Bowles. With heels, I'll tower over him."

"So?" She turned to the clerk. "Enjoy your height, my dear. Consider it an asset, not a flaw."

"*Hmmph!* I might forget if the male species could."

She looked at me in surprise. "Certainly you don't believe the measure of a man is his height, do you?"

"Well, no . . ."

"Then why should you belittle Mr. Bowles by thinking he evaluates your worth by your height?"

I sighed. I didn't have an answer. I eyed myself in the mirror one more time before agreeing to try on the two-inch heel on the kidskin slippers.

I slipped my foot into the shoe. *So soft,* I thought. I grimaced at the sight of my gray cotton stockings next to the delicate shoe on my foot. A pair of white silk hosiery would complete the ensemble, even if my ankles were all that anyone could see. I closed my eyes and tried not to imagine the cost of this extravagance.

Chloe Mae instructed the clerk to package the outfit. "We'll take it with us." That evening while CeeCee and Ashley dressed for the party in the guestroom where they were staying, Chloe Mae and I played sisters in my room. For me, the party had already begun. It was all that I dreamed.

"You and Hattie must have had such fun together," I commented as Chloe Mae piled my curls on the top of my head and pinned them into place.

"We did. But remember, parties in Shinglehouse were few and far between. Mostly we dressed up only to go to church each week and to grange meetings."

"What fun! Though Hattie can be a stick-in-the-mud sometimes . . ."

"My dear sister, Hattie, had good reason to be more sober than some young people. Her bad leg bothered her more than she admitted. And yes, she was more serious-minded perhaps than I was. I guess it's good she married a preacher."

I chuckled to myself. Henry was anything but serious, preacher or not. "He makes her laugh. When she gets too serious, he makes her laugh."

"I'm glad to hear that. Obviously, living in California I've not gotten acquainted with my brothers-in-law like I should."

"Hey, how could you? There are so many of them." We laughed together.

After spraying my neck and wrists with her favorite perfume and using rice paper on our cheeks, we were ready to descend to the parlor. As we passed the girls' room, Chloe Mae asked if they were ready to go down as well. "Oh no." Ashley's blond curls danced about her face. "Mama says it's important for a young lady to make an entrance, Aunt Chloe."

"Fine." Chloe kissed her daughter on the cheek. "We'll see you both down there in a few minutes then. I can hear the first of Grandma Julia's guests arriving."

Cy met his wife at the foot of the stairs. He planted a gentle kiss on her cheek and whispered in her ear. She smiled and blushed. James E. and Julia were greeting four young men who arrived together. She introduced me.

My stomach gave a flutter when Franklin Bowles arrived. I patted a few stray curls into place. After giving his hat to the butler, Franklin took my arm and escorted me toward the parlor. When I saw that my two-inch heels made me at least one inch taller than he, I slouched a trifle to hide the difference.

We hadn't stepped from the marble foyer onto the parlor's lush Persian carpet before CeeCee made her entrance at the top of the stairs. The spring green dimity dress she wore suited the delicate blush in her cheeks. I smiled to myself as the four young men circled around her before she reached the bottom step. *What a lovely princess,* I thought.

However, when Ashley paused at the top of the stairs, then gracefully floated down the staircase, all conversation stopped. Every male in the room held his breath; I was sure of it. I cast a glance toward Franklin. He, too, stared, agog at her beauty, along with the suddenly annoyed old me and the rosy-cheeked college boys.

As Julia proudly introduced her granddaughter, Ashley's giggle sounded like the proverbial tinkling crystal. Already, I could tell that by the end of the evening, the sound of her laughter would begin to annoy me. Lawrence's timely announcement that dinner was served ended Ashley's magical moment. One of the young men who didn't wait to be introduced to her commandeered her to the table.

Throughout the evening, Franklin couldn't keep his gaze off her. Neither could the other male guests, for that matter. At first I felt miffed. I couldn't believe that a professional man of his stature would act like the schoolboys acted over a simpering blonde. I must admit that he didn't trip over himself all evening trying to win her favor like three of the four young male guests did. My irritation turned to amusement as I watched the social interplay surrounding the blond beauty throughout the evening. I tried not to like her, but somehow I did anyway. I had the feeling CeeCee and one or two of the young married women present felt pretty much the same way.

After the last guest departed, James E. gathered the family into the parlor. "Cyrus has an announcement to make this evening before we head off to bed."

Cy took Chloe's hand and drew her close to his side. Their son, Rusty, edged next to his mother, and CeeCee slipped beneath her father's other arm. "I received a telegram I've been expecting for weeks now. It seems that I've been commissioned by the president to go to London to help with the war effort. Of course, my wife and my lovely children will be coming, as well. We'll be leaving immediately after Thanksgiving."

My heart sank. I was just getting used to having my big sister close by me, and I'd almost made up my mind to take the job Mr. Collingsworth offered. With Cy and Chloe Mae heading for England, moving to New York City was definitely out for me.

That night as I slipped into my dimity nightdress, I glanced at my Bible resentfully. I'd been praying for God to give me direction as to what I should do. *He certainly did that,* I thought. *But He didn't have to slam the door of opportunity on my fingers!*

The holidays passed. Our Thanksgiving was complete when Chloe received news that her stepson, Jamie, was safe and recovering in a French hospital. He'd been missing for several months.

A train ticket to Pennsylvania was my Christmas gift from Julia and James E. It was great seeing Pa again, as well as the rest of the family. Hattie opened her house to the family on Christmas Day. All but Chloe's family in England and Joe's family in California made it to Christmas dinner. The crowd was so big we had to set up a table in the parlor for all the children and grandchildren under twenty. Whew! I just made it to the adults' table.

The noise around the two tables was so loud that we didn't hear Mr. Winchell, Hattie's nearest neighbor, and the town's telegraph operator banging on our front door until he peered into one of the kitchen windows. As Hattie placed a bowl of mashed potatoes on the adult table, she looked up in time to see Mr. Winchell's face peering in at us. She dropped the bowl of potatoes onto the table and screamed a blood-curdling scream. The men around the table leapt to their feet while we women echoed Hattie's fright. Wailing children thundered into the kitchen, along with the family's barking dog, Sidewinder. As to where Muffin, the yellow-and-white tomcat disappeared to, no one knew or cared.

Hattie's husband, Stanford, opened the front door. Mr. Winchell burst inside. "A telegram from England," he shouted. "You have a telegram from England!"

Telegrams always seem to spell bad news. We all held our breath and glanced toward Papa. "Here, Ed," Pa said, extending his hand toward Mr. Winchell. "I'll take it."

No one spoke as Papa opened the yellow envelope and removed the matching sheet of paper. "Dear Family—stop Have a Merry Christmas—stop We miss you—stop Love, CeeCee, Rusty, Chloe, and Cy—stop.

Excited cheers erupted from the family. When the shouting

subsided, Stanford said, "Hattie, break out the apple cider, and give Ed a cup. This is cause for celebration!"

"Preacher, this wouldn't be the hard stuff, now, would it?" Ed asked.

Stanford threw back his head and laughed. The rest of the family laughed as well. "Why, Ed Wilson," Stanford said, "that you could suggest such a thing, and me, the president of the Shinglehouse Prohibition League!"

Hattie handed Mr. Winchell a cup of cider. "Shame on you teasing the preacher like that, Ed. And you a church deacon."

CHAPTER SIX

On the Move

During the last weeks of my freshman term of college, I changed my mind several times a day about spending the summer in New York City. Everyone I talked with had a different opinion. My college professor thought I was being foolish. James E. agreed. Julia was for it, however. So much, in fact, she talked her son, Ian, and daughter-in-law, Drucilla, into inviting me to stay with them throughout the summer months. Drucilla seemed pleasant enough, but her daughter, Ashley? An entire summer of Ashley? *I will make it work,* I thought, since the generous invitation did solve my housing problem.

When I wrote to Chloe Mae in Europe about my plans, she encouraged me to give it a try. Her letter included a letter of credit to meet any needs I might have during my stay. All I had to do was go to her bank, and I would be issued the amount I requested.

One after another, the obstacles fell, though the opposition came from many other directions. My father told me that I was chasing "fox fire," as he put it. "First college, now New York City? I should make you come home where you belong . . ." The thought that by law he could make me return to Shinglehouse unnerved me.

When I showed my father's letter to Franklin, we'd been tossing bread crumbs at the ducks in the Boston Commons' pond.

"Could he do that?" I asked.

"I suppose so," Franklin admitted.

I shuddered. "Can you imagine my father having that little faith in me? One minute the man is as progressive and insightful as the best of Harvard's thinkers; the next, he's absolutely antediluvian in his thinking."

Franklin took my hand and led me to a park bench. "Dorothy, I must confess that I, too, think you're making a terrible mistake. You're too . . ."

"How long have you felt this way?" I looked at him in surprise. Previously, he'd listened to my plans without comment. "I had no idea you felt so strongly. Is it that you think I'm not good enough to make it as a writer?"

He shook his head sadly and continued to hold my gloved hand. "You know better than that. You're an excellent writer. As I told you last winter, I don't think a young lady like yourself belongs in such an environment."

"What environment? The world? Should I stay in my parlor and tend to my knitting?"

"I didn't say that. But you are entirely too innocent and too lovely to come into contact with the seedier side of life."

My mouth dropped open, but no words sprang to mind.

"Perhaps I'm being selfish, but I wish you'd stay here in Boston. Perhaps I'm afraid that when you go to New York City, I'll lose you forever."

I continued to stare in surprise.

"I care for you, more than you might think. I haven't said anything because I've been trying to respect your wishes to keep our relationship as friends."

"Franklin, what are you saying?"

"I don't know for sure. But I do know that you are the most

attractive woman I've ever met."

I laughed aloud and tried to withdraw my hands from his. "Why, Mr. Bowles, you are making me blush."

"I'm serious, Miss Dorothy."

I sighed and shook my head. I knew plain when I saw it, and I was plain. "It's very nice of you to say so, but our friendship has always been based on truth. I think we should maintain that basis."

"I didn't say you were the most beautiful woman in the world. What I said was, you are the most attractive woman in the world to me. Your eyes sparkle with intelligence and compassion and wit." With his finger, he traced over the shell design in my white hand-crocheted wrist-length gloves. Then he lifted his head and unnerved me by gazing directly into my eyes. "I love the way the corners of your mouth turn up with humor. Your face reflects the honesty and beauty of your character, Miss Dorothy. And that's what true loveliness is all about."

"I-I-I," I stuttered, carefully slipped my hands from his grasp, and glanced away. *Oh no,* I thought, *I hope he's not doing what I think he's doing.* I'd never been in this position before. And I certainly wasn't ready for him to declare his love for me. Not that Mr. Franklin Bowles hadn't become one of my dearest friends. He had. But nothing more that that. I swallowed hard. "Mr. Bowles, I think . . ."

"Don't misunderstand me, Miss Dorothy. I realize that I am in no position to engage your affections seriously. Public servants are seldom wealthy. And, as you know, I come from humble roots. So, I am hardly prepared to . . ." He let out his breath slowly. "I'm really bungling this, aren't I?"

I didn't answer, for at the moment I found the stripe in my dimity dress extremely fascinating.

"Look, I guess I'm afraid for you, going to the big city and dealing with all kinds of lowlife."

"I won't be alone, you know. I've prayed this through, and I know God is in this plan. He's the one who's made all the pieces fit."

"Um, yeah, I guess."

"You don't believe me about God, do you?"

"I believe that you manipulate your God to fit your circumstances."

I shot a surprised look at Franklin. "Oh no, you have it backward, Mr. Bowles. Before I make one step any direction, I take my situation to God and wait for Him to show me which way to go. I know He'll be with me regardless—that's what He promises—but I've learned that I will be much happier if I wait for Him to direct me instead of plowing ahead on my own. Do you see?"

He shrugged. "Does it matter?"

"It matters more than you can know." I glanced away then back again. "Thank you for caring, Mr. Bowles. You are a dear, dear, friend."

He tossed a handful of bread crumbs at a gaggle of adventurous ducks but said nothing.

I tried to coax a smile out of him. "I'll be back in the fall."

His lips narrowed to a thin line. "Much can change in three months."

I tipped my head teasingly to one side. "You could visit New York, you know. Perhaps to investigate a case or something?"

"I could, maybe, if I knew that such a visit would be welcomed."

"Of course your visit would be welcomed." I was surprised to see a hint of uncertainty in his eyes. Franklin Bowles always seemed to be the most confident man I'd ever know, even more than Pa. "And we could write. The postal service makes regular deliveries both ways, so they say," I teased.

He took a deep breath then exhaled. "Yes, I suppose you're right."

"Of course I am." I dared to lift my hand and touch his drawn face. "Stop worrying. I'll be just fine."

He sighed again. "I certainly hope so."

A cool breeze disturbed the moist wisp of curls on each side of my face. If I inhaled deeply, I could almost detect the aroma of the open sea on this unseasonably hot June morning. I brushed the loose curls aside with my gloved hand and smoothed the starched collar of my cotton blouse. I stirred against the padded leather cushions of the hansom motor cab. I hated to think what the oppressive heat was doing to the back of my blue-and-white striped seersucker suit.

The vehicle stopped in front of the *Tribune* building. The cab driver opened the door and helped me out onto the sidewalk. As my gaze scaled the impressive gray stone building, one hand went to my throat. My other hand held my portfolio of all the articles I'd written and gotten published. The driver cleared his throat and held out his hand. After I handed him his fee, the driver climbed back into the cab and left me standing alone on the busy sidewalk.

People rushed past, intent on their destinations—most of them men. A woman, pushing a wicker baby carriage, smiled at me and continued on her way. Did she know how out of place I felt? I wondered. An older man and a woman who reminded me of Julia hurried by, worry lines mapped on their faces. A boy in short pants cycled up to the front door of the building, leaned his bicycle against the wall, climbed the steps to the building, and disappeared inside.

"You're finally here, Miss D. M. Spencer," I told myself. "You can't back out now. You have an appointment with Mr. Matthew Brewster Collingsworth Jr. in five minutes."

My stomach lurched as I stared at the imposing gargoyles above the building's massive oak doors. I was thankful that my gloves absorbed the sweat in my palms. "Oh, dear Lord, help me not to fall flat on my face, neither proverbially or in actuality."

I took a deep breath and straightened my shoulders. Patting the crown of my hat, I dragged a wisp of a curl from the side of my face and fastened it behind my ear then marched up the stairs.

As I reached for the brass door handle, a tall, well-dressed and clean-shaven gentleman in his midthirties climbed the stairs behind me. When he opened the door and held it for me, I thanked him. He smiled and tipped his bowler hat at me. That's when I

4—S.D.D.S.

noticed his height. I had to look up in order to meet his gaze. He towered over me by a good three inches, and I was wearing two-inch heels! My approval must have shown in my face, for his eyes sparkled down at me as if he knew a secret that he didn't intend to tell. In one hand he carried a leather briefcase and in the other a rosewood cane, its golden head shaped like a hawk.

The man hurried past me into the cool beige-and-white marble-encased lobby. I noticed that he walked with a slight limp. He tapped a button on the wall, and two brass doors slid open, and he stepped inside a metal cage. The doors closed behind him.

A wiry little man sitting at a large mahogany reception desk glanced up from a stack of papers lying before him on the desk-top. As the corners of his mouth broke into a smile, his mustache ascended to his sallow cheeks. His eyebrows arched above his thick, wire-framed glasses. I had the feeling he was unaccustomed to welcoming females to the establishment, but then, maybe I was being overly sensitive.

"May I help you, madam?"

I smiled and tilted my chin defiantly upward. "Yes, please, I have a two o'clock appointment with Mr. Collingsworth?"

"Which Mr. Collingsworth? Mr. Matthew or his brother, Mr. Giles?"

"Mr. Matthew."

The man pointed toward the elevator. "Third floor, to your left as you exit the elevator."

I looked at the imposing brass doors and gulped. I'd never before ridden in an elevator, and I wasn't sure I was ready to start today. Instantly I had visions of the iron-barred cage plummeting into the basement the moment the doors closed behind me. "Sir?" I asked. "Do you have stairs?"

He eyed me over the rim of his glasses. "Of course, Madam, but it's quite a climb."

"I don't mind."

"You'll find the stairs down the hall and through a door to your left. Mr. Matthew Collingsworth's office will be straight ahead as you exit the stairwell. Mr. Giles's office is to your right."

"Thank you so much. You've been most helpful." Remembering Chloe Mae's advice to stand tall, I straightened my shoulders and lifted my chin. My heels clicked on the marble floor and echoed off the marble pillars as I walked down the hall to the stairwell. I didn't need to steal a glance over my shoulder to know that the little man behind the desk was watching every step I took. "Dear Lord, don't let me turn my ankle or stumble and make a fool of myself."

I successfully traversed the foyer, entered the stairwell, and started up the stairs. Sunlight shined in through the leaded windows, causing the stairwell to heat up like a silo. I paused at the second landing and seriously considered taking the elevator to the third floor. Tiny beads of sweat popped out around my hairline and on my neck. "I'm going to arrive at Mr. Collingsworth's office smelling like a barnyard in August." I removed a linen handkerchief from my small white leather purse and dabbed at my face and neck.

Resolute, I climbed the second flight of stairs to the third floor. Before opening the stairwell door, I opened a tiny vial of lavender scented perfume I carried in my purse and dabbed it on my neck and wrists. I tucked loose curls around the edges of my white linen hat then inhaled deeply. *What if Mr. Collingsworth throws me out of his office, or worse yet, laughs in my face? What if he demands that I give back all the monies he's paid me for my articles, or what if he has me arrested for fraud or something?*

From somewhere beneath me, I heard the reassuring rumble of the presses cranking out the next day's edition of the paper. I could smell the familiar smell of newspaper ink. I hadn't realized how much I'd missed it over the last year.

"Don't be silly! He won't have you arrested." My voice rang off the walls of the empty stairwell. I glanced at the watch dangling from the brooch on the neck of my blouse. 1:57 p.m. "You can't back out. If you do, you'll always wonder what might have happened if you'd had more courage."

I closed my eyes and tried to calm my breathing. "Though I walk through the valley of the shadow of death . . . Dorothy Spencer, you are being ridiculous. Pull yourself together."

I reached for the stairwell door only to have it shoved toward me. A man in his forties, with ink-stained hands and a green visor on his forehead and clutching a fistful of papers, rushed past me with barely a nod and hurried down the stairs. *Yes*, I thought, *I miss the bustle of the newspaper office.* I straightened my back and opened the door.

Beside the door in the small lobby, a brass pedestal ashtray and a matching spittoon greeted me, along with a massive oak desk. The desk was piled high with newspapers, file folders, and yellow papers. The door behind the desk stood open. The sign on the door read, "Matthew B. Collingsworth Jr. Editor-in-chief."

I peered in and knocked on the open door at the same time. Books lined three of the walls of the office. The fourth contained a double window edged with maroon velvet draperies. Two men, one with graying hair and a bushy white mustache and the other, the man who opened the door for me earlier, leaned over a cluttered mahogany desk. With his hat removed, his sandy brown hair had been greased back to control the curls.

"What?" The younger man growled. "What is it now?" He glanced over his shoulder and quickly straightened. The older man did the same. By the look on their faces, I was an unwanted interruption. "Miss, are you looking for someone?" the younger man asked as he strode toward me.

"Yes, in fact, I am." I glanced around the younger man toward the gentleman I assumed to be Mr. Collingsworth." I am D. M. Spencer, and I have an appointment to see Mr. Matthew Collingsworth at 2:00 p.m., I believe?" They stared at me in disbelief. By the question in my voice, even I wasn't sure I had the time of the appointment right.

"D. M. Spencer?" the gentleman I supposed to be Mr. Collingsworth asked. "D. M. Spencer? The reporter from Boston?"

"Yes, sir. My name is Dorothy Mae Spencer. I go by D. M. Spencer professionally." I smiled at the two men, their faces frozen with consternation. "I brought the portfolio of articles I've written as you requested."

The two men looked down at the leather portfolio in my hand as if it were a poison adder then back at my face.

"Bu-bu-bu-but—" the younger man sputtered.

"Miss Spencer, there's been some sort of mistake here. We were not expecting you to be a-a-a female."

I laughed out loud. "Neither was my father before I was born. He swore I would be a boy."

"Bu-bu-bu-but—" The younger man again tried to speak. He wore the expression of a thieving raccoon staring down the barrel of pa's shotgun.

I directed my comments toward the older man. "Sir, I assure you that I meet all the requirements necessary to do the job. And," I added with a twinkle in my eye, "you won't need to worry about my quitting to join the army, unless women are enlisting this year, that is."

The men looked at each other then back at me. The older man crossed the green Persian carpet and extended his hand as if to guide me to the door. "Look, Miss Spencer. Obviously we here at the *Tribune* appreciate your writing. You are a truly talented young lady. But, I'm sure you can understand why we could not hire you on at the paper."

Standing inches from the man, I stared him down. "No, I can't. My writing style is neither masculine nor feminine. It is simply good journalism. And as you said, you have a need for good journalists, with so many of your male employees leaving for the Paris front. Those were your words."

The older man turned around to face the other. "Is that what you told her, Matthew?"

Now it was my turn to be surprised. I looked from one gentleman to the other. "Now that you know who I am, would you be so kind as to tell me who you both are?"

The younger man snapped awake as if he'd been caught cat-napping. "Sorry, where are our manners." He stepped closer to me. "I am Matthew Collingsworth, and this is my half brother, Giles Collingsworth. Giles is the head of editorial. Please, won't you be seated?"

I nodded and seated myself in one of the two leather and mahogany winged-back chairs in front of the desk. "A pleasure, gentlemen." Giles took the other chair beside me, while Matthew rounded the desk and sat in the leather padded desk chair.

"Well"—Matthew Collingsworth straightened a stack of papers on his desk—"It looks like we have a little misunderstanding."

I smiled determinedly. "Misunderstanding? I can't see any misunderstanding. You've been publishing my work for several years now."

"Bud never told me you were a woman!" Matthew growled.

I turned to Matthew's brother. "Mr. Collingsworth, from your editorials you strike me as being a liberal, progressive thinker. Nary an issue goes by but that you report on the progress of the women's movement. For some time now I've admired your intellectually persuasive way with words." I deliberately tipped my head in deference to the older man. "Ask your brother, if a woman can do the job, shouldn't she be allowed to do it? And I've proven I can do the job."

Giles Collingsworth sputtered a series of buts and looked pleadingly at Matthew.

"When I went to work for the *Shinglehouse Sentinal*, Mr. Ames didn't believe I could do the work either, so he hired me on a trial basis. Perhaps such an arrangement would work in our situation."

Matthew shot an indignant glare at his brother then forced a smile. "Our situation? We have no situation. Manhattan is hardly Shinglehouse, Pennsylvania, Miss Spencer."

"Miss Spencer," Giles said, adopting the condescending tone I so much hated hearing from older adults, "I am sure you have the ability to do the job, as you put it, but frankly, I'm worried about the reaction of the news staff having a woman working alongside them."

I'd heard all the arguments before, and I could see that my hopes were quickly dissipating before these two antediluvian thinkers. So, I decided to throw caution aside.

"Why, Mr. Collingsworth"—I tipped my head to one side and batted my eyelashes innocently—" Do you mean to tell me that the cleaning done in the building is performed by men?"

I continued to stare at Giles while he bent to adjust one of his patent leather spats. Out of the corner of my eye, I saw a smirk teasing the corners of Matthew's lips.

"Um, er, no." Giles's face reddened. "We do hire cleaning persons, which do happen to be female."

I pursed my lips. I felt like a spider capturing a hapless fly. And it had been so easy. "Oh, I see. Your male employees don't mind having ladies around to empty their trash or sweep up after them, but they might strongly object to having a woman perform a similar job as theirs? Is that it?"

"That's not what I meant!" The man glared at me then at his brother. "Say something! You're the editor-in-chief. Tell her we can't hire her, no matter how well she writes!"

The sound of Matthew's laughter started in his shoulders and belly then reached his mouth. He threw back his head and laughed until his whole body shook. Wiping a tear from his eye, he rose to his feet and walked to the window behind his desk where he continued laughing.

This infuriated Giles. He leapt to his feet. "Stop laughing, you hyena. I don't see anything funny here."

Matthew turned around. "You, Giles, are what's funny. I've never seen anyone best you in an argument." He withdrew a handkerchief from his pocket and blew his nose. "She's got 'ya. If we don't hire Miss Spencer, she can prove you to be a hypocrite to all your readers. All she'll have to do is tell her story to our competitor."

"What?" Giles glared down at me. "You wouldn't."

I gazed up at him with my innocent, wide-eyed look.

"You would! This is extortion! Blackmail! I won't stand for it."

"Hold on," Matthew interrupted. "I don't think Miss Spencer intends to do any such thing. I just think she's right to hold us to our principles."

"But she's a woman. She can't work in the newsroom. You know—"

Matthew blew his breath through his teeth. "Unfortunately, you're right. Maybe someday women will be accepted in the news-room. Until then, I have an alternative, which will do the *Tribune* a great service."

My eyes widened expectantly. "Do you mean I have a job?"

"Wait a minute. Wait until you hear the conditions." Matthew paced across the room to the left then back again before speaking. "No one but us in this office knows that D. M. Spencer is a woman, right? What if we hired Miss Spencer as a reporter-at-large? Now, hear me out, Giles." He paused a moment to think then continued. "She would report directly to me. We would keep her identity a secret. This would allow her to go where the press would not be welcomed. By your articles, you've proven you have access to and are comfortable with a variety of social classes. I think it would work, Giles."

"You're out of your mind!" Giles stared in horror. "When father hears about this, he'll have another stroke."

Matthew winced. "Miss Spencer, our father, Matthew Collingsworth, the first, owns the *Tribune*. While he's recuperating from a stroke at his place in the Hamptons, my stepbrother, Giles, and I are running the operation."

"I'll tell you, he won't like it." Giles reiterated.

"Then keep quiet about this. He never needs to know. We're not breaking any laws nor are we running a financial risk. So why would he complain?"

Giles closed his eyes and wagged his head back and forth. "I want to go on record as being against this hare-brained idea."

Matthew strode around the corner of the desk. "Giles, you

can go on record for anything you like as long as you vow to keep D. M. Spencer's identity a secret."

"Fine! As long as you know I'm against it, I'll keep quiet." Giles walked to the door and opened it. "And now, I don't want to know anything more. I'll be in my office if you need me."

"Sounds fine to me." Matthew rounded the desk and sat in the chair his brother vacated.

I set my jaw and tilted my chin upward. "Mr. Collingsworth, you need to know that if asked, I won't lie."

The editor-in-chief shook his head. "I would never ask you to lie. A reporter's honesty is his, er, excuse me—this is going to take some getting used to—or her greatest weapon."

"I'm glad you understand that."

"To begin, I want you to get acquainted with New York City. Maybe do a series on the immigrant population's response to the war. Or their adjustments to America. Or whatever strikes your fancy." He pursed his lips and pressed his fingers together spirelike. "I know I can trust your judgment in this area, having read your earlier pieces."

We talked about what would be required of me and about my salary. "You choose our weekly meeting time and place. Don't contact me otherwise unless there is some emergency. You will exchange your story for your weekly pay at the determined location. Send me a note once you establish a safe meeting place."

I bit my lower lip and frowned. "Sir, the only flaw I see in the plan is, there are only so many places a young single woman can be seen without causing a scandal, which would reflect on both of us and the paper as well."

"We'll work out the logistics. I want you to report on everything from child labor practices to women's issues to prohibition and attitudes about the war. Anything newsworthy. But be careful to preserve your identity. There are some nasty scoundrels out there. Your anonymity will be your best defense."

I didn't speak for several seconds.

"Perhaps I misread you, Miss Spencer. Perhaps your talents

would be better utilized reporting for the society page or "Hazel's Household Hints."

I bristled. "No! You know and I know that I can do this job."

A smile eased across his face then dissolved into a scowl. "Good. If a situation becomes dangerous, leave. No story is worth risking yourself for. And when at all possible, take someone with you."

I nodded in agreement. At that point I would have agreed to swing from a circus trapeze from one of the towers supporting the Brooklyn bridge if he'd asked. I had a job as a writer on the *Tribune*. It didn't matter to me that no one could know it was me. I knew, and that's what counted.

"We'll give our arrangement a three-month trial," he continued. "June through August. On September five, we'll meet to reevaluate the situation to be certain it's working for both of us. That should work out well for you, since you mentioned that you may want to return to college in the fall."

I shrugged. College seemed thousands of miles away at that moment.

"Do we have a deal?" His gray-green eyes bore into mine.

"We have a deal."

He extended his hand to me. I took it. We shook hands awkwardly. Neither of us were familiar with taking the hand of the opposite sex. He rose and helped me to my feet as well. "You're quite a woman, Miss Spencer." A quirky grin tugged at the corners of his lips. "When you came in here and identified yourself as D. M. Spencer, I had no intention of hiring you. And now, I've not only hired you, but I've done it flying in the face of tradition, my brother, and frankly, my better judgment." He shook his head. "How did you do it?"

I looked up into his face with guileless gratitude. "Thank you. Thank you, Mr. Collingsworth. You won't be sorry."

He bowed and touched my gloved fingers to his lips. "I hope not, Miss Spencer. I truly hope not."

I danced out of the *Tribune* building into the bright sunlight. What an opportunity! Finally I was doing what I loved doing and getting paid for it. And all with a dash of adventure. When my feet touched the sidewalk, I twirled in a circle then waved my arm signaling for a nearby taxicab.

I could hardly wait to tell my father and Franklin and Mrs. McCall—"Oops!" My hand flew to my mouth. No one must know the true nature of the job, I reminded myself. No one except Papa, Chloe Mae, and maybe Franklin. Everyone else—what will I tell everyone else?

CHAPTER SEVEN

A Secret and a Mysterious Boy

All the way home from the *Tribune* office I wondered what I would tell my host and hostess regarding my employment situation. Obviously, I couldn't remain in New York City for the summer without purpose. Ian and Drucilla McCall were kind enough to open their home to me, and I couldn't deceive them.

Automobiles jockeyed for position among horse-drawn carriages, delivery wagons, and pedestrians as the cab in which I rode inched its way up Fifth Avenue. I rested my head against the black leather seat and closed my eyes. "Lord, I need Your wisdom here. What I do must be done first and foremost for You. But I do not accept the philosophy that the ends justify the means—I cannot lie even to preserve my identity."

I jerked alert at the sound of a police whistle outside the vehicle. When I assured myself that all was well, I resumed my prayer. "Father, You told Your children to be 'as wise as serpents and harmless as doves.' And You also promised to give us wisdom when we ask for it. Well, Father, I'm asking; no, I'm begging. I don't know what to do."

The cab driver eased his vehicle to a stop in front of the McCall's gray stone townhouse that overlooked the south end of Central Park. "We're here, Miss. Miss?" the cab driver said in a lilting Irish-American burr.

I opened my eyes. My head snapped forward. "Oh, so we are." I was no closer to a solution than I'd been five blocks ago. As I rummaged through my purse for change with which to pay the driver, I whispered, "In Your time, Lord. In Your time."

The driver helped me from the cab and thanked me for the tip I gave him. He waited as I ran up the front steps and rang the doorbell.

Sarah, the family's parlor maid, answered the door. "Welcome home, Miss. Sir and Madam are not at home at present. They said to tell you they will see you at dinner, which will be at seven." The maid closed the door behind me. "Madam also said to tell you that the cook will prepare a light repast should you be hungry before then."

"Where's Rolf?" I'd expected to see the rotund form of the family butler greet me at the door."

"He's running errands for Madam."

I glanced toward the white marble staircase that led to the sleeping quarters on the second floor. Two black wrought iron filigree banisters edged the broad white staircase that narrowed to a small landing then divided into two staircases the rest of the way. "And Miss Ashley?"

"Miss Ashley is spending the evening with friends."

"Thank you, Sarah. I would enjoy a sandwich and a lemonade if that is convenient."

The middle-age woman smiled graciously. "Will you dine in the solarium or in your room?"

"The solarium will be fine. Let me take my briefcase up to my room, slip into something a bit more comfortable, and then I'll be right back."

"Very well, Miss." The maid tipped her head in respect.

I dashed up the staircase to the guestroom where I was

staying and kicked off my pointed-toe pumps as quickly as possible. *Pointed toes might be in vogue this year, but my feet don't know it,* I thought, as I paused to rub the circulation back into my feet.

Casting my linen dress, soiled gloves, and cloche hat onto the bed, I paused to appreciate the soft welcoming ambiance of the room. Pale pink brocade satin covered the walls. Matching draperies edged the two floor-to-ceiling windows. A swag valance of the same fabric topped the multipaned window. White silk sheers had been drawn back in Prisscilla fashion to allow the sunlight access to the room.

Two small bedside tables and a marble-topped credenza matched the wood-inlay design of the richly embossed mahogany bedstead. A white marble fireplace with plaster wedding-cake swirls filled the wall opposite the bedstead. A bust of Julius Caesar accented the marble mantle.

I especially like the beige brocade, satin-upholstered settee and two matching side chairs that warmed the cold feeling of the fireplace's marble façade. A large bouquet of fragrant pink roses filled the center of a massive marble-topped, gold-embossed, heavy Baroque sofa table in front of the fireplace. A couple of leather tomes on Greek philosophy and architecture sat at one end of the table.

I opened the massive, hand-carved mahogany armoire and chose a lavender-and-white cotton plissé tubular dress Chloe had insisted on buying for me before she left for Europe. I slipped the garment over my head and secured the drop waist white patent leather belt at my hips.

I sat down at the mahogany ladies' secretary where I'd dropped my portfolio upon entering the room and released an exhausted sigh. Subterfuge was so exhausting. And I still had no answers regarding what I would tell my host and hostess.

I took out a couple of sheets of linen rag stationery. It was time I wrote to Chloe Mae. If nothing else, putting my thoughts on paper might clarify them for me.

Dearest Chloe Mae and Cyrus,

Here I am, settled in Drucilla's guestroom for the summer. I met the indomitable Mr. Collingsworth II, actually two of the three Collingsworths. Mr. Collingsworth senior is recuperating from a stroke. He and his wife live at the family's summer cottage on Long Island. Matthew Collingsworth is an interesting gentleman, but Giles, the older stepbrother, despite his liberal "pen," seems like a stuffed shirt. As to Matthew, time will tell. I have a job, and I don't have a job . . .

I laid my fountain pen aside at a knock on my door. "Miss Dorothy?" Maria, the upstairs maid called. "I brought your lunch upstairs for you."

"Oh!" I'd forgotten about the food I'd requested. I rushed to the door and opened it. The olive-complexioned maid, barely sixteen-years-old, balanced a silver tray in her hands.

"Where would you have me place this?" she asked. "At the desks or on the sofa table?" I considered how clumsy I knew I could be and opted for the marble-topped table.

My eyes lighted up at the beautiful array of food before me. "This was so nice of you, Maria. You didn't have to bring it upstairs, though. I would have come down to the solarium to eat."

"I was glad to do it, Miss Dorothy." She giggled nervously. "It gives me a few minutes escape from the endless gossip in the staff kitchen. When the cook and Mrs. French, the housekeeper, get together, ah, there's no rest." The girl cupped her ears as if in pain then giggled again. "Besides, if you ate in the solarium, the staff would have to stop gossiping for a while, since the kitchen is right next door to the sunroom, you know."

I laughed at her animated chatter. Her luminous dark eyes and wide, friendly smile flashed when she spoke. I found her enchanting. I watched her pour milk from a heavy crystal pitcher into a matching crystal goblet.

"So, where was home for you before coming to America, Maria?"

"Naples, Italy."

"You're a long way from home," I admitted.

Her eyes misted for a moment. "Yes, but I'm thankful to be here. My older brother, Luigi, came over to the states before me. He's a silversmith, like my father."

"Luigi sponsored you? How long have you been in this country?"

"A year. Luigi is good to me. We are saving to bring more of our brothers and sisters to America."

"Really? How many brothers and sisters do you have?"

"Seven are still in Naples, as well as my mama. Papa died two years ago. Bad lungs, you know." She tapped her chest as she spoke. "He dreamed of coming to America from the time he was a teenager. So sad."

"Yes, it is. My father has an unfulfilled dream to go gold prospecting in Alaska, but he still has a couple of younger children at home." Tears came to my eyes when I thought of Papa and his dreams. I sighed as I remembered my brother Joe in California and Chloe Mae in England. "I, too, come from a large family. And like you, we're scattered all over the globe."

I sat down on the edge of the beige brocade sofa. As I watched Maria remove the silver-domed lid from my sandwich plate, I felt a kinship with the young woman. And I hoped we would become as good of friends as I'd become with Agnes at Julia's place. I'd quickly discovered that being a "poor relation" sometimes has its advantages. One advantage was that the household staff felt closer to me than they did the regular members of the family.

I eyed the freshly baked croissant stuffed with watercress, mayonnaise, and cheese. I knew I could never finish it alone. The oatmeal cookies stacked on a side plate would fill me so full that I would not be able to eat dinner at seven. "I can't eat all of this, Maria. Could you help me?"

The girl looked at me in horror. "Oh no, Miss Dorothy. That would be improper. The cook would have my scalp."

I winced. I'd moved too fast. *It will take time to win this girl's trust and friendship,* I thought. My friendship with Agnes had sprung up almost immediately. *I can't expect Maria to respond as quickly,* I reminded myself. *But, I will keep trying.*

Knowing dinner was as formal an affair in the McCall household as it had been at Julia and James E.'s table, I chose one of the dresses Chloe Mae had insisted I take from her wardrobe.

I slipped the pastel blue silk-tubular dress over my head and shoulders. The smooth, cool fabric hung from my shoulders to my ankles. A matching fabric rose, and sash resting on my right hip accented the long line of the fabric. I brushed the snarls out of my hair, piled it high on my head, then pinned it into place with a set of ivory combs my parents had given me for my fifteenth birthday. As I looked at my reflection in the mirror over the bureau, my eyes softened as I thought of how proud my father had been to be able to give me such a valuable gift.

A wave of nostalgia washed over me. So much had happened. I studied my face. At the moment, I felt younger than Maria and very much alone. The carved-oak grandfather's clock at the top of the stairs gonged seven times. I clutched my stomach. Ready or not, I had to go down those winding stairs and tell my host and his wife something, but what?

"Oh, dear God"—I exhaled sharply—"where are those words You promised to give me when I needed them? Now would be nice, You know."

Drucilla and Ian met me at the top of the stairs. "My, aren't you looking fresh and lovely this evening," my host said as he took my arm to escort both his wife and me down the stairs. "And how did your day go?"

I mumbled something about the weather and fell into step beside him. Drucilla glanced around her husband, eyeing me questioningly.

"Mrs. McCall, I love that shade of yellow on you," I cooed, hoping to change the subject. "Not many women have the complexion to carry it off, but you, it's breathtaking on you."

"Why, thank you, Dorothy. But, please, it's Drucilla, remember? Ian and I don't go for all that formality. We spent too long in the wheat fields of Kansas to be impressed by formality." She paused a moment then continued. "Of course, there are times it's fun to . . ."

I smiled to myself. I'd succeeded in getting them off the topic for a few moments. However, sooner or later, preferably sooner, I would have to level with them regarding my employment arrangements.

The three of us entered the high-ceilinged dining room. Rolf waited behind Drucilla's chair. While he seated her at the nearest end of the table, Ian drew a chair for me about midway. I seated myself and thanked him graciously. He continued to the far end of the table, where Rolf stood waiting to seat him as well.

Of all the rooms in Ian and Drucilla's home, I liked their family dining room the best. The walls, covered with white brocade silk, contrasting with the aqua-colored, brushed-silk draperies and white-plaster detailing in the walls and ceiling, produced a cool, light, and relaxing atmosphere. Two three-tier crystal chandeliers, wired for electricity, hung above the black walnut dining table for twelve. Matching three-candle sconces illuminated the wall area between each floor-to-ceiling window and on each side of the marble fireplace. I wasn't yet sure how I felt about my hostess, but I did appreciate her taste in interior decorating and in fashion.

The conversation between Ian and Drucilla flowed freely during the meal as Rolf served course after course of carefully prepared food fit for royalty. I waited in agony for the subject of my job interview to be introduced, still not knowing what I should say.

Needing only to answer short Yes or No questions, I analyzed the filigree etched in the sides of the silver bowl filled with white magnolias sitting in the center of the table. Smoke wafted from the ten long white candlesticks anchored in the silver candelabras on each end of the table.

". . . isn't that right, Dorothy?"

I started.

"Dorothy?" Drucilla repeated my name.

"Oh, I'm so sorry. I guess I was daydreaming for a moment. Please forgive me."

Drucilla laughed. "Of course I will, darling. Dear Ian and I have been so busy discussing our day we've neglected to ask you about yours. Please tell us about your day. Did you go for your interview?"

I cleared my throat. I could hear Mr. Collingsworth's words, "Truth—your best weapon!"

"Well, it was quite interesting . . ." I told them how surprised the newspapermen were to learn I was female. Then I told them about the arrangement I'd made with Matthew Collingsworth. "It is important that no one discover my identity as D. M. Spencer. Being a woman, no one will suspect I work for the *Tribune*. I told him I would not lie." I paused to study their reactions. Drucilla's mouth hung open in surprise, while Ian's face remained inscrutable.

"I felt, as your houseguest, I should reveal to the two of you what was happening. How else could I justify living here if I didn't have any employment? As you can see, this is a secret that mustn't go any farther than the two of you. That includes Ashley."

"Absolutely!" Ian scowled at his wife. "Ashley mustn't know. She's a dear, but her mind is a sieve at times."

"Ian, to say that about your only daughter!" Drucilla clicked her tongue in censure then grinned slowly. "Of course, you're right. How exciting! Like living in a dime novel."

Ian's frown deepened. "Won't this be dangerous?"

I shrugged. "I don't think so. I'm not going out looking for trouble. I'm only recording life in New York City as I find it."

"I know Matt very well. He attends our church, in fact. And I can't imagine him agreeing to an arrangement like this if danger were involved. Are you sure your sister would approve?"

I straightened my shoulders defiantly. "I am of age, you know."

He chuckled. "You reminded me of your sister right then.

That's the same way she would have reacted to my question. Would you mind if I talked with Matthew about this?"

I arched one eyebrow. "I would rather you didn't. I acquired this position on my own, and I'd like to prove I can handle it on my own as well."

"She's right, Ian dear. Don't go sticking your nose into places where it doesn't belong." Drucilla sent a conspiring grin toward me then glared back at her husband. "Why don't you sign up for a class or two at the Brooklyn Women's College? Then if anyone asks what you do, you can tell them you're a student."

"Brilliant, my dear." Ian warmed to the subject. "One class would be enough."

I thought about Drucilla's suggestion. It was a good one.

We dropped the subject when Rolf entered the room carrying a large silver tray laden with slices of cherry pie and cheesecake. And while I thought I was stuffed before, I couldn't resist a slice of cherry pie.

I could get too used to this life, I thought as I devoured my dessert. At home in Pennsylvania, I was chief cook for the family. And while I disliked cooking, I hated baking.

I allowed the light, flaky crust to melt in my mouth. My piecrust always resembled leather, salty leather, in fact. If I never had to bake another pie or cook another stew, I would be delighted. I couldn't understand why, when I visited Chloe Mae at her Cape Cod cottage, I often found her and her Chinese companion, Au Sam, elbows deep in pastry flour. Chloe Mae didn't have to make her own pies; she chose to. Incredible!

When we finished eating, the McCalls and I retired to the family drawing room to discuss my situation. I was relieved at their encouragement. Drucilla liked being privy to my adventure, and she liked the fact that I would be the first female reporter on staff even if no one would know it. Ian, while more reserved about my job, promised to reserve judgment for a while.

"But the minute I believe your safety to be in danger, I will march right down there to Matthew Collingsworth's office and let him have it," Ian promised.

I laughed at his ardor. He reminded me of Papa.

It wasn't until I was alone in my room that night I realized that Ian had given Matthew and me a natural way to meet—at the church. While I didn't necessarily want to make the actual church service a place of commerce, we could become regulars at the midweek young people's meeting. In the morning I would send Mr. Collingsworth a note to that effect.

As I dressed for bed, I thought, *perhaps I can encourage Ashley to attend, as well.* If I could convince her that it would be a great place to meet eligible young men . . . I looked in the mirror as I brushed the snarls from my hair. "Dorothy Mae Spencer, you are a devious young woman, do you know that?"

Is being deviously honest an oxymoron? I wondered as I reached for my Bible. I turned to Proverbs 3:6. I'd turned to this text so many times since I decided to leave Shinglehouse. And it never failed to encourage me. "In all thy ways acknowledge Him and He shall direct thy paths."

"Lord," I said as I knelt beside the bed, "Help me never to forget to acknowledge You. Please direct my paths and help me to trust Your leading. Amen."

During the next week, I nosed around Ellis Island's immigration offices, where I discovered all kinds of interesting statistics about the people clamoring to enter the country. I talked with a few who passed all the requirements to enter and listened to the heartache of those being sent back to Europe for one reason or another. While I pitied those forced to return to their homelands, I let the stories speak for themselves.

At church that weekend, I walked past Mr. Collingsworth without so much as a nod. Ian spent a few minutes after church speaking with him. I hoped they didn't discuss me.

I spent time getting better acquainted with Ashley. By the following Wednesday, Ashley had convinced herself that it was her idea for the two of us to attend the youth meeting. "We could have a splendid time together, Dorothy, just like sisters. I'm sure Mama and Daddy would allow us to attend without them, you being an adult and all. We could even stop at the 'Village Tea House' for hot chocolate on the way home from the service." Ashley's enthusiasm almost had me convinced. "Have you seen the way Scott Sebastian looks at me across the sanctuary?" She clapped her hands together like a seven-year-old and giggled. "This is going to be so much fun. I've really missed dear, sweet CeeCee since she left for Europe. We were so close, you know."

Yes, I thought, *this is truly going to be quite the adventure.* I wrote my first couple of articles, passed them on, and received payment without detection.

One evening Ashley picked up her father's copy of the *Tribune.* She ran across my article on a sixteen-year-old Italian-American boy who'd come to America, to have his only relative in the country die within six weeks of his arrival. The story told how he'd looked for work, but no one wanted to hire a "Wop," as the employers called him.

I, along with the McCalls, was sitting in the drawing room when Ashley read the story. "Look, Dorothy, the author of this article is named Spencer too. Isn't that a scream? Imagine, you sharing the same last name as a real writer!"

I glanced toward Drucilla. She grinned then returned to her needlepoint. Ian pretended not to hear.

Our weekly forays to the church's youth meetings proved to be beneficial to everyone concerned. With Ashley so absorbed in the attentions of Scott Sebastian, she failed to notice Mr. Collingsworth and my brief encounters. After a few weeks, the two gentlemen sat with us during the meeting. From there, after the proper amount of time lapsed, they began to escort Ashley and me home after the service.

One Wednesday evening, Ashley and Scott lingered significantly behind us as we walked. This gave Mr. Collingsworth and me the opportunity to discuss article assignments.

"D. M. Spencer is receiving a bundle of mail each day," Mr.

Collingsworth told me. "I brought along a sampling for you to enjoy. Your fans declare you to be a champion crusader for the working class. Your detractors have other descriptions for you."

"Like what?"

"Oh, anticapitalist, Bolshevik, a Kaiser-lover." He studied my reaction.

"I don't understand. All I do is tell the stories of real people. I'm not on a crusade for labor or for big business."

He smiled. "Wasn't it the apostle Paul who described truth as a two-edged sword? Such a weapon is bound to draw blood every now and then."

"I suppose."

"What do you tell your subjects when you interview them? They're likely to hear about their story being told in the paper."

"When anyone asks, I tell them I'm gathering stories for a friend who works for the paper."

"Hmm." We strolled in silence for a moment, my gloved hand in the crook of his arm.

I glanced up at him as we approached the stone steps leading to the McCall's gray stone townhouse. "I've been thinking of doing some articles on the prohibition issue. I thought I would drop in on the Women's Christian Temperance Union offices to start then talk with some of the Irish immigrants I've gotten to know. They have strong opinions on the subject. What do you think?"

He paused at the base of the steps and turned to face me. "The topic sells papers, to be sure. But be careful. Feelings run high on prohibition."

I patted his arm with my other hand. "I'm always careful, but thank you for caring. You know," I reminded him, "We're almost to the end of August. When does my temporary status come up for review?"

"Why don't you come down to the paper on Monday? We can meet with Giles. I want to be certain I include him in any decision I might make. It's wiser that way."

I understood. If anyone didn't approve of what I was doing, it would be Giles Collingsworth. And like it or not, his opinion would be important to my future as a big-city reporter.

Cy and Chloe sent a letter from London with the good news that they and their children would be boarding the ship, *Luxembourg,* for New York by the end of the week. I knew the crossing would take a month during peacetime. But no one could tell how long it might take in wartime. Visions of enemy torpedoes racing toward the luxury liner haunted my sleep the night after I received her letter.

Somewhere in the wee hours before dawn, I fell to my knees at the side of my bed and asked my Father to forgive me for fretting and worrying. "You promised to be with us, and that includes my loved ones wherever they go, including on the high seas. I will trust You, Father. I will praise Your holy Name for Your compassion and goodness. I love You. Amen."

A letter postmarked Boston arrived every Friday afternoon. Franklin never missed a one. Each letter told about the happenings in his life, especially at work. Occasionally he told about attending a dinner party or an opera. He never mentioned who his date may have been, and I never asked. Besides, the longer I stayed in New York, the farther from Boston I felt. The outcome of Monday's meeting at the *Tribune* would determine the kind of letter I'd be sending the next week.

On Thursday I headed for the Women's Christian Temperance Union offices. They supplied me with an armload of materials for my articles. After dropping them off in my room, I boarded the subway for the Irish community in lower Manhattan. I felt the most relaxed among these people since my hair color stood out the least, thanks to my mother's Irish roots. On my first visit to the neighborhood, Margaret, a withered old woman, had claimed I was the daughter of her long-lost cousin in Downpatrick, Ireland.

Emerging from the subway tunnel into the bright sunlight blinded me for a moment. My vision was still adjusting to the intense light as I crossed the street and rounded the corner by

121

O'Mally's Meat Market.

Thunk! A mighty bundle of energy slammed into me, catching me at the waist and propelling me backward into the side of a brick wall. To keep from falling on the slate sidewalk, I clung to my attacker.

"Let go, lady! Let go!" The scruffy boy shouted. "They're after me. Let go!"

He struggled to wrench free while I clutched his skinny arms to prevent his escape.

"Where do you think you're going so fast?" I asked, as he struggled to break free of my grasp.

A gang of teenage toughs thundered around the corner, their angry shouts filling the midafternoon air.

"Here! You take her!" The young boy shoved a tiny bundle of dirty rags at me. Instinctively, I released him and caught the object in my hands. A middle-age male pedestrian leapt out of the way as the young boy dashed up the street. Morgan, the owner of the meat market, shook his fist and shouted at the child.

The older boys darted past me, intent on catching their prey. They charged past poor Morgan, leaving him in a frenzy of frustration. "Hooligans! All of you!" he shouted.

In all the excitement, I'd forgotten the bundle I still clutched in my hands. I unwrapped the layers of soiled rags until I reached a small, deep red velvet drawstring bag. Loosening the strings, I emptied the contents of the bag into my other hand, and I gasped.

CHAPTER EIGHT

On the Trail of a Tale

"Hey! Come back." I shouted. But the boy had vanished among the pedestrian shoppers jostling with horse-drawn carts and wagons for space in the narrow cobblestone roadway. Colorful vegetable carts, rag collectors, and a street-size carousel charging a penny a ride created a circus atmosphere. The horn from an occasional motor-driven vehicle punctuated the general pandemonium of day-to-day business in the Bowry district.

I started in the direction I'd last seen either the small boy or his predators. A gaggle of pedestrians intent on their destinations clogged the sidewalk.

"Where did he go?" I called to the owner of the meat market.

He wagged his head and turned his attention back to a large red-faced woman customer who was badgering him to give her a deal on yesterday's pork chops.

I glanced down at the object in my hand. The unblinking emerald eye of a medieval dragon stared up at me. Sunlight sparkled off the creature's deep red ruby body that was encircled by tiny diamond chips. The pin's silver filigree setting needed polishing.

By the clasp and the style of brooch, I knew the exquisite piece of jewelry must be very old. While I knew little about quality jewelry and even less about antique pieces, I had no doubt that this pin was worth a king's ransom.

Slipping the pin into my jacket pocket, I strode to where I'd last seen the boy. As I passed a sidewalk fruit vendor, I asked if he knew the child being chased by a gang of older boys. The man with thick brown hair and a matching mustache shook his head and brushed me aside. I asked a woman sitting on her steps holding a small baby.

"No speak English." She shrugged and glanced away. Exasperated, I continued up the street. As I crossed a blind alleyway between brick buildings, a high, squeaky voice called out to me from the shadows.

"Lady?"

I glanced about. There were several female shoppers nearby. When I failed to see the source of the voice, I resumed walking. "Lady," the voice called a second time.

I turned and again saw no one. Shrugging my shoulders, I started walking once more.

"Lady. Over here!" The voice came from behind a stack of discarded wooden fruit crates. "I'm right here." The speaker's *r*s rolled off his tongue in a thick Irish brogue. The boy stood and extended his hand. "You have my brooch?"

"Yes, but I'm not sure it's yours." I arched a skeptical brow.

"It's my ma's. Please, lady, give me the brooch," he insisted.

The shuffle of heavy leather boots alerted me to the fact that we weren't alone. The small boy dipped behind the boxes once more. The gang of boys who'd been chasing him skidded to a stop a few feet between me and the busy street.

"OK, kid. Give us the pin," the tallest of the four boys demanded. ". . . and we won't beat you up."

The younger boy popped up from behind the boxes. "No!" His lower lip protruded defiantly. "It's not yours. It's my mother's!"

"You lie. It's mine, and you know it," a second tough charged.

I scowled at the defiant little boy. "Is that true? Is the brooch theirs? Did you steal it from them?"

"No, ma'am." His eyes widened convincingly. "The pin belongs to my mother. She brought it from the old country. It's her last piece."

I scowled and glanced at the other boys. They stood with their brows knitted, their legs spread, and their fists planted firmly on their hips. The tallest of the gang swaggered toward me. I towered over him by a head. He leaned forward until his nose was inches from my chin and glared up into my face. "What do you want, Lady? This ain't none of your business."

I narrowed my eyes and returned his glare. "It is, as long as you're threatening this child."

He snorted then glanced at his buddies. They chuckled. "Are you afraid we might hurt the hustling little Mick, eh, Red?"

I arched an eyebrow and ignored his effort to intimidate me. "I'm not afraid of anyone, least of all, you and your rowdy friends."

"Well, maybe you should be." He bent down and pulled a shiny hunting knife from his boot. The blade glinted in the sunlight.

"Jimmy, it's broad daylight," one of his friends hissed. "Someone will see you."

"I'm not afraid," he bragged.

I whispered a quick prayer asking for wisdom. As a child growing up on a farm, I'd encountered a raging bull, a rabid dog, a cornered skunk, and more than one skittish stallion. And more recently, I'd survived the human stampede in Boston. But I'd never stared down the razor edge of a six-inch blade. I decided the best thing for me to do was maintain my fearless façade.

"You are buying yourself more trouble than you might imagine," I growled at the insolent boy. "If you continue to threaten me or this child with that weapon, I will shout for the nearest policeman." I looked beyond the boys toward the main street and waved. *Dear Lord, now would be a nice time for you to send that wisdom I requested,* I breathed silently. I started abruptly and pointed over the young man's shoulder. "Oh, there's one now. Officer? Officer!"

"You don't think I would fall for that trick, do you?" the boy snarled.

"Officer?" I called again. "Could you come here, please?"

The boys stared at me incredulously.

"Yes, ma'am? May I help you?" The cop replied.

When the boys glanced over their shoulders to check out my story, the child in question darted past them and disappeared around the corner of the building. When I looked at the leader of the gang again, the knife had disappeared from the boy's hand.

I smiled and nodded impudently at the boy then placed a hand on his shoulder. "Yes, sir, I believe you can. It seems these young men have lost something of value. I wonder if you could help them find it?"

I felt the young man's body stiffen. He shot me a glance then shook his head violently. "No, no, that's OK." He darted a look at his buddies.

The policeman's eyes narrowed at the sight of the boys. "Ah, you fellows again. Haven't I warned you to stay away from this neighborhood? You don't belong here."

Without a word, the leader slipped free of my arm and ran past the police officer and disappeared around the corner. His three abandoned compatriots charged after him.

The officer smiled. "They won't be back for a while. Now, what is this all about?"

"It seems I got into the middle of a skirmish between those young men and the boy who dashed out of here when you arrived. I don't completely understand what it's all about. I'd like to find out.

"I've seen you around here before, haven't I? Askin' lots of questions."

I smiled innocently. "Do you know the little boy's name?"

"Aye, that's the Reilly boy, the son of Bobby and Rosalie. He's a little pip, that one." The officer shook his head sadly. "Gonna bring trouble on his saintly mother's head, he will."

"Do you know where he lives?" I asked.

"Just up the street in 221, fourth floor back. Why do you want to know?"

"He gave me something to hold for him, and I want to return it," I said.

"Ah, the brooch." the policeman nodded.

"How did you know?"

"It's the wee lad's only claim to fame in the neighborhood. It seems his ma was a member of the royal family back in England— way down the line, of course—when she married the boy's father, a potato growin' Irishman. Her family disowned her. She and Bobby used her collection of antique jewelry to come to America. The brooch is the last of the lot, so I hear. And every once in a while, when Mum's at work, the lad brings it out to brag."

"Doesn't the mother object? It's very valuable, you know."

The policeman scratched the side of his head with his billy club. "The mum don't know. She works twelve to fourteen hours a day to support the family."

"And her husband, Bobby?"

The officer's face screwed with consternation. "Ah, Bobby spends his days soused out of his gullet at Paddy's Bar or sleeping one off in the city jail."

I blinked in surprise. So *this* was the crusader's cry against selling alcohol.

The police officer studied my face and knew what I was thinking. "Now, don't go judging poor Bobby. He'd work if he could. But no one wants to hire him."

"Why?"

"Haven't you read the signs on the front of the factories along the waterfront? HIRING! NO Spics, Wops, Micks, Chinks, or Niggers need apply. As a Mick, Bobby doesn't stand a chance."

I had seen the signs but never stopped to think much about them or what they meant for the people referred to by those ethnic slurs. The officer smiled at my ignorance. "That's Spanish,

Italian, Irish, Chinese, and Coloreds. The only immigrants the bosses want to hire must be natives of England or northern Europe."

"I know! And that's terrible!"

He shrugged and stuffed his billy club into its holder. He took my arm and led me back to the main street. "Unfortunately, that's human nature."

"Does that make it right? Can't we as an enlightened society stop it?"

"You one of those blue-stocking suffragettes, Miss?" I bristled but remained silent as he continued. "Those do-gooders think they can change what's always been. Females and their uncontrollable emotions! Enough to drive a man to drink, if you know what I mean."

My steely glare brought a blush to his cheek. "No offense meant, ma'am."

My lips smiled, but my eyes snapped with anger. "Which direction did you say was the Reilly's tenement?"

"The middle of the next block. Can't miss it." He tipped his hat and grinned.

"Thank you, officer." I smiled and headed north. By the time I crossed the intersection, the police officer had disappeared from my view. I felt the brooch in my pocket and asked myself why I hadn't given it to him to return.

A woman barely into her twenties sat on the steps of number 221. Her blond hair hung in greasy strings around her face and shoulders. An infant lay nursing in her arms. I smiled and asked about Bobby Reilly's apartment.

"Apartment?" She laughed. Time had replaced the sparkle of youth in her laughter with the steely edge of cynicism. "It's a room with access to the water closet down the hall. Sorry, fourth floor in the back."

I thanked her, climbed the steps to the front door, and reached for the doorknob.

"Just go on in. It's not locked." As an afterthought, she added,

"But no one's home, you know, except the kids, that is."

"I appreciate your help, ma'am. What did you say the children's names were?"

The woman's eyes narrowed. "I didn't. Why do you want to know?"

"I have a little something to return to them."

My answer seemed to mollify her suspicions of me. When I realized she would say nothing more, I pushed open the front door and entered the dark and dank hallway. Stained wallpaper hung in loose strips on the stairwell. The odor of urine accosted my nostrils. I retrieved a linen hanky from my purse and held it over my nose as I climbed the squeaky stairs to fourth floor. As a child growing up in a relatively impoverished community, I thought we had it bad. But that day I decided I'd rather be country poor than city poor anyday. Trees, grass, and clear blue skies are just a few of the benefits in the country, regardless of one's financial status.

I heard the sound of tiny feet scrambling over a wooden floor when I knocked on the Reilly's door. The door swung open by itself. The latch hadn't caught. "Hello?" I called, peeking inside at the cramped and gloomy room.

A table with dirty yellow paint peeling from the legs sat on one side of the colorless room. Behind the table, wooden crates stacked against the wall served as storage cupboards. Mismatched flour sacks were tacked across the front of each crate. Instead of chairs around the table, there were four wooden crates. And in the center of the table, an amber bottle held one limp and wilted brown rose.

"*Yoohoo,*" I called. "Anyone home?" I peered around the edge of the door. In front of the windows on the other side of the room, a brown, tattered wool blanket almost covered the springs and lumpy mattress. The yellow-brown shades, intended to provide privacy from the people living in the tenement house across the trash-strewn yard, hung curled and torn from the rods.

Curled up on an overstuffed gold brocade club chair that looked as if it had been rescued from the trash cart, a gray-and-white kitten sat hunched and ready to spring should I trespass much closer. "Oh, you beautiful little thing," I cooed, inching closer. "Will you let me hold you?"

Suddenly, two scrawny arms shot up from behind the chair and snagged the animal from its perch. "No!" a tiny voice snapped. "You can't take Lily. Go away!"

I paused midstep and stepped backward. "Hello? My name is Dorothy. I didn't come here to take away your kitty cat."

Two steps farther and I peeked over the arm of the chair into the intense blue eyes of a terrified five-year-old girl. She held the kitten tightly against her chest and neck. "Lily's mine! You can't take her!" Her eyes narrowed defiantly.

"Lily certainly is a beautiful kitty. You are a very lucky little girl to have a pet like Lily," I assured her.

The child's face softened as she stroked the animal under the chin. "Mum says we can't afford to feed her. But Lily doesn't eat much. And I share my food with her."

A glance at the girl's gaunt little form told me she barely got enough to eat as it was. Her faded dress couldn't hide her scrawny arms and legs. The bulky high-up shoes on her feet looked to be two sizes too large. *Probably hand-me-downs from her brother,* I thought. To a woman overwhelmed by the responsibilities of being a mother and the family breadwinner, I imagined that even a wee kitten could seem like more than she could bear.

"I'm not here to take Lily from you. I'm here to see your big brother. Is he home?"

"Bobby?" Her eyes grew suspicious. "Why? Why do you want to see Bobby? Has he done something bad?"

"No, I don't think so. By the way, what is your name?"

"Molly . . ."

"What a pretty name. Do you know that my mother and father usually called me Dolly, even though my real name was Dorothy?"

"Really? Dolly? I wish my name was Dolly. Sylvie, she lives downstairs, has a real dolly named Lillibelle. Lillibelle has a painted face and eyes that open and shut."

"*Ooh,* I'm sure she's beautiful, Molly."

"She is. And you know what? Sometimes Sylvie lets me hold Lillibelle."

"Sylvie sounds like a good friend."

"She is, and she's seven years old. I'm only five." Molly held up one hand, her fingers spread for me to see.

"Wow! I remember being five years old."

Molly giggled and eased out of hiding to the edge of the bed. "You were never five like me."

"Yes, I was." I knelt beside the bed and pet the animal's head. "And I had a kitten named Pester. Pester had fluffy yellow-and-white fur and the biggest green eyes you ever saw."

"Really? You were five? And you had a kitty too? Did you live in one of the big houses with the fancy curtains at their windows?"

"Oh no, I lived with my family on a little farm in Pennsylvania. Do you know where Pennsylvania is?"

Molly's eyes widened, and she shook her head sadly. Then she brightened. "You really lived on a farm? With chickens and pigs and cows and horses and sheep and . . ."

I laughed. "That's right, all except for the sheep and the pigs. We had seven cows and a bull we named Bully . . ." Molly and I giggled. "And we had lots and lots of chickens and an old rooster named Boo . . ."

"Boo?" Molly asked.

"That's right, Boo. Boo was frightened of everyone except my pa. He'd run and hide whenever my mother or we kids would enter the chicken yard."

"What else?" Molly shifted her weight on the bed. Lily scrambled from her arms and disappeared beneath the bed. "What other animals? Horses?"

"Two mares—Princess and Duchess."

The girl's eyes widened again. "Duchess? Did you know that my mother is a real duchess, or at least, she was before she married my da."

"A real duchess? I'm impressed."

"There you are." I felt a small hand touch my shoulder. "I've been looking all over for you. Where's my mum's brooch?"

I reached into my pocket for the intricately designed pin and placed it in the boy's hand. "I would advise you, Bobby, never to take this out on the street again. If you lose it or someone steals it, your mother will be heartbroken."

The boy hung his head. "The boys were calling me a runt Mick. And I wanted to prove to them . . ."

"I know what you were trying to do. But what if I'd been a bad person and kept your mother's pin?"

He brightened. "I knew you wouldn't. Everyone says you're a good lady, even if you don't live here in the neighborhood."

"Hey!" A voice shouted from the doorway. "Who are you, and what are you doing here?"

Little Bobby surreptitiously slipped the brooch in my hand. "Da? What are you doing here?"

"What am I doing here? I live here, you addle-brained bummer."

Slipping the brooch inside my glove, I stood and turned to see a red-faced man with bloodshot eyes leaning on the doorjamb for support.

"Mr. Reilly, my name is—"

"I don't know you, do I?" He staggered closer to where I stood. "Hey, aren't you the crazy lady that comes around here asking a bunch of questions?"

I stood and pasted on my most gracious smile. "My name is Dorothy Spencer. Your daughter's been showing me your beautiful kitten."

"Good thing! That useless cat's gotta go."

"But Da," Bobby wailed, "Lily will soon be big enough to catch the rats. You know how you're always complaining about the rats."

Mr. Reilly staggered over to a big bucket sitting near the table. He lifted a dipper from the pail and took a drink. The water slobbered down his chin. The water in the pail splashed as he dropped the dipper back into the pail. He whirled about, staggered somewhat to regain his balance, then crossed the room toward the bed. Bobby grabbed his sister's arm and shoved her behind him. The two children moved toward the door as their father continued his uneven dance toward the bed. "Gotta sleep. You kids get out of here. You too, fancy lady. I gotta get some rest."

Outside in the hall, Bobby asked for the brooch. I handed it to him. "Thanks, ma'am. For both times. You're a good person."

"Why, thank you, Bobby. But I don't think I understand what just happened."

He sighed and slipped the brooch into his hip pocket. "My da doesn't know mum still has the brooch. He thought she'd pawned off everything. If he knew, he'd sell it and spend the money on ale. He loves his ale."

Molly took my hand into hers. "Miss Dorothy, if Da makes me give away Lily, would you take her? I know you'd be nice to her."

I knelt down beside the little girl. I could see in her eyes that her little heart was breaking at the thought of being separated from her precious Lily. I thought for a moment. I was certain Ian and Drucilla wouldn't be too thrilled if I lugged home a kitten.

"I'd be glad to, Molly. But Lily would be sad if I took her away from her home, don't you think?"

Molly nodded solemnly. Bobby peered under the bed. "I'll find her for you." He dragged the reluctant kitten from under the bed and tenderly placed her in my arms. The moment I stroked Lily's head, she started purring.

"Tell you what, I can't keep a kitten at my house, but I'll pay you to keep Lily for me. How does that sound? I'll give you money for her food and for taking good care of her. Then I'll come to visit her here at your house. Do you think you could do that for me?"

Molly's head nodded enthusiastically. She clapped her hands gleefully. "I could do that! I could do that!"

"I'd help her," Bobby added. "You know, go buy the food and

such. She's not allowed to leave the building when mum's at work. But I can."

"You're not supposed to either!" Molly hissed.

Bobby made an ugly face at his sister.

"All right, but Bobby, only if you promise not to take your mother's brooch out of the apartment again. "OK! I promise." He grinned up at me. "And I'll take good care of your cat for you."

"No!" His little sister interrupted. "I'll take good care of Lily. She was my kitty, not yours!"

I placed Lily in Molly's hands and gave the cat one last stroke on the head. "Isn't she beautiful? Take good care of her now." I reached into my purse, withdrew a leather change purse, and took out two dimes. I placed one dime in Bobby's hand and the other in Molly's. "I'll pay you twenty cents a week for caring for Lily. Whatever you have left after feeding her each week, the two of you can keep. Is that fair?"

The children stared at the shiny dimes in their hands. Their eyes danced as they nodded enthusiastically. I told them Goodbye and promised to come to see Lily soon.

My steps were light when I left the tenement building. As I passed the young woman sitting on the steps and holding her baby, I blew a kiss to the young child. The delight I saw in Molly's and Bobby's faces stayed with me the rest of the week.

I was pleased with the results of my article that week for the paper. I reread it while preparing to attend the midweek youth service. Using several stories I'd heard in the Reilly's neighborhood, I ended the article with, "People come to America expecting to find the 'Promised Land.' But the golden promises turn to vapor when they look in vain for work to sustain their families. Signs that read "Help Wanted—No wops, spics, niggers, or chinks need apply," leave most to fend as best they can without work. One immigrant shoveled snow from the sidewalks all winter, the only work he could find. Others turn to alcohol to soothe their injured pride and deaden the pain of their discouragement. At a time when our country is at war and our brightest and best young men are dying on a foreign battlefield, how can we allow jobs to go begging when we have strong and eager men and women willing to do the work?"

I smiled to myself. I'd been careful not to take advantage of the people who trust me enough to share their stories. I hoped I might change at least one employer's mind about hiring immigrants. I put the article into an envelope then stuffed it into my purse. Pulling my beige linen cloche hat over my hair, I adjusted the fabric rose attached to the side and then examined myself in the mirror to be certain my beige-and-mint-green linen suit was straight in the back. I frowned at the hobble skirt buttoned to one side at the narrow, ankle-length hem. How I'd allowed Ashley to purchase such an impractical piece of clothing, I'll never know.

Ashley popped her head around the corner of my bedroom door. "Oh, you look lovely, Dorothy. Mr. Collingsworth is going to absolutely drool over you."

I laughed. "I certainly hope not. What a disgusting idea."

"Oh, silly. You know what I mean. That outfit is absolutely the cat's meow."

I thought of Lily, who'd quickly made up to me, and I laughed again. "The cat's meow, huh?"

"And those linen pumps—perfect!"

"You look quite lovely as well, my dear. That shade of blue truly becomes you."

She twirled before the mirror. "Do you think Scott will like it?"

"I'm sure he will." I wanted to tell her that her liking it is enough, but I knew she wouldn't, or possibly couldn't, understand. Her whole world was wrapped up in pleasing men. I smiled to myself, knowing that my father would approve wholeheartedly of Ashley's way of thinking.

However, if I'd learned anything from my older sister, Chloe, it was to learn how to be content with yourself and not to look to others for vindication. She suggested I read Psalm 139—that we are ". . . fearfully and wonderfully made." Most evenings before going to bed, I practiced walking tall. Of course, I found it a pleasure to walk tall beside Mr. Collingsworth. When I realized that his presence made a difference in my posture and that I planned for days what I'd wear to the next youth meeting, I admitted to myself that I wasn't so different from Ashley.

The meeting at the church ended with us gathered around the piano singing our favorite hymns. The pastor's wife, Ottalie, could make that piano jingle on "Seeking the Lost." We drew closer to one another as we lustfully sang the four-part harmony on the chorus. At one point, I felt a hand resting on my shoulder. I turned to discover its owner, Mr. Collingsworth, smiling at me. I returned his smile. As a result, he almost missed his bass part on the beginning of the chorus.

Over the summer, I'd purposely refused to think of my employer by his first name. I'd done that with Mr. Ames and lost my heart in the bargain. I wouldn't be such a fool again. But having thought that, I knew I cared more for Mr. Matthew Brewster Collingsworth Jr. than I should.

If only I could have similar feelings for Franklin Bowles, I thought. *Who can explain the heart of a woman?* From Franklin's letters, I knew that if I encouraged him in the slightest, he'd be on the next train to the city. He was a good man. He'd make a fine husband for some woman, someday, but instinctively I knew I would never be that woman. But Matthew Collingsworth—he was a different story.

I looked forward to our weekly appointments. He was the first man, besides Pa, to whom I could express my true opinions on almost any topic, and he'd listen whether he agreed or not. Of course, if he disagreed, we were in for a lively debate, which often ended in a draw and the two of us sharing a strawberry ice-cream soda at a small sweet shop on the way home after meeting. I think the owner stayed open a little late on Wednesdays, to accommodate the youth from the church.

Lately, our topics of conversation were becoming more personal than political. I told him about my family, about Joe in California, and Chloe in London. "She and her family are on their way home as we speak. I can hardly wait to see them. You'll have to meet both Chloe and Cy. You'll like Cy. He's quite an intellectual, you know." I purposely failed to mention why I left the *Shinglehouse Sentinel.* Mr. and Mrs. Ames belonged to another portion of my life.

One Wednesday evening, Mr. Collingsworth mentioned that he'd been married before and that his wife, Lyssa, had died in childbirth, along with their son.

"How long ago? " I asked.

"Seven years." A look of overwhelming sadness flooded his face.

I glanced away. "You must have loved her very much."

"No," he replied, "I didn't. I married her so that our fathers could merge their newspapers. We were married a little over a year."

"I'm so sorry. My mother died during childbirth too. My father still grieves for her. And it's been almost ten years."

"I grieved, because I didn't love her. She deserved better. Sometimes I think I will never again marry and put a wife through the experience of childbirth. Even now Lyssa's screams haunt my dreams."

I glanced up at him in surprise. For a man to admit to having such strong feelings, I admired him more than ever. His admission left me feeling a tiny pang of regret, not that I expected our working arrangement to go any farther than friendship. Yet, a tiny whisper from my heart desired more from him than mere friendship.

"Giving birth to a child is dangerous, even in these modern times. I witnessed the birth of my youngest sister, as well as several of my older sisters giving birth to their children, and I've never seen such joy on a mother's face as when she's introduced to her newborn. There's nothing like it."

Scott and Ashley caught up with us, which squelched any further discussion. "Are we stopping for an ice-cream soda?" Scott asked.

"Miss Spencer? May I entice you into sharing an ice-cream soda with me?" Mr. Collingsworth's eyes twinkled.

"Why, yes, Mr. Collingsworth, that would be nice." I gave a little curtsy.

"Wait!" He stopped and held me back from entering the shop. "Only if you will stop calling me Mr. Collingsworth. My friends call me Matt. And I consider you a dear friend, Miss Spencer."

"As you wish, Matt. And my friends call me Dorothy."

"Miss Dorothy, very formal. Do you have a nickname? I told you mine."

I sighed. All this time I'd been trying to bury the childish nickname. Between clenched teeth, I said "Dolly. My family calls me Dolly."

"Dolly . . . Oh, I like that. Would it be too presumptuous of me to call you Dolly?" He leaned forward within a breath from my cheek. An unfamiliar quiver ran the length of my spine. I swallowed hard.

"Yes, that would be fine," I gulped.

"Are you sure?" He drew a fraction of an inch closer.

I couldn't speak, only nod my approval.

CHAPTER NINE

One War Ends, Another Begins

My meeting on Monday at the *Tribune* with Matt and his brother, Giles, went well, at least the business part. While Giles still had reservations about my status with the paper, he had to admit that my column had stimulated sales and advertising. And for a newspaper, sales and advertising are the bottom line. Reluctantly, he agreed I'd passed "muster" as he put it. "I still hate to think what Father will think when he learns we hired a female reporter. No offense, Miss Spencer. Our father would love you as a daughter-in-law but not as an employee."

I blushed at the inference. "No offense taken, Mr. Collingsworth."

"Come to think of it, he wouldn't be too happy to have you as a daughter-in-law unless your parents are well-seeded."

"Well-seeded?" I looked to Matt for definition.

"Money." Matt's eyes remained at a disinterested half-mast. "My father respects only money, no matter how it is made."

"I, for one, agree with him, little brother. You, of all people, should be grateful. Without his filthy lucre, you would never have graduated from Yale, and you wouldn't have been able to start at the top of this business instead of in the pressroom," Giles reminded him, then turned toward me. "Forgive us, Miss Spencer, for airing family laundry in front of you. Though, from what I've heard, I suspect you know more about my family than I know about yours."

This time Matt reddened as well. Over the months, Matt and I had both shared information about our siblings and their lives, as well as information regarding our own. *What has Matt been saying about me to his brother,* I wondered. That Giles thought our professional relationship had become more of a friendship baffled me. If anything, Matt and I had purposely behaved disinterested toward each other in front of his brother.

Without warning, Matt's secretary called him from the office for several minutes. Giles took advantage of the opportunity to say the things he never would have said in his brother's presence. "Miss Spencer, you are a lovely and intelligent woman. I don't blame my brother for being smitten with you. But you should know he is still in mourning for his wife, Lissa."

"Yes, I know. But what does that have to do with me? My spine stiffened. "Where is this conversation leading?"

"What I'm about to say may sound cold. You need to know that if and when my brother marries, it will be to a woman of means who can further the family fortune. This is just the way it's done in our family."

"Mr. Collingsworth, while you may be my employer, you have definitely overstepped the bounds of propriety." I straightened in the chair and tilted my chin defiantly. "I assure you that while I treasure the growing friendship between Matthew and me, that is all it is. No one is smitten with anyone. We are friends, that's all."

Giles smiled a tight, smug smile. His eyes indicated he knew something more. "Just so you know, Miss Spencer. It's nothing personal. And please forgive me for overstepping my 'bounds' as you put it, but I did so for your benefit."

"You may not believe this, but I did not come to New York to find a husband. I am serious about my writing, I assure you."

Giles gave me a condescending smile, but under his breath he added, "This is exactly why women don't belong in the work place."

"Excuse me?" I asked. "Did you say something to me?"

He cast me a withered smile. "No, I believe you may go now. I am sure Matthew will be contacting you in his usual manner next week."

I left the office feeling totally humiliated. In my haste to leave the building, I climbed aboard the elevator, sputtering to myself about Giles and his insensitive advice. I didn't realize my mistake until the gates clanged shut. I shot a glance toward a middle-age man wearing the rubber apron of a pressman over his work clothes. The curled ends of his mustache arched upward. "First floor?"

I nodded helplessly. I gripped the bars on the sides of the cage as we descended to first floor. The box jerked to a stop, and the gates swung open. I stepped out onto the hard marble surface and heaved a giant sigh of relief. Hoping to catch a glimpse of Matthew before I left the building, I looked around the foyer as I headed for the front door. He was nowhere in sight.

Later that afternoon, my heart skipped several beats when I received a phone call from Matt apologizing for his brother's tactless remarks. "Dolly, I'd like to see you, to clear up any misunderstandings."

"Everything is fine, Matt. Your brother only told the truth as he saw it."

"Please, may I take you to dinner to reassure myself that everything is all right? Nothing fancy, just a small mom and pop place in Little Italy."

I thought for a moment, knowing how badly I wanted to go. "Will Giles mind?"

"Giles? This dinner has nothing to do with Giles. It's for us."

"All right, then, I'd love to."

"I'll pick you up at six, if that's OK."

"Six will be fine." I glanced at the small timepiece inside the locket on my suit lapel. If I hurry home, I thought, I'll have four hours to—*What are you saying?* I scolded myself. *You are sounding less and less like the practical spinster Dorothy Spencer and more and more like the flighty debutante, Ashley McCall.*

When Ashley learned of my "date" with Mr. Collingsworth, she insisted on helping me dress. "It's not a date, Ashley," I insisted. "We have some business to discuss."

"What business?" Her big blue eyes reminded me of her ignorance of the situation.

"He's helping me with my writing."

Ashley giggled. "Oh, that's a good one."

Ashley decided I should wear a pale green linen dress that I'd bought when I first arrived in New York City. Styled in the popular shift cut with a matching draped jacket that buttoned on the right hip, the dress hung free from the shoulders. Ashley insisted I borrow a cream-colored, wide-brimmed hat abloom with soft yellow silk roses and pale green satin ribbons. I wasn't sure about the hat. It added four inches to my height.

"You have to wear it, Dorothy. You just have to," Ashley insisted. "Here, you need to borrow my ecru lace gloves as well."

Arguing with Ashley was impossible. I can hold my own against wit, against logic, against most intellects, but against Ashley? I collapsed to the mat during the first round. After meeting Julia, her grandmother, I knew from whom the girl had inherited her skills. I did draw the line against the rouge pot she tried to put on my cheeks.

"Ashley, take a good look. Does it look like I need color in my face? I don't want to look like Clara Bow, you know."

She giggled. "I can just see you with those rosebud lips. Who knows? Maybe your Mr. Collingsworth would find you irresistible."

"He isn't *my* Mr. Collingsworth. We are friends, that's all." When I saw a look of feeling rejected cross Ashley's gentle face, I realized I'd spoken more crossly than I intended. "It's all right, Ashley. You aren't the first to make assumptions about Matt and me."

She brightened. "See? I knew it! Now, for a spritz of my very favorite perfume, straight from Paris, France."

Before I could object, the icy liquid hit my neck. I sneezed.

From my bedroom window overlooking the street, I saw Matt's cab ease to a stop in front of the McCall's townhouse at two minutes to six. I slipped on the gloves and grabbed the matching crocheted purse Ashley had insisted I use.

"Wait!" Ashley insisted. "You want to make a dramatic entrance."

"I don't think so. With my style and grace, I'd more likely step on the hem of this dress and do cartwheels down the stairs."

She laughed, clutching my arm as if such a tiny wisp of a girl could hold me back if I chose to leave. "Nonsense. That's what the handrail is for."

Maria knocked on the open door. "Miss Dorothy, your escort for the evening has arrived."

"Thank you, Maria."

Ashley fluttered about, checking me from head to toe. "Take a deep breath. Shoulders back, chin elevated."

"And I'm supposed to walk like this?"

"Absolutely."

When I started down the stairs, Matt stood at the bottom of the stairs talking with Ian. But by the time I reached the landing, I had his full attention. "Oh, dear Lord," I whispered. "I can't fall. Please don't let me fall." I'd barely breathed my prayer when my heel caught on the edge of the carpet. I heard gasps from the top of the stairs where Ashley and Marie stood watching.

Seeing me stumble, both Matt and Ian darted up the stairs to my aid. I caught myself before the two men reached me. I laughed nervously as Matt took my arm and escorted me down the rest of the stairs.

Ian rushed to my defense. "I need to get someone to repair that carpet edge. It could be dangerous."

Matt and I escaped the McCall place without further incident. He helped me into the waiting cab then climbed in beside me. After telling the driver our destination, Matt leaned back against the seat and glanced my way. I grinned in spite of my nervousness.

"I feel like a high school boy picking up his first date," Matt confessed.

"It was a little awkward, wasn't it? It could have been worse, I suppose. I could have fallen at your feet."

Matt gave a little chuckle. "I've always wondered what would happen if when these lovely socialites made their grand entrances, they stumbled."

"I am hardly a lovely socialite, Mr. Collingsworth," I reminded him with a rueful smile.

"No, you're not a socialite, thank God. But, lovely, ah, Dolly, you are incredibly lovely, even when you threaten to tumble down a flight of stairs wearing two-inch heels."

"Two-inch heels? How did you—"

"My dear Dolly, I notice every detail about you."

I gulped.

"For instance, I know that while your eyes are usually periwinkle blue, they become deep pools of midnight blue when you're worried and saffire blue when you're angry. And your hair . . ."

My hand shot up to the chignon at the back of my neck. "What about my hair?"

"Oh? Looks like we're here already. You are going to love Mama De Angelo's pasta. *M-m-m-wa!*" He kissed his fingertips in the manner I'd seen Italian immigrants gesture.

The cab eased to a stop beside the curb. The driver opened our door, and Matt helped me out of the cab. Taking my arm, he placed it on the crook of his elbow and escorted me into the quaint little restaurant.

"Matthias!" A short, round, balding man burst through a set of shuttered doors. "So long since you've been to see us!"

"Papa De Angelo!" Matt called.

The owner of the restaurant rushed to Matt and engulfed him

in his arms. "I have missed you, son. Where have you been?"

"Busy, as usual." Matt pounded the man on his back as if he were a long-lost brother.

"Mama mia, and who is this lovely goddess?" The old man eyed me appreciatively. "Mama," he called over his shoulder, "come see Matthias and his beautiful ladyfriend."

An equally short and round woman, with graying hair pulled back into a tight bun, scurried through the kitchen doors and over to where Matt stood waiting with open arms.

"Matthias, where have you been? We missed you." she shook her short chubby finger in his face.

"I know, and I am sorry." He planted a kiss on the woman's cheek. "It's been diff—"

"Don't explain. We're just glad to have you back." She led us to a table covered with a red checkered cloth. "Now, sit and eat! Eat! You're too skinny."

"Yes, Mama, you always say that." He turned to me. "Mama, this is my friend, Dolly. She's from Pennsylvania."

"Ah, what lovely skin. I can tell she's not a city girl. Too wholesome, like the girls back in my Calabria."

"Mama," Matt explained, laughing as he spoke, "always has an opinion and is not afraid to voice it."

"Ah, but you love me, anyway, don't you, Matthias?"

Matt gave the woman an affectionate squeeze. "You bet! You're my gal, but don't tell Papa. I wouldn't want him to take after me with his trusty butcher knife."

"And don't think I wouldn't," Papa gestured. "I know a good thing when I see it." Casting a slow approving glance my way, he continued. "I trust you are as wise with this one, Matthias. What a woman!"

I blushed and glanced toward the scattering of paintings mounted on the red brick wall behind our table.

Matt grinned at my discomfort. "Trust me, Papa, I know a good thing when I see it. Look at Mama."

The old man whooped with laughter then gave his wife a kiss

on the cheek. "You are a wise man, indeed. You will try my Rosa's Pasta e Fagioli. You will love it."

Matt winked at Mama De Angelo. "If Mama made it, I know I'll love it."

"Good, good! Just make yourselves comfortable. I'll be right back. Mama bustled off to the kitchen while Papa lighted the wick of the candle melted in the wine bottle in the center of our table. Without further comment, he, too, disappeared through the slatted doors into the kitchen.

"As a boy," Matt began, "I visited Italy. That's where I met Papa and Mama De Angelo, at their restaurant in southern Italy. They wanted to come to America."

"And you helped them?"

"I talked with my father. He actually facilitated their immigration. Since then they've been very special to me. The De Angelos have seen me through all the major changes in my life." Matt paused for several seconds. "When I brought Lyssa here for them to meet, Papa cautioned me against our engagement. He could see what I couldn't. When she died, Mama and Papa were here to console me. I, uh, haven't been back much since."

He glanced toward the kitchen. "I wonder where Mama is with her Pasta e Fagioli?"

"What is, may I ask, Pasta e Fagioli?"

"Soup. Pasta and bean soup. That's just the first course. Wait until you taste her stuffed artichokes and stuffed green peppers."

"Artichokes? What's an artichoke?"

A slow grin spread across his face. His eyes twinkled as if he harbored a tasty secret. "You've never eaten an artichoke?"

"No, not that I can remember."

"You are in for a treat, my dear." Mama De Angelo entered the room carrying a tray. "Mama, this woman has never tasted an artichoke, can you imagine?"

"No? Never? Ah, the fruit of the gods," she exclaimed. She placed the bowls of soup on the table, along with a small saucer of green chilies and a cup of grated cheese. "Don't let Matthias fool you, dearie. These peppers are very hot." She cuffed Matt alongside the head as she might a ten-year-old ruffian. "My Matthias loves to tease." She shook her finger in his face. "You be good to her, do you hear?"

"Yes, Mama." A devilish grin shined through his humble expression.

I laughed and shook my head. "You are incorrigible, Mr. Collingsworth. I am definitely seeing a side of you I've never seen before." *And,* I thought to myself, *I like it.*

I loved the soup, the plate of spaghetti with maranara sauce, and the stuffed pepper, but the artichoke? I wondered to myself, as I scraped a leaf between my teeth, who was the first person to try eating this oversized thistle? They must have been terribly hungry.

I ate it all. How could I do less with Mama De Angelo filling my plate the moment I could see the bottom of it? And Papa De Angelo standing by my shoulder and saying, "Eat! Eat! Too skinny! The wind will blow you away. Eat!"

As we were finishing our meal, a group of tough-looking men entered the restaurant and chose a table next to the wall. I had the feeling that Matt knew the men and they knew him. Their loud laughter drew the attention of the other diners. At one point, the man who appeared to be the leader of the pack shouted at Papa. "Food!" he demanded, banging his fist on his table. "We want food!"

Matt frowned and started to his feet. A warning look from Papa settled Matt down once again.

The leader of the pack called out to Matt. "Hey, preacher man, out slumming tonight?"

Matt glanced in the man's direction then turned his attention back to me.

"Preacher man?"

"A long story."

The congenial mood we'd been enjoying had been broken. Matt remained tense and distant throughout the rest of the meal.

Even the rich, creamy cannoli couldn't elevate his dark mood.

As we left the restaurant, Papa De Angelo drew Matt aside. While waiting, I glanced toward the offending table of men. One man winked at me and leered suggestively. I might be a country girl, but a leer is a leer whether it is given in Shinglehouse, Pennsylvania, or Manhattan, New York. I arched one eyebrow and glared down my nose at him—a definite advantage for tall women. He laughed, said something I presumed to be in Italian, and looked away.

Once settled in a cab and heading home, I asked Matt about the intruders. "Oh, just some bounders I knew from the docks. I spent a summer as a dock worker before entering the news business. They're bad news, to be sure."

"They could be trouble for the De Angelos."

Matt nodded his head. "Vinnie Rullo, the leader, was once my friend. In the last few years, he's gotten into everything illegal—a real wise guy."

"A wise guy?" I'd never heard the term.

Matt lifted one corner of his lip into a sneer. "That's the term for a little punk who thinks he's tough. An underground crime syndicate, established in the old country, is slowly developing in America's big cities. Boston, New York, Chicago, you name it. And my ex-friend, Vinnie, and his brother, Joey, are wanting a piece of the pie, so to speak."

"It's strange, but I'd swear I've seen the same type of characters lurking around the Irish pubs down by the Bowery. Different nationality but similar attitudes."

"Most of the immigrants to this country are hard-working citizens like Mama and Papa De Angelo, but, unfortunately, a few bad apples of every nationality slipped through Ellis Island. They're going to become real trouble for the government in the next few years, mark my words." He turned toward me. "I hope those thugs didn't ruin the evening for you."

"Oh no, I had a delightful time. Even the artichoke I would try again." *Oops!* My gloved hand flew to cover my lips. *What had*

I said? That I wanted him to ask me out a second time? "I didn't mean—"

"I hoped you did. I certainly intend that there be another time, and soon." He tenderly removed my gloved hand from my lips and touched my fingers to his lips. Suddenly, without warning, his face darkened, he placed my hand on my lap, and withdrew into himself. After several seconds, he cleared his throat. "I'm sorry. That was too forward of me. I had no right."

I wanted to say that I didn't mind, but I sensed that would be the wrong thing to admit to him.

"I wouldn't want to mislead you, Dolly. I do want your friendship, but that's where my intentions stop. I do not want to deceive you in any way."

I didn't reply. I couldn't think of what to say. Instead, I stared out into the gathering night beyond the automobile window.

When the cab pulled up in front of the McCall's residence, I gasped. A familiar, sporty Pierce-Arrow convertible was parked there. Matt insisted on walking me to the door, and Drucilla was equally insistent that he come inside for a few minutes. "Ian would love to introduce you to a guest of ours, an attorney from Boston. I am sure you'll have lots in common."

I glared at her. She smiled sweetly in return. "They're discussing the Volstead proposal. So, did the two of you have a pleasant evening?"

"Lovely," I simpered, following her into the parlor where Ashley sat next to Franklin Bowles on the silk damask sofa and Ian sat across from him in a matching armchair. Both men rose to their feet when I entered the room. Franklin rushed to my side.

"Miss Dolly, it is so good to see you again." He ignored the presence of Matt. "Your last letter disturbed me greatly, so when I had business in the city, I decided to stop by to be certain everything was all right with you." He took my hand and led me to the sofa. Ashley reluctantly made room for me to sit between them. Ian shook hands with Matt and introduced him to Franklin as my employer.

The two men eyed one another suspiciously, like two roosters in a hen yard. Drucilla saved the day.

"How would you gentlemen like a cool drink? Ashley, why don't you play hostess while Dorothy and I prepare some lemonade in the kitchen."

Kitchen? Drucilla? Were the kitchen staff on holiday? Drucilla never prepared her own food or drink. I wasn't sure she even knew the way to the kitchen. "Yes, ma'am." I followed her from the room.

"What is going on?" she asked, the moment we were out of hearing range. "Who is this gentleman? I do hope you are not leading two men on at the same time. That would be quite unseemly."

I choked in surprise. Didn't she know how her own daughter keeps six or seven men on a string at the same time? Besides, I certainly hadn't led Franklin to think there was more between us than friendship. And Matt, he'd made it quite clear that friends were all we could ever be.

Life isn't fair, Lord, I thought. *Here I am, the woman who no man wanted caught in such a weird predicament.* At the slightest hint of romantic interest on my part, I suspected that Franklin would declare his love for me. But I didn't love him. And over time, my feelings for him wouldn't change. But Matt . . . Given the slightest encouragement, I would fall in love with him. Giles had seen it the other day in the office. His warning had been given in kindness.

Oh, Chloe, I thought, *get home soon! I need some big-sister advice.*

"Dorothy? Dorothy? Did you hear me?" Drucilla's voice broke through my reverie.

I glanced over at her in surprise. "Sorry, did you say something?"

"I said, 'what's going on here with these two men?' "

"Nothing that I know of. I can't imagine what I might have said to Franklin to prompt him to come here. And tonight, of all nights!"

Her eyes narrowed. "Tonight? What's special about tonight?"

"Nothing, I guess." When we reached the kitchen, the butler had the lemonade poured and ready for us to carry back to the parlor.

"Well, something happened. You both looked so pensive when you entered the house," Drucilla insisted.

"Really? Imagine that." I picked up the silver tray and hurried from the room before she could ask any further questions.

By the time I entered the parlor with the tray, Ashley was examining her nails while Ian, Matt, and Franklin heatedly discussed the proposed prohibition measure.

"America needs to return to the family values of old," Matt insisted. "The consumption of alcohol destroys families."

"Man has been drinking spirits since the dawn of time. It's human nature. You can't legislate against human nature." Franklin took an icy glass of lemonade from the tray and mumbled Thank you to me.

Ian lifted his hand to say something, but Matt didn't give him a chance. "Along that vein, one could say that it's human nature to get angry and kill others—Cain, the firstborn son of Adam and Eve did, yet we legislate against murder."

"That's a bogus argument." Franklin waved his hand in the air.

"No more bogus than your human-nature position, Mr. Bowles." Ian interjected. "The concept of alcohol prohibition isn't exactly new, either. Kansas banned the sale of liquor in 1886. The Dakotas, Maine, Vermont, and New Hampshire followed four years later."

"And is there proof that their families are stronger as a result?" Franklin looked from one man to the other.

"Having lived in Kansas for a time," Ian said, "I'd have to say that Yes, family life on the prairie is stronger."

"Ah," Franklin interrupted, "but is the improved family life due to no alcohol or to the fact that life is difficult and their survival depends on working together?"

Matt smiled a crooked smile. "You have a point there, Mr. Bowles."

"And" —Drucilla handed her husband a glass of lemonade— "it's not a topic that will be solved in my parlor, so I suggest we discuss something more pleasant such as how did you and Dorothy first meet, Mr. Bowles?"

Franklin glanced over at me. "At one of your mother-in-law's famous dinner parties. But we became much better acquainted at the famous concert in the park." His gaze flickered toward Matt then returned to our hostess.

Matt glared into the partly empty glass in his hands.

"In the riot, we got separated from the McCalls. Later we found your mother-in-law at the local police precinct, in handcuffs."

"Leave it to my mother," Ian added. "If she's not in the middle of one crisis, it's another. Last time, she dragged her granddaughters into the fray."

"That isn't completely accurate, Papa," Ashley said. "Grandma took CeeCee and me shopping, and we accidentally got drawn into the demonstration. She really didn't mean—"

"The end result is the same, is it not? She and my niece CeeCee ended up behind bars for a time. And you, Ashley, were left to fend for yourself in the streets of Boston."

"Oh, Papa, I was never in any danger. You know that." Ashley batted her long, dark lashes at her father. "Besides, it was great fun!"

"Mrs. McCall sounds like a delightful woman." Matt smiled at me.

"She is." I smiled back. "Julia's one of the most genuine individuals I've ever met. I hope you meet her one day."

"I would like that." Matt set the tumbler on one of Drucilla's wooden coasters and rose to his feet. "I really must be going, Mrs. McCall. Nice to meet you, Mr. Franklin. I would enjoy discussing the prohibition issue with you again sometime." He took my hand and touched my fingers to his lips. "I'll see you on Wednesday night, Miss Doll—er—Dorothy?"

I gave him a weak smile. "I'll be looking forward to it."

The Battle Begins

"Am I reading this situation right?" Franklin asked after the rest of the family retired for the night. He gazed at me from the opposite end of the damask sofa. "Is there something developing between you and Matthew Collingsworth?"

"No, not really." I sighed and thought, *I wish there were.*

Franklin reached across the empty space between us and took my hand. "Dorothy, tell me the truth. Am I wasting my time being here?"

I gazed at his drawn, ashen face and sighed again. "Franklin, I don't know what to say. We've shared so many lovely times together, but—"

"I should never have let you leave Boston."

"Let me?" My nerves bristled.

He shook his head. "I didn't mean that the way it sounded. I meant I shouldn't have let you leave without declaring my intentions to you."

"Franklin, wait. I do love you, but not in the way you would like. I love you like I love my brothers. You're a wonderful man.

Some woman is going to be thrilled that I'm saying this to you tonight."

His gaze scanned the room. He swallowed hard. "Then it is Collingsworth."

"No, if I'd never met Mr. Collingsworth, I would still be saying what I'm saying to you tonight. As for Matthew, he has made it clear to me that there is no future for us." I took a deep breath before continuing. "I must be equally as honest with you. While I hope we'll always be friends, I don't have romantic feelings toward you."

"Friends! The death knell to every romance." He released my hand, leaned forward, and placed his head in his hands.

I felt his devastation. Hadn't I experienced similar feelings just a few hours earlier? Why couldn't I feel for Franklin as I did for Matt? And why couldn't Matt have the same feelings for me as Franklin had? I didn't know what to say. "I'm sorry."

He shrugged and got to his feet. "I guess I'm wasting my time." He helped me to my feet, holding my hands for several seconds before speaking again. "You did mean we would remain friends?"

I nodded.

"There's no chance of anything more?" His eyes bore into my soul.

I ached to say "Yes, of course, there's always a chance." My cautious self screamed at me. "You foolish woman! He's a good man, and he loves you. You are ending your chances for marriage and a family of your own. Do you really want to do that?" But another part of me knew it would be unfair to Franklin to hold out hope. He deserved better. He deserved a woman who could give him her all, not one who only held warm affection toward him. I shook my head. "Sorry, I am so sorry."

He nodded and let himself out of the house. I remained in the parlor for several hours, until the first rays of morning sun silhouetted the townhouses across the silent avenue.

During the weeks that followed, I had little time to think about Franklin or Matt. First, Chloe and her family came home. We had so much to talk about that we talked all night the first night she got home. When I told her of my dilemma regarding Franklin and Matt, she laughed. "And you were the spinster lady whom no man would ever love? Remember saying that?"

I blushed and changed the subject to my living arrangements and whether I should move in with her and Cy or stay with the McCalls.

"You know you're welcome to live with us as long as you like, and I'm certain Dru and Ian feel the same way. But if I were you, now that you know you'll be staying in the city, I think I'd choose to become independent. I'd rent a couple of rooms at a respectable boardinghouse. That way no one will be looking over your shoulder at every turn."

I stared in surprise at my sister. "You think I should—" I couldn't believe it. I'd thought of striking out on my own many times, but I was afraid of what people might think.

"Yes, I do. Cy and I were discussing this one night aboard ship. As much as I would like to be selfish and keep you with us, I think you need to build your own life. You need to stop thinking of yourself as a spinster aunt and recognize yourself as the creative and productive woman you are."

The next morning I intended to catch a few hours of sleep, but my mind was in too much of a turmoil. All I could think about was Chloe's suggestion. Did I have the courage to take such a step? Could I make it on my own? I didn't know.

It was two days after Chloe's arrival from Europe that I received a note from Mrs. George Randolf Claiborne telling of the death of their son. "He died a hero," Mrs. Claiborne wrote. In the last paragraph, she added, "In his last letter, Georgie asked me to give you this." A silver medallion with Queen Victoria's image engraved on one side fell into my lap. Tears flowed down my face as I ran my fingers over the metal coin. I vowed that I would make an appointment to see the Claibornes in the morning.

Our meeting went as expected, difficult but necessary for us both. Mrs. Claiborne told me the story of George's bravery. "In the middle of an attack by the Germans, Georgie saw two of his friends fall. Rather than leave them on the field to die, he dragged them to safety. While bringing the second man to safety, a German shell exploded behind him. The shrapnel caught him in the back of the head, and . . ."

I asked permission to share Georgie's story with my newspaper friend, and the Claibornes agreed. That evening I wrote about my friend and his desire to make a difference in the world. As I folded the pages of the article and placed them in an envelope, tears spilled out yet again. The light from my desk lamp illuminated the medallion. I picked it up and ran my fingers over the embossed surface. "George, my old friend. I know you would tell me to move ahead, to dare to live."

When I told Drucilla and Ian the next morning at breakfast of my decision, their faces dropped. "Dorothy, are you sure about this? Ian and I have enjoyed having you here. You've been a good influence on Ashley."

"I've enjoyed being here. You made me feel welcome immediately. And it's been fun having a little sister again."

Ashley breezed into the sunroom. "Who's little sister?"

Ian sighed. "Dorothy has decided to get herself a room at a boardinghouse."

"Why? Don't you like us anymore?" Ashley asked.

"Of course I do. I love each of you like family." I glanced from face to face. "I think I need to branch out on my own a little."

"How does Chloe Mae feel about this decision?" Drucilla asked.

"She's the one who suggested it."

A frown knitted Drucilla's brow. "I must admit that I'm surprised."

"I'm not." Ashley buttered a piece of toast and took a bite. "It will make it much easier for you to pass your newspaper articles to Mr. Collingsworth."

I choked on a spoonful of oatmeal. "Excuse me?"

"Your articles that you give to him each Wednesday night? And the envelope he passes to you in return?"

Drucilla, Ian, and I shot surprised looks at one another. Ashley saw our consternation and laughed. "You didn't really think I didn't know what's going on, did you? This is terrific. I won't have to walk home with Scott anymore."

We continued to stare in surprise. "You didn't think I really liked him, did you? He's OK, but not for a boyfriend, kind of like you and Mr. Bowles."

Again my lower jaw dropped open.

Again, Ashley giggled. "How blind do you think I am? And how stupid, D. M. Spencer? I didn't need a Harvard degree to figure that one out. By the way, I liked your article on the Italian fellow who had to shovel snow in order to have enough money for food and lodging."

I was dumbfounded. By the looks on her parents' faces, they were as well.

"Do you think I could go with you on a story and help you sometime? It sounds exciting." Her eyes glistened with excitement. "And can I visit you at your boardinghouse occasionally?"

"Well, yes, I'd like that," I stammered.

"Good." She took another bite of toast, slurped down a glass of milk, and excused herself. "CeeCee and I have a great shopping excursion planned for today, so please excuse me? Papa, can I have a little extra money to spend? I know I've spent this month's allowance, but CeeCee and I haven't gone shopping together in such a long time." She fluttered her eyelashes and put on her best little-girl pout.

"This month's and next!" He reached in his vest pocket and withdrew a silver money clip then counted off several large bills.

"Oh, Daddy, you're a darling!" Ashley kissed his cheek.

"Ian!" Drucilla started, then sat back in her chair and sighed. "You're spoiling her."

Ian shrugged and gestured his surrender. "Ah, what can I do? She turns my will to tapioca pudding."

"Oh, Daddy," Ashley cooed. "I love you so much." She pressed another kiss on his cheek and then planted one on her mother's as well. "Don't worry, Mommy, I love you too."

"*Shoo!* You spoiled child." Drucilla grinned and clicked her tongue. "Ian, you spoil her so."

He sighed and nodded. "I know. But how much longer will I have her before some dashing prince sweeps her off her feet? Besides, seeing her happy gives me pleasure, as well."

The next few weeks passed quickly. Chloe and I visited a number of boardinghouses and found the ideal furnished room just four blocks from the church where I met Matt and two blocks from the subway. The room had a heavy black-walnut bedstead with matching dresser and dressing table, as well as a well-worn green velvet sofa and rose velvet upholstered armchair in front of a massive marble fireplace. A large black-walnut armoire filled the far corner of the room. A small writing table and straight-backed chair sat in front of the window. My necessary room, which I would share with three other tenants on the floor, was down the hall and to the right. My meals would be taken downstairs with the landlady, Mrs. Stahl, and the other tenants.

Slubbed rose-satin draperies edged the floor-to-ceiling windows of my new home. Below was a cityscape worthy of an artist's canvas. Across the street from the boardinghouse was a French cafe with red-and-white striped awnings and tables on the sidewalk. CeeCee said the place reminded her of the one in Paris where she located her artist friend, Thaddeus. Next door to the cafe was a small general store where I would be able to buy the occasional odds and ends I might need.

On my first night in my new home, I took out my Bible and read from Philippians 4:19: "And my God will meet all your needs according to His glorious riches in Christ Jesus."

Beside the massive bed with its downy-soft mattress and the brightly colored crazy quilt Chloe Mae gave me as a house-warming gift, I knelt and gave thanks for my new home. "You have promised to meet all my needs, Father. And as usual, You have kept

Your word. I rejoice in You and Your love for me."

I climbed into my new bed, punched the down-filled pillow, slid beneath the covers, then turned off the lamp on the stand beside the bed. Darkness settled around me like a comforting friend. I thought of George, of his parents, of Franklin in Boston, of CeeCee waiting to hear from her friend, and of Papa and the kids back home. And as much as I missed them all, I knew I'd found a home.

In the next few weeks I added little knickknacks to the room and flouncy pillows for the sofa. I tossed one of my crocheted shawls over the worn spot on the arm of the sofa.

Autumn passed quickly. Franklin's letters arrived less frequently. My relationship with Molly and Bobby, and, of course, Lily, grew with each visit. I found ways to pay Bobby for introducing me to people I could interview. I arranged to visit Little Italy, as well, and the De Angelos. Mama and I became great friends.

The prohibition movement gained momentum that fall. Henry Ford and many other industrial giants threw their influence and their money behind the movement. While I didn't write either for or against the issue, I let my stories of heartache and despair I encountered in the neighborhoods of New York City speak for themselves.

I only saw Matt at church. We kept our communication brief and businesslike. He told me that my column had easily become the most popular one in the paper. I asked him how Giles felt about this development. Matt avoided answering my question.

On November 11 there was dancing in the streets. The Great War had ended. Our boys would be coming home. Sirens wailed, bells clanged, and people screamed when the news was announced. As part of the throng of revelers on the streets of Manhattan, I'd never been kissed so soundly or so frequently before in my life. When the alcohol began to flow, I headed for the safety of my little home. I'd seen enough riots in Boston; I didn't need to be involved in a Manhattan-style one as well.

A week before Christmas, I visited the Claibornes. Matt asked to go with me, since he knew George's story. I took them a copy of a photograph I'd taken of George while he was at our home in Shinglehouse. My father found it in my room and mailed it to me once he heard of George's fate.

Matt, the Claibornes, and I talked for some time until Mr. Claiborne invited Matt to view several rare coins he kept in his study. This left Mrs. Claiborne and me in the parlor.

Katherine, as Mrs. Claiborne insisted I call her, had dark rings around her eyes. She coughed a lot into her embroidered linen handkerchief.

"Have you seen a doctor? You don't look like you're feeling well." I touched her arm gently. "Are you taking care of yourself?"

"I haven't been sleeping well." She smiled, her eyes revealing the sadness in her heart. "You are right. I haven't been well. Now that the war is over, George is taking me to Italy immediately after the holidays. There is a health spa in northern Italy . . ."

"I'm so glad. I worry about you."

She smiled again. "You are a sweetheart, Dolly. Sorry, I understand that you go by the name of Dorothy now, but to me, you'll always be Dolly."

"I don't mind. Matt, er, Mr. Collingsworth, calls me Dolly too."

Katherine leaned closer. "Your Mr. Collingsworth seems to be smitten with you, young lady."

I blushed. "Oh no! We're just friends."

She pursed her lips. "Mark my words. He'll propose before a year has passed."

I laughed, but inside my heart, I hurt.

"Dorothy, I hope I'm not imposing, but I need to ask you something. It's rather personal."

I gulped.

"May I?" Lines of worry filled her forehead.

"Of course. I'll answer as best I can."

"I know you will." She paused for a moment and pursed her lips as if trying to organize her thoughts. "Georgie told me about the talks you and he had about God and heaven. He said 'Dolly is the first person I've ever met who knows her Bible. She talks with God every day.'"

I blushed and mumbled a Thank you. Knowing all the hours we spent sitting on the porch discussing God's Word and sharing our experiences for the day, sometimes with Hattie's husband and sometimes with Papa, had made such an impact on George, and it warmed my heart.

"I went to my parents' church as a child, but after marrying George . . . well, my husband has always been self-sufficient, at least until we lost Georgie. God wasn't in his plan for living."

I nodded, encouraging her to continue.

She stopped speaking for several seconds. When she resumed, her words came out in a burst of emotion. "Where's my son, Dolly? Is he floating on a cloud and playing a harp, or is he rocking in Abraham's bosom? Is he gone forever? Where does the Bible say my son is right now?"

I glanced about the parlor for a Bible. There was none. How I wished I had mine with me. "Whew," I admitted. "You've asked questions theologians have argued about for generations. Where do you think he is?"

"I don't know. As a child I believed the dead had to spend time in a never-never land until someone prayed them into heaven. I pray for him. All the time." She wrung the life out of her linen handkerchief. "But I'm so afraid I won't pray enough and my son will be stranded in some God-forsaken place."

Gently, I placed my hand over one of hers. "God is a God of love. He loves your son more than you ever could."

"Is that why He took Georgie from me?" Her eyes swam in tears.

"You don't have a Bible handy, do you?"

She shook her head. "No, I don't think so. My husband wouldn't tolerate what he calls 'a book of suspicion and lies being in the house.'"

"I can answer every one of your questions right now, if you'd like, but I'd feel better showing you the answers in the Bible. You need to take God's Word for it, not mine."

The woman lurched forward, her eyes pleading with me. "If I buy a Bible, could you show me?"

I broke into a smile. "Oh, Katherine, I'd love to. Maybe we could plan to meet next Thursday evening. Would that be convenient for you?"

Katherine blinked and reddened. "I was hoping we could meet tomorrow afternoon."

"Tomorrow afternoon?" I thought regularly about my scheduled visit to Little Italy.

"We could meet wherever you like. I could come to your place, if it would be more convenient. That way—"She cast a frightened glance toward the parlor door—"George won't necessarily know." While I knew what her words said, I wondered what they didn't say. Was she so fearful of her husband that she didn't even want him to know about our meeting?

"Tomorrow afternoon sounds perfect. And I'd love to have you visit my place." I found a pen and scrap paper in my purse and scribbled out my address. "Would four o'clock be convenient?"

"That would be perfect." She grasped my hand between hers. "Thank you so much. This means a lot to me."

"Me too." I was surprised how much I was looking forward to our meeting. *To share the peace I felt regarding the state of the dead with Katherine, what a privilege,* I thought. Would you mind if I prayed with you?"

"I'd love it. Can you do that?"

"Oh yes, God hears us anytime, anywhere."

"Then please . . ."

We bowed our heads together. "Dear heavenly Father, we love You so much. We are thankful that You are more than a God and the Creator of the universe; You love us like a Father. Katherine, here, is filled with worries and fear for her dear son. Quiet her mind. Soothe her pain. And fill her with Your promised peace so that she can sleep tonight and truly rest in Your love. Amen."

"Oh, that was lovely. Thank you so much."

"You are so welcome." My eyes brimmed with tears. I sniffed. "In the meantime, know that dear Georgie is not languishing in some never-never land waiting for your prayers to release him. When you pray tonight, thank God for His marvelous love and His compassion to you and to your son."

"All right." She nodded her head enthusiastically. "I'll do that."

The men entered almost immediately after I finished praying, as if on cue from a Master Director. I smiled to myself as I watched the pompous George pose with pipe in hand before the imported marble mantle of the room's fireplace. What a powerhouse for the Lord this man could be if he knew Him. In my mind I said, "You, dear sir, have no idea how much your life is going to change now that you have a praying wife."

The day was far gone when Matt and I stepped out of the house onto the front steps of the Claiborne estate. By the look of clouds overhead, we were in for one big storm. An icy breeze whipped around the corner of the main house. I drew my heavy beige wool coat about me. The beaver pelt about the collar tickled my chin and neck.

I'd been thrilled when Chloe asked me if I could use a good coat. Being one of the youngest girls in the family, I was used to, and definitely appreciated, hand-me-downs. But lately, clothes from Chloe were hardly in that category. While she was nowhere near as extravagant as her in-laws, her closets burst with an array of new clothing. Hence, my wardrobe seemed to be expanding as well, since she returned from Europe.

I tugged on my gloves. Matt helped me into the automobile then cranked the car to life. I was glad that his little Pierce Arrow had a canvas roof. We'd barely entered the Sunday-afternoon traffic when the first snowflakes splattered on the windowsill. Big, lazy flakes drifted down around us, sticking to tree limbs, porch railings, and the boulevard, isolating us from the people walking along the sidewalk and from the vehicles inching along the roadway. We were cocooned in a magical world of our own.

"Isn't it beautiful?" I whispered, almost afraid to break the captivating silence of the moment.

Matt seconded my opinion. "I love the city during the year's first snowstorm. All the filth and dirt and evil is blanketed with a covering of white." We'd barely driven ten blocks before the snowfall intensified to the point where Matt had to stop to clear the windshield. When he climbed back into the car, snow fell from the brim of his hat. He brushed the flakes off his coat collar and sleeves. I squealed with delight as the melting flakes pelted my face.

I wrinkled my nose when he brushed a melting flake from my nose with his gloved hand. He laughed and brushed a second flake from my chin. "You are so beautiful, do you know that?"

He leaned closer. His smile faded as his gaze focused not on my eyes but on my lips. I froze. Seeing my reaction, he recovered quickly. "I'd better get you home before we become snowbound in this vehicle."

"Oh no!" I pointed to the windshield. "It's all covered again with snow."

He opened the car door to get out. I did the same on my side. "I'll get it," he called.

"Let me help." I brushed my gloved hand across the windshield. Scooping up a handful of snow from the car's fender, I threw it at him. It landed on the back of his neck.

"I can't believe you did that!" He looked up in surprise. "Of all the dirty—"

I giggled and tossed another handful of snow at his right cheek. *Splat!* The snowball hit its mark. I ducked when I saw his first snowball coming toward me. It skimmed the top of my cloche hat. I threw another snowball and then scurried around the rear of the automobile. I didn't expect him to do the same on his side of the car. *Thunk!* We collided full force, sending both of us onto our backsides, laughing.

I threw a huge glob of snow at him, hitting him on the forehead. I then scrambled to my feet and ran. By now the grass in the small neighborhood park near where we stopped was lightly covered with snow, as were the tree branches.

"You'll pay," he shouted, gathering snow in his hand as he ran toward me. I slipped and skidded as I ran. My city-style boots gave me no traction. For the first time in my life, I wished I were wearing my heavy leather farm boots. I continued running. I could sense him right behind me.

Without warning, I skidded to a stop under the branch of a tall pine tree. I grabbed the snow-laden branch and turned to face my pursuer. "Come one step closer, and I—"

Splat! A snowball hit me full in the face. Stunned, I pawed at the snow covering my eyes. Realizing that he was gently removing the snow still clinging to my face, I appeared to relax. "I'm sorry!" He brushed a clump of snow from my left cheek. "I hope I didn't—"

He didn't have time to finish his sentence before I snagged the branch over his head. Snow cascaded down on both of us, our own private snowstorm.

As it fell about us, he removed his glove and gently brushed his fingertip along one side of my face. I couldn't breathe. I sensed he had trouble breathing, as well. His voice was husky as he brushed a stray curl from my face. "Dolly, Dolly, Dolly . . ."

I also sensed I was out of my league. I'd never felt such strong feelings toward anyone before. I wanted to run away—far, far away—yet I longed to stay trapped in the moment forever. I couldn't explain it. "*Um* . . . The snow is falling faster. Maybe we'd better be on our way."

"*Uh-hmm,*" he muttered, his fingers still entwined in the stray curl. "That would be wise." Yet he did not move, and I couldn't. We gazed at one another for several seconds.

"May I kiss you?"

I looked up at him, certain he could see straight into my heart. There was nothing I wanted more at the moment. At the last moment, reality returned. "Do you think that would be prudent?"

His eyes narrowed. A frown line deepened in his forehead. He took a step away from me. "You're right. Thank you for reminding me, but you're right. Until I can come to you without the guilt of Lyssa's death haunting me, I would be out of line."

"Matt, I-I-I." What could I say? My lips felt dry and parched. How I wanted to welcome his kiss, his embrace. How I wished he were free to make a declaration of love for me. I couldn't play at love. I respected myself and Matt too much to turn our relationship into an adolescent game.

We drove home in silence, stopping when necessary to clear the windshield. The car eased to a stop in front of my boardinghouse. He turned off the engine and turned to face me. "I feel like such a cad. I wish I could offer you more than my friendship right now. Honest, I do . . ."

"I know. I do appreciate your friendship." I thought of Franklin. "More than you could possibly know."

"I don't know if—"

"Sh . . ." I touched his lips with my gloved hand. "Don't. I admit that I cannot understand the burden of guilt you carry, but I do know our Burden Bearer. Sooner or later, you'll have to trust God enough to let Him carry it for you."

He glanced away. "I know you're right. I've told myself the same thing dozens of times." He climbed out of the car and came around to my side to help me out as well. He escorted me into the porch of my boardinghouse and quickly said Goodbye. Seeing the boarders gathered around the big oak table for dinner, he asked, "Did you miss dinner? I should have thought to get you something to eat." He removed his watch from his best pocket and glanced at the time. "We still could go—"

"No, no. I'm sure I'll be able to get enough to eat. Mrs. Stahl is a very generous woman." I stepped aside so he could open the front door for me. "Thank you for wanting to go with me to the Claibornes. And good night."

He released the door behind me after I stepped inside the house. With a heavy heart, I watched Matt brush the snow from his car windshield and hop inside. I watched until the vehicle inched down the snowy roadway, lost in the swirl of steam coming from its exhaust.

"Oh, dear Miss Spencer," my landlady called. "We're all in here. Come, come. Steaming hot stew and fresh bread. I made plenty."

I heaved a deep sigh, replaced my concerned frown with a smile, and entered the brightly lighted dining room. *If I weren't so hungry, I'd forget supper and go straight to my room,* I thought. But the aromas of homemade bread and hearty stew set my stomach to growling.

That evening, alone in my room and watching the snow fall, I talked with God about my friend Katherine and about Matt. How different they both were; Katherine had never known a loving God and dear, sweet Matt knew Him but didn't really understand Him to be a forgiving Father.

When I awoke the next morning, the world was transformed into a sparkling dream world. Around noon, I received a call from Katherine. "I haven't been able to get to a store for a Bible this morning. Perhaps we'll have to postpone our visit until Tuesday."

"Katherine, I have a spare Bible you can use for a time, if you'd like. I'll be glad to lend it to you, if you still want to meet."

"Really? Oh, that's wonderful! Yes, I'll come by subway. That will be fun. I seldom travel by subway, you know." The excitement in her voice was contagious. "I'll see you soon then."

"Be careful. The streets are slippery."

"I'll be careful," she assured me. "By the way, last night I slept so soundly I didn't hear George get up this morning. And he let me sleep. Imagine! I've eaten breakfast with him every day he's been home for the last twenty years."

I chuckled.

"I'll see you later this afternoon. Do you think we could meet at three instead of four, since I want to get home before dark?"

"That would be a good idea, I think."

"Wonderful! See you then."

As I puttered about my room, preparing to entertain my first guest, I prayed for wisdom to answer Katherine's questions. The two Bibles lay atop the small cherrywood sofa table. During the morning hours, I'd reread all the texts I needed to share.

Half an hour before she got there, I hurried downstairs and asked Mrs. Stahl if I could heat a pot of water on her kitchen stove. I told her about Katherine's visit. "Of course, child, anytime. At least, when your visitors are ladies, of course." She removed the lid of a big round Dutchman cookie jar and offered it to me— "take several to serve with your tea."

"You are such a dear." I gave the ample woman a big hug. Carefully I carried the tray of hot mint tea up the stairs, along with the cookies and Mrs. Stahl's porcelain tea cups and saucers. I'd barely arrived in the room when I heard the front doorbell ring. Then I heard Katherine's voice in the rooming house vestibule.

I greeted my friend at the foot of the stairs and introduced her to Mrs. Stahl. I could tell, as my landlady helped Katherine off with her expensive camel-hair coat, that the woman was impressed with her guest. Mrs. Stahl talked and talked, first about the weather then about riding on the subways. I wondered how I could politely break away.

"Mrs. Stahl, Katherine and I are having a little Bible study upstairs in my room. You are invited to attend if you wish."

"Oh? Really?" For a second, the woman seemed interested and then shook her head. "No, thank you for the invitation, but I don't think so. Too much to do, you know."

"Well, should you change your mind, you are welcome."

"Thank you so much, Dorothy. You are such a sweetheart." The landlady excused herself, and we climbed the stairs to my room. Once inside, Katherine said all the right things about my humble abode, though I know for her it must have seemed sparse and cramped.

"You have a perfect little nest here, Dorothy. I've never been on my own. My parents were wealthy, so I went from one mausoleum to another." She ran her gloved hand along the back of the sofa. "I'm not complaining, mind you. George is good to me, a

168

little overbearing at times, but good. And I do love him."

"But?" I knew she wanted to say more.

"But, I think I resent him for bullying Georgie first into running away then into joining the army." An edge entered her usually mellow speech. "My son might have been alive today if . . ." She stopped, shook her head, then displayed her socialite smile. "*If onlys* are quite worthless, don't you think?"

"Indeed I do. Please come over here and make yourself comfortable. Would you like a cup of peppermint tea? A cookie?"

CHAPTER ELEVEN

Beyond the Brink

"Please understand, Katherine, I don't have all the answers, but I'll do the best I can." I handed Mrs. Claiborne an extra Bible I found among the books I'd brought from home.

"Georgie said that you were the wisest woman he ever met. I think he had a mild crush on you, if the truth be known." She smiled the smile of a mother who would never realize the love of a daughter-in-law. "He came home from Pennsylvania a changed boy. He had a faith in God that even his father couldn't shake. And if you don't think that frustrated George!" She laughed. "OK, where do we begin?" She flipped through the first few pages of God's Word. "Genesis?"

I laughed. "No, at least not today. I think we should begin by answering your questions. Let's begin in the book of Ecclesiastes. Psalms is the middle book then Proverbs, Song of Solomon, and then Ecclesiastes." I directed her through the Bible. "Find Ecclesiastes 9."

"Here it is! Here it is." Katherine's excitement was contagious. "The whole chapter?"

"No, skim down to verses 5 and 6."

"Yes! Here it is."

"Why don't you read the verses aloud?"

She removed a pair of wire-rimmed spectacles from her purse and perched them on the bridge of her nose then cleared her throat. " 'For the living know that they shall die; but the dead know not any thing, neither have they any more a reward; for the memory of them is forgotten. Also their love, and their hatred, and their envy, is now perished; neither have they any more a portion for ever in any thing that is done under the sun.' " She looked up from the Word, her eyes filled with horror. "That's terrible. Is my Georgie gone forever? That's what my husband believes."

"No, no, that's just one text. With God's Word, it is important to cross reference what He says in order to get a complete picture." I placed my hand on her arm for comfort. "Let's turn to 1 Thessalonians 4." I helped her locate the New Testament then the first of the two books of Thessalonians. "Verses 13 to 18. Here, I'll read this one aloud. 'But I would not have you to be ignorant, brethren, concerning them which are asleep, that ye sorrow not, even as others which have no hope. For if we believe that Jesus died and rose again, even so them also which sleep in Jesus—' Did you get that? '. . . sleep in Jesus will God bring with him."

"Is that saying Georgie is in heaven?"

"Let's read a little farther, verses 16 and 17."

She took a deep breath. " 'For the Lord himself shall descend from heaven with a shout, with the voice of the archangel, and with the trump of God: and the dead in Christ shall rise first—' "

" 'Rise first?' I'm confused," she admitted.

"Here's what verses 17 and 18 say: 'Then we which are alive and remain shall be caught up together with them in the clouds, to meet the Lord in the air: and so shall we ever be with the Lord. Wherefore comfort one another with these words.' "

Katherine knitted her brow. "Then let me see if I understand what this says. The dead are asleep until Jesus comes. They're not suffering in any way." She paused a moment, lost in her thoughts.

"And when Jesus comes, He will take those of us who are alive, as well as those sleeping in the grave, to heaven with Him. Is that it?"

"Pretty much, at least as I read it."

"That certainly is a lot clearer than I thought it would be."

Katherine sipped her tea and nibbled on a sugar cookie for several seconds. From where we sat, we could see the late afternoon December sun dipping below the western horizon. "Do you think you have the time to answer other questions from God's Word for me? Perhaps another day?"

"I would love to, Katherine. Same time next week? Perhaps I should come to your house next time?"

She shook her head vigorously. "I'm not ready to share this with George. Let me scribble these texts down on my note pad so that when I get my Bible tomorrow, I will be able to find everything we talked about." She wrote down the verses, and I thought of Georgie's eagerness once he became on fire for God's Word. They were so much alike—mother and son.

I watched Katherine make her way to the corner then disappear from view. *What a gentle soul,* I thought. I hoped we'd become good friends in time.

As Katherine and I continued meeting each week, her confidence in God's faithfulness grew. Her timidity and feelings of ineffectiveness lessened. I wondered if her husband, George, was noticing the changes as well. How would he react to the new woman his wife was becoming?

At Christmas I visited my family in Pennsylvania. Pa, especially, appreciated my presence there. Chloe and her family spent the holidays visiting Cy's family in Baltimore. However, the rest of the family, except for Joe's branch in California, gathered around Hattie's shiny oak trestle table for Christmas dinner.

Tears came to my eyes at seeing Mama's favorite Irish linen tablecloth. The bowls of food before us took me back to my childhood days. All Mama's best holiday recipes.

"It's beautiful, Hattie," I whispered reverently.

"Thank you." She beamed with pleasure. For a long time, I'd known that my big sister's greatest joy was pleasing others. And all too often her efforts went unnoticed and unappreciated.

The family joined hands for the blessing. I looked around the table at the faces of so many people whom I loved, and a wave of homesickness swept through me. I hadn't realized how much I'd missed them. But I'm home, I reminded myself.

After the meal, Papa and I walked into town. The snow crunched under my stylish leather boots. I held onto my father's arm for support. I realized I would have been wise to borrow my younger sister's Arctics. They would have been much more stable on the unplowed roadways.

We talked first about national politics, including the prohibition issue. We discussed the postwar situation in Europe.

"Our newspaper editor, you remember him, don't you?" Papa asked. "He had a leg blown off during cannon fire. He and his wife and baby are living back East somewhere at his wife's family's place."

Stunned, I could hardly breathe. "Bud? Bud Ames?"

"Sad. He was doing great things for this town."

"Bud?" My mind refused to accept what my father had said. "What's going to happen with the *Sentinel*?"

"His cousin is running it right now, but who knows? There's rumor it's on the market. I hope it doesn't close altogether."

"I'm sure someone will come along to run it." I had to change the subject until I could sort out my confused thoughts. "So, how is Grandma Bixley's arthritis this winter?"

"Bad. She can hardly get around now." Grandma Bixley was eighty years old. Papa had been treating her arthritis since long before I was born.

"That's too bad. She was always in the middle of every church party game. I can't imagine life at the old church without her."

My father laughed. "Don't worry. She'll outlive us all."

Papa asked about my job, even though I'd been sending him copies of my published articles all along. I told him I loved it.

"And do you like living in the city?" he asked.

"Sometimes yes. Sometimes no," I admitted. "I enjoy the vibrancy of the city, its throbbing pulse." We crossed River Street in front of Foote's Department Store. "On the other hand, the peace I feel here, I never feel in New York."

"What about your employer?" Papa assisted me as I stepped onto the wooden sidewalk. "You never say much about him. Matthew Collingsworth, isn't it?"

"Actually, the paper is operated by two brothers, Matthew and Giles Collingsworth. They're good men. They operate the paper for their father, who had a stroke some time ago."

"*Hmm.* What about the lawyer you met while you were in Boston?"

I smiled and patted my father's arm tenderly. "Papa, are you trying to ask if I'm seeing anyone, personally?"

"Well . . ." My father reddened. "Yes, I guess I am. I still look out for my little girl, you know."

I laughed. It had been a long time since I felt like anyone's little girl. At the sound of sleigh bells, we both turned. Mr. Simons, the local Ford dealer, and his wife were out for a Christmas afternoon ride the old-fashioned way. Their matching sorrels pranced in the crisp almost pristine snow. The Simons waved. We returned their greeting. "Need a lift home?" Mr. Simons asked.

"No, thank you," my father called, "just walking off Christmas dinner."

Mr. Simons nodded and shook the reigns, causing the bells to jangle. The sleigh pulled forward.

"There's something to be said for bygone days." I turned and caught a last glimpse of the shiny black sleigh.

"You must see that all the time in the city."

"I suppose. The rag man and the ice man still operate wagons and teams of horses. Much of the freight hauling is still done with a team of horses, as well as the fire wagons. And, of course, the city maintains horse-and-buggy rides through Central Park, but it's been a long time since I've seen a horse-drawn sleigh, accompanied by silver bells." I knew I was rambling, possibly hoping to prolong the beauty of these moments with my father.

"Times are certainly changing . . ." Papa patted the back of my hand in the crook of his arm. "What a time to be alive and see the changes! And my baby is a part of it." He glanced down at me with fondness and pride in his eyes.

"You really don't mind my living alone in New York City, Papa?"

"Darling Dolly, as long as what you are doing is respectable, honest, and brings you happiness, I salute you. Too few people ever pursue their dreams. I'm proud that you have the courage to do so. So tell me about this Matthew Collingsworth."

"Papa! How did Mr. Collingsworth get into this conversation?"

My father chuckled. "You don't think I can see the glow in your face whenever his name is mentioned? Give your poor old dad credit. Besides, your face is an open book—don't ever change that."

I laughed. "You are incorrigible."

"My, my, fifty-dollar words. You *are* becoming worldly-wise."

I gently slapped him on the arm. "Papa, stop teasing."

The late afternoon sun cast long icy shadows across our pathway as we trudged the last miles back home to the farm. It had been a good day. Warmed by my father's encouragement and support, I fell into bed that evening at peace with my world. I pulled my mother's hand-stitched, down-filled quilt up under my chin. In the unaccustomed darkness of country living, I could hear my little sister snoring in her sleep instead of the constant city noise I heard in my little room in the boardinghouse.

"Dear Lord, thank You for all these people who love me and want only the best for me. Sometimes in the city, even with Chloe and Cy and their children less than two miles from me, I feel terribly alone. Everyone but me has someone." Matt's face drifted across my consciousness, and I realized that all the loneliness wasn't erased by being back home. I wondered what he might be doing

176

out on Long Island at the family estate. Would he be walking along the beach? At a dinner party? Perhaps discussing the operation of the newspaper with his father and brother? "Be with him, Lord. Keep him safely in Your care."

Before drifting off to sleep, I prayed for Bud and his little family. I wondered about his future. I never would have imagined my life taking the turns it had, and I'm sure Bud never imagined his.

By the day after New Year's, I was eager to get back to the city and to my friends, especially to see Matt, since I knew he'd be back from visiting his parents' home. I'd purchased several toys for Molly and Bobby from Shinglehouse's main industry, a toy factory.

My arms were loaded with suitcases, shopping bags, and various-sized packages as I stepped off the train at Grand Central Station. I asked a porter to help me to the taxi stand with my packages. We were walking across the marbled floor of the station's magnificent rotunda when I heard someone call my name. I turned. There was Matt, shouting and waving at me from across the rotunda. He bounded toward me, acting as eager to see me as I felt seeing him. For a moment, hope rose within my heart, but then my reason took control.

He skidded to a halt inches in front of me. He acted like a gangly teenage boy struck dumb by a pretty girl. I laughed at the incongruous analogy. "Here, let me help you with those packages." He took most of the things I carried from my hands. "I have my car waiting outside."

I laughed aloud. "Begging your pardon, sir, but where do you plan to stash all these packages?"

"No problem," he insisted, waving for the porter to follow him. "There's plenty of room in the 'boot.'"

To my surprise, Matt managed to get all but two shopping bags in the trunk of the Pierce-Arrow. After helping me into the car, he ran around the vehicle to the driver's side and hopped in. "Where to?"

"My place, I suppose."

"Nonsense! You must be starving. I know how abominable train fare can be. Let's go visit Mama and Papa De Angelo."

I gazed at him in surprise. I'd been to see Mama and Papa several times since our one visit there together. But I suspected he had not.

I remembered the toys I had in the trunk of the car. "Matt? Would it be possible to swing around to the Bowery? I have a few Christmas gifts to deliver to friends of mine."

"Sure, I'd love to. So who are the mysterious recipients of your generosity?"

I laughed at his verbosity. "You are certainly feeling rhetorically fit today, aren't you?"

"Indubitably, my dear." He grinned and eased into the stream of traffic heading away from the station.

His lighthearted mood baffled me. It was a side of him I'd never before witnessed. He kept me laughing by sharing stories of his bizarre holiday visit with his parents. Matt could turn any event into a comedy routine. No matter what his family was like, I was certain they couldn't be as hilariously funny as he made them sound.

"You are incorrigible." I dabbed at the tears of laughter brimming in my eyes.

Suddenly, his mood changed. "I told Dad about you."

"Excuse me?"

"Dad was waxing verbose about D. M. Spencer's column, which set poor Giles squirming in Mama's Louis XIV settee. After about fifteen minutes of accolades for the mighty Spencer, I decided Dad was ready to know the truth."

"And?"

"And he ordered me to fire you."

"What?" The two packages on my lap slid to the floor.

"I, of course, told him that was out of the question." Matt shrugged and tipped his head nonchalantly to one side. "It made a grand finale to a miserable week."

"Matt! Don't be mean!"

He laughed. "You weren't there, so you can't know."

"By what you say, I can imagine."

"One thing is certain. There's no hyperbole that can overstate the experience." He exhaled through his teeth. I knew that while he might joke about his family's idiosyncrasies, his relationship with his folks pained him more than he'd ever reveal to anyone.

I pointed to the right. "Here's the street. Third house on the right. That's the O'Reilly's place."

The two children saw the Pierce-Arrow pull up in front of their home. Before we could get out of the car, they were bursting through the front door of the tenement house.

"Miss Dorothy! Miss Dorothy! Merry Christmas!" They shouted as they bounded down the front steps and into my arms.

"Guess what. I got Lily a catnip mouse for Christmas. She loves it!" Molly chatted.

"And I saved some of the money you gave me to buy Mama a pink-and-white gingham apron. She looks so pretty in it." Bobby danced in synchronization with his speech.

Matt opened the trunk. It was the first time Molly had spotted the tall stranger. She cowered in the folds of my coat. Bobby eyed Matt suspiciously.

"Don't be afraid," I encouraged them. "This is my friend Matt. He helped me bring a few little presents to you. I brought them all the way from Pennsylvania." Reaching into the trunk, I extracted two large shopping bags filled with brightly wrapped packages. "This bag's for you." I handed the first one to Bobby. "And this bag's for Molly. Let's go upstairs and open everything up!"

The children flew up the stairs, three steps faster than Matt and I. When we stepped into the dingy little one-room apartment, I was surprised to see a man and a woman sitting on wooden vegetable crates on each side of the rickety table.

"Mama! Daddy! Look!" Molly dumped the contents of her bag on the floor. She dropped to her knees to inspect the individually wrapped presents.

Bobby did the same, leaving the adults to introduce themselves.

It was the first time I'd met both parents together. The only time I'd met their father was when he was ready to pass out from liquor.

The two shook our hands cordially. "I appreciate the attention you've given my children, Miss Dorothy," Mrs. O'Reilly began. I looked at the sad, listless face of the children's mother. The woman couldn't have been much older than I was.

I introduced Matt as my friend and not as the *Tribune* editor. "I hope you don't mind my bringing little gifts now and then to your children. I appreciate them caring for my Lily too. My landlady would frown upon my keeping a cat, you know."

The woman smiled at me. "I know what you're doing. Before I left Ireland, I would have been insulted by your charity. But . . . " Her eyes misted. "Here, in America, beggars can't be choosers."

"Oh no, Mrs. O'Reilly. Bobby and Molly do much more for me than I ever could do for them. I'm one of several children in a family. And every now and then I get homesick for them. Bobby and Molly give me someone to love when my arms feel empty."

Mr. O'Reilly gazed at the table in front of him without speaking.

"Bobby tells me that your mother was Irish, Miss Spencer," Mrs. O'Reilly said.

"That's right. She was a second-generation American. On the parlor windows, Pa still has handmade panels of lace that my grandmother brought with her from Ireland."

I glanced at Bobby. He'd torn into the packages with the curiosity natural to a boy his age. He was busy assembling a wooden train set, complete with engineer, porter, trees, and a brightly painted wooden depot.

Molly, on the other hand, sat gently caressing the brightly wrapped packages, first one then another.

"Go ahead." I dropped to my knees beside her. "You can open them."

The little girl shook her head slowly. "They're too pretty to open. I love the pictures of the pretty candles."

I picked up one of the packages. "Here, let me help you. I think we can unwrap it without tearing any of the pictures."

"I've never had anything so pretty."

Slowly, I removed the red satin bow and looped it over her head. It fell to her neck. "That will look pretty in your hair, won't it?" Unfolding the rest of the package was easy. I left the last fold for her to undo. She lifted the paper and looked inside.

"A baby doll dress," she cooed. As she lifted from the wrappings a tiny pink taffeta dress with row upon row of white lace around the skirt, the room grew silent. As she examined the tiny frock, her eyes grew sad. "It's very nice, Miss Spencer. Thank you."

I looked toward the child's mother. Her eyes glistened with tears. The girl's father continued staring at the table.

"Let's open another package," I suggested. This time Molly undid the ribbon and paper and out fell a tiny yellow hand-crocheted sweater set with matching bonnet and booties. The child caressed the soft lacy bonnet for a second before opening the third package. The third package contained an undershirt and layette set. My sister Hattie had taken a few minutes and embroidered light blue ducklings around the hem of the layette saque and diaper. By the time Molly reached for the fourth and largest package, I could sense Matt, as well as the girl's parents, holding their breath.

As Molly lifted the fourth package, her eyes shone with excitement. She rattled it next to her ear and glanced my way, unable to speak. Quickly, without regard for the wrapping, she tore off the gold satin bow. The paper flew into many pieces until she reached the shoebox beneath. She paused for a moment at the sight of the shoebox. Slowly, she lifted the cover from the box and squealed.

"A doll-baby. My very own doll-baby!" She lifted the yellow flannel-blanketed, porcelain-faced doll from the box and cuddled it in her arms. "Mommy, look!" She leapt to her feet and ran to show the doll in the pink-and-white flannel nightie to her mother. "It's just like the one you had when you were a little girl. Remember?"

The mother nodded then glanced toward me. "Thank you," she whispered.

Without warning, Mr. O'Reilly shot to his feet. "Give it back! Give it all back. We don't need it. We don't need charity!"

We stared at the man as he snatched the doll from the little girl's arms and threw it across the room. Molly screamed. Then he started on the wooden train set.

"Robert! No!" the mother shouted, yanking on his shirt-sleeve. "Don't do this! Stop!" Bobby snatched the engine and red caboose into his arms and cowered in a corner.

"We don't need no do-gooder coming around here with gifts for the kids, gifts that we, as their parents, can't afford to buy them ourselves." He swung his arm back, which sent his wife flying across the room. She landed in a heap beside the bed and then buried her face in her hands and sobbed. Molly ran to retrieve the doll from where it landed.

At Mr. O'Reilly's violent action, Matt wrestled his arms behind his back and shoved him, face first, into the wall.

"Let me go!" the man shouted. "This is my home, and that's my wife. Let me go."

Matt shoved his face against the wall. "Not until you settle down and behave yourself. Miss Spencer is only bringing gifts to her friends. It's a holiday tradition in America, you know."

Mr. O'Reilly quieted. "All right. I give. I give."

Matt pulled up on his arms, tightening his grip. "Are you sure?"

"Yeah, I'm sure."

Slowly, Matt released Mr. O'Reilly's arms, and he hurried to his wife's side. "Darling, I am so sorry. I never want to hurt you." He helped her to her feet and onto the edge of the bed. He glanced toward us. "I'm sorry. Sometimes I get so frustrated I lose control, especially when I've been drinking some. I should be the one buying my little girl dolls. I should be the one buying trains for my son." He leaned forward, burying his face between his knees. His shoulders heaved with heart-rending sobs. "Forgive me."

Matt walked over to the young father and put his arm around

the man's shoulders. "Mr. O'Reilly, why don't you and I take a short walk? Get some air? Talk?"

Matt helped Robert O'Reilly to his feet and out the door. We listened to the sound of their footsteps as they descended the staircase. Molly crawled out of the corner, holding her doll. Her lower lip protruded dangerously far. Tears brimmed in her eyes. "Look, Mama, Daddy broke Mary Elizabeth's toe."

"Oh, honey," the girl's mother examined the doll's injury. "I think Mary Elizabeth will be just fine. Why don't you put the booties on her to keep her sore foot warm?"

Molly frowned for a moment and then nodded, her face solemn. "Yes, maybe that will make Mary Elizabeth feel better."

My surprise must have shone on my face, for when the young mother glanced my way, she confided in me. "I had a china-doll from France when I was a child, and her name was Mary Elizabeth."

Mrs. O'Reilly gathered her two children to her and comforted them for a few seconds. Then she distracted them from the memory of the painful scene by examining their new toys. Both of us were on the floor playing with the children when the two men returned.

Mr. O'Reilly's face beamed with happiness as he took his wife into his arms and asked her forgiveness. "Guess what, Mama? Mr. Collingsworth has offered me a job at the *Manhattan Tribune*. Of course, I'll have to stay off the sauce now. But a job, a real job, in America!"

I shot a surprised glance at Matt. He grinned and shrugged his shoulders. "Just a janitor in the pressroom."

I wanted to give Matt a giant hug and plant a great big kiss on his cheek. Instead, I grinned and said, "You never cease to surprise me, Mr. Collingsworth." Before Matt and I left the O'Reilly home, Mr. O'Reilly apologized again for his actions.

At the De Angelo's restaurant a few minutes later, I asked, "Do you think he'll be able to stay sober?"

"I don't know. But the first time he comes to work loaded, he knows he's out of there. I can't risk having an inebriated worker near the presses."

I gazed at the menu in my hands. "Well, if this prohibition bill passes in Congress, it might be a moot point."

"I wish that would be true, but I'm afraid we're in for some troubled times. I'm already hearing rumors from the lower elements in the city." Matt frowned. The criminals are planning for a heyday. They're already scouting out smuggling routes from Canada and from the Caribbean."

"But surely, the authorities . . ."

"Only time will tell."

I didn't realize then how right Matt was. By January 16, 1919, the three-fourths of states necessary to ratify the Eighteenth Amendment had done so. It was to go into effect one year later. The prohibition victory parade down Fifth Avenue easily rivaled the one held a few months earlier announcing the end of the Great War. Big money and big industry won what had seemed impossible. The law banning the trafficking and sale of alcohol in America would go into effect the following year.

Life in the big city proceeded normally. No one seemed worried about the coming restrictions. During the months following, people talked openly about the preparations being made to accommodate the "natural appetites" of mankind, as they put it. The nation's newspapers switched their attention to the riotous attitudes of the young men returning from France and the scandalous styles of clothing worn by the younger women of the age. A new form of music swept the cities of America, something called jazz. All this and more gave D. M. Spencer much about which to write.

It was a magical time. I loved the throbbing vibrancy of the city. People seemed alive and carefree after the doldrums of war. Social rules and regulations of the nineteenth century lessened, for good and for bad.

For me, it was good. As a woman, I could come and go about the city more freely. I continued meeting Matt every Wednesday evening, and then after the youth meeting, we often shared a chocolate frappe at the cafe across from my boardinghouse before saying Goodnight. We talked until we saw Mrs. Stahl preparing to lock up for the night, then I'd run across the street and into the boardinghouse. Matt would wait on the sidewalk until I turned on a light and waved to him from my second-floor window.

Chloe and Cy had us over for dinner several times. Matt and Cy's friendship grew until they were meeting for lunch occasionally when Cy was in the city. But with me, Matt stayed at arm's length. Sometimes when I'd see other young couples strolling in the park at sunset, I'd think about what I was missing. However, most of the time, I appreciated being in his company enough that I would do nothing to risk the comfortable balance we had.

Matt went with me to visit the O'Reillys when their third child was born. When Mrs. O'Reilly placed Megan, their newborn, in my arms, my breath caught in my chest. *Will I ever hold a child of my own,* I wondered? Out of the corner of my eye, I caught Matt staring at me and the baby. I wondered what he might be thinking. Was he thinking about the child he lost? The wife who died? I didn't know, and I knew I could never ask.

When I handed the tiny bundle back to her mother, I reminded myself that I'd chosen the life I led. If I'd wanted children, I could have married Franklin. A few days previous, I'd received a note from Julia McCall telling me of Franklin's engagement to Judge Meyers's granddaughter, Sophia. The couple would be married in August.

The summer came and went in a flurry of picnics, concerts, and boat rides on the East River. Chloe Mae and Drucilla vied with one another to introduce me to a succession of eligible bachelors, as if all I had to do was to troll for a husband! My writing skills sharpened, as did my nose for news. I visited the De Angelos at least once a week. They made me feel like one of their family. The shopkeepers in the neighborhood became so accustomed to seeing me around they'd call me by name as I passed and offer me a handful of grapes or a fresh piece of biscotti. The older men would tease, and the women would pinch my cheeks and tell me I needed to gain weight. And always, someone would have a story to tell.

One Thursday afternoon, I was talking with Anthony, the local tailor. He was telling me about his dream to save enough money to move to Los Angeles, where he'd make costumes for the film industry. Suddenly, the front door of his shop burst open and three swarthy looking men swaggered in. Anthony stiffened and moved rigidly behind the small glass case where he displayed several items of men's clothing. His voice broke as he spoke. "What do you fellows want?"

"Hey, Anthony, we're paisanos, remember? Vinnie's been noticing how many customers you've had lately, and he's decided to up your insurance policy."

"Look . . ." His eyes shifted from the men to me then back again. "I'm paying you guys as much as I can afford. I can't give you more and still keep the shop open." He gestured with his hands.

The leader of the group shrugged and gestured with his hands too. "Aw, Anthony, remember you have a beautiful wife and three gorgeous babies. You wouldn't want anything bad to happen to them, would you?"

The tailor ripped around the edge of the glass case. He grabbed the lapels of the leader's suit coat with one hand and leveled a large pair of tailoring scissors at the man's throat with the other. The other two men hauled him off their leader.

Undeterred, Anthony spit out his words. "If you or your thugs touch one hair of my family, I will personally gouge out your eyes."

The leader seemed unruffled by the tailor's outburst. He glanced toward me and shrugged. "Sorry you have to see this, lady, but that's what you get for hanging around with the likes of Anthony." He nodded to one of the men. One man held Anthony while the other punched him in the stomach several times. Anthony doubled over, retching on the floor.

Furious, I started toward the front door. The leader grabbed my arm and tossed me back against a shelf of fabric bolts. "Where do you think you're going, lady?"

"To find the constable, of course."

The leader threw back his head and laughed. "I don't think so."

I felt a rush of heat on my neck and face. I'd never been so angry in my entire life. "Three men against one! *Ooh,* I'm impressed." I straightened to my full height and glared down my nose at the man. "You are nothing but a disgusting schoolhouse bully. You should be taken to the woodshed and walloped!"

"You and what army?" The leader leered up at me.

I wrinkled up my nose. "You're despicable."

"Despicable? Did you hear that, Vince? The lady says I'm despicable." The man laughed then turned to the tailor, doubled up on the floor. "This lady's mouth just got you an additional $35 a month. That brings your monthly bill to $100 even." He gently cuffed Anthony's face. "See you in two weeks."

"You can't do that. This is America," I cried.

"Yes . . ." The leader sighed contentedly. ". . . America, the land of opportunity." The three men swaggered out of the shop but not without the leader turning and giving me a lecherous wink.

"I'm going for the constable." I helped Anthony struggle to his feet.

"No, please, forget what you saw here."

"But the police can help!"

He shook his head. "They already know, but they just look the other way."

My mouth flew open in surprise. "But that's extortion. There are laws—"

"Yes, there are laws . . ." He paused for a moment as he staggered to a stool. "And then there are laws. Unfortunately, we must live by Vinnie's laws to stay in business in this neighborhood."

"I don't understand. What would happen if you refused to pay?"

He massaged his stomach. "First, they'd vandalize the shop,

then they'd go after me and my family. No, it's not worth it."

"Do they do this to all of the shop owners here?"

He nodded.

"Why don't you band together and fight him?"

Anthony gave me a sick smile. "You don't know what you're asking. Please excuse me, but I need to rest."

"Of course." I helped him to a day bed in the work area behind a blue-and-white striped dividing curtain. "I'll turn the sign on the door when I leave. This has to stop! Anthony, I know someone at the newspaper who might be able to make a difference. Would you mind if I tell him about Vinnie and his thugs?"

Fear filled the man's face. "If Vinnie ever found out, I—"

"Don't worry. He won't. I promise you that." I seethed with anger as I made my way on the busy sidewalk. My outrage grew as, at each shop, I asked about Vinnie and his "insurance" plan. While no one would speak openly about it, their fear and fury screamed silently out of their persons. It wasn't until I reached the De Angelo's place that I realized Mama and Papa must have been paying those hoods as well, just for the privilege of operating their restaurant.

I wondered if the Irish community had a similar problem. They did. I couldn't believe it. I hopped a subway back to my boardinghouse. Within a couple of hours, I had written drafts of a series of articles for the following week, articles revealing the corruption plaguing the immigrant population of New York City.

The following Wednesday evening, when I delivered my weekly articles to Matt, I still couldn't talk about what I'd uncovered without raising my blood pressure. "Can you believe such a thing can go on in America?" I asked.

Matt chuckled. "Dear Dolly, you are such a child in so many ways."

I glared at him.

"It's one of the traits I most appreciate about you." He smiled down at me.

I folded my arms across my chest and scowled. "Are you

complimenting me or making fun of me? I can't tell."

"Complimenting you, of course. Your naive view of life is what makes your writing so unique. You see the world through innocent eyes, which makes those of us whose eyes are jaded remember our lost innocence." He glanced down at the envelope of articles I'd handed him. "Ethnic gangs are not a new phenomena nor did they originate in America. Unfortunately, when good people emigrate to America to better themselves, the leeches and parasites of their culture do too." He pursed his lips and frowned. "It's this criminal element in society that will most benefit when the prohibition act takes effect next winter."

"I don't understand."

"Like vultures, they feed on society's weaknesses."

My next visit to Little Italy gave me an idea how strong these gangs really were. Papa De Angelo and I were talking at a table when my favorite two thugs swaggered into the restaurant.

"Oh, lookee here!" Joey, the younger of the two Rullo brothers, chortled as he headed toward the table where I sat. "Our favorite pig-tailed tattletaler. Let's find out how loud she can squeal."

Vinnie narrowed his spite-filled eyes at me. The broad smile on his lips didn't reach his cold steel-gray eyes. "Joey, you don't think such a prissy little lady would write such nasty things about me, do you? Trying to get me in trouble with the constabulary?"

"I don't know, Vinnie. Who else could have done it? Could it be a mere coincidence that those slanderous articles appeared in the *Tribune* a week after our little disagreement? Written by a D. M. Spencer?" He took the chair on one side of me. His friend forced Papa out of his chair to sit down on the other side of me. "So you have an inside source at the *Trib*, a source whose last name happens to be the same as your own, so I hear."

"I go call the cops!" Papa turned to leave, but Joey grabbed his coattail.

"You stay put, Pops." The younger man yanked Papa De Angelo back to his side. My hands flew to the old man's defense. Vinnie captured my right hand midair and refused to let go. He had it cupped, which rendered me helpless.

"I can't quite figure this out," Vinnie said, increasing his grip on my fingers. "Is D. M. Spencer your husband or your brother?" He eyed me critically, as he increased his grip.

"I'm D. M. Spencer." Tightening my lips into a thin line, I stared insolently into his eyes. I didn't want to give him the satisfaction that he might be hurting me.

"Yeah, sure you are." He threw back his head and laughed. When he stopped laughing, he stared into my eyes. "You're lucky I have a sense of humor, Miss Dorothy." He drew out the syllables of my given name as if it were a bad joke. "No self-respecting newspaper hires a female to write their stuff. Did you hear that, Joey? Red here is playing funny with us." He tightened his grip on my hands. I could hear my finger bones pop from the pressure. "*Hmmph!* Tough little lady. Not even a grimace," he muttered then released my hand.

I slipped it back into my lap, thankful for the kid-skinned gloves that buffered some of the pressure.

"Look, babe, you take this message back to your employer. Stay out of Vinnie's life, you got it? I don't want no more heat coming down on my head, understand?"

I grinned and raised one brow. "As we little ladies would say, 'If you can't take the heat, get out of the kitchen.' "

Suddenly, he pounded his fist on the table in front of my face. I jumped in surprise. "My mama taught me not to hit a lady. But I represent some fellas whose mamas failed." Vinnie rose to his feet and shoved the chair he'd been sitting on. The chair toppled over and slid across the floor. His brother did the same, sending his chair in the opposite direction. "So keep your perky little nose out of my business."

Perky nose, I thought, *how ludicrous! My nose is anything but perky.* Slowly, I stood to my feet, towering over both of the men by five or six inches. My fists balled, I gazed down my patrician nose at them. "I am not intimidated by either you or your bully bosses."

Vinnie curled his lip into a sneer. "Then you, Miss Dorothy, are not as intelligent as I gave you credit for being."

I maintained my composure until the restaurant door slammed shut behind them and then sank into the chair. Hidden by the red-and-white checkered tablecloth, my knees shook like gelatin. My teeth would have chattered, but I'd locked my jaw in defiance of the men and couldn't seem to unlock it.

"Are you all right?" Papa asked, his face ashen.

"I'm fine, thank you. Why shouldn't I be?"

Papa rattled off several words in Italian. Mama De Angelo rushed from behind the kitchen doors carrying a cup of hot peppermint tea, my favorite. "My poor bambina." She handed the cup to me. "Here, drink this. You shouldn't mess with Vinnie or his kind. They are a bad lot."

"My wife is right, Miss Dorothy." Papa righted the toppled chairs. "When Mr. Collingsworth hears about this, he will be livid."

I started at the mention of Matthew. "No! Please, Papa De Angelo, we mustn't mention this to Mr. Collingsworth. Let me take care of it my own way."

"I don't know." Papa knitted his brow.

"Please?"

CHAPTER TWELVE

In Harm's Way

January 16, 1920, dawned sunny and biting cold. Newly fallen snow crunched beneath my boots as I trudged to the subway station. Signs in the bars and restaurant windows along the way read "Liquor sellout before midnight!" A young couple, carrying their infant, pushed a baby carriage loaded with whiskey bottles up the street. People carried armloads of amber-colored bottles, the pockets of their overcoats already stuffed with similar bottles. Everyone was stocking up for the "drought."

When I emerged from the subway tunnel at the Bowery station, I could see worry and frustration on the faces of the people living there. A solemn pall hung over the patrons of Paddy's Bar. The sign in the window read, "Drink while you can. Tomorrow it will be against the law."

While it made sensational copy, the sign wasn't entirely accurate. The Eighteenth Amendment didn't outlaw the drinking of alcohol, only the selling of it or the transporting of it across state lines. People could drink without fear of breaking the law, but Paddy and other bar owners like him couldn't sell it.

Matthew could see problems that I could not imagine. We discussed the situation at length during the weeks leading up to this time. What began as an altruistic ideal for humanity opened doors to corruption never imagined by the Anti-Saloon League or the Women's Christian Temperance Union. Physicians could write prescriptions for liquor "as a medication." Priests and rabbis could freely purchase alcohol for religious purposes. Loopholes within loopholes, the government had passed a law without determining how it would be enforced.

The next morning, on January 17, 1920, the *Tribune* headlines read, "Booze Is Dead!" Headlines across the nation echoed the sentiment. The people most affected by the law were the immigrants from the European countries where alcohol was core to their culture. Yet, that very core destroyed families and individuals like very few enemies outside America ever could, including the hated Kaiser himself.

The city changed in the weeks and months that followed. It was as if people played a giant game of hide-and-seek with the police. New York City became known as the "City on a Still." Speakeasies sprang up overnight, more than 5,000 within the city limits before the end of the first year.

Ashley kept me informed on the happenings at the speakeasies. From what had been the corner pub to the privileged people's "21," hidden stashes of alcohol were available. The trick was to get past the doorkeeper by using the correct code words.

Ashley loved shocking her parents and relatives with tales of police raids, "shimmy" dancers, and bootleg whiskey. "One evening, my date and I left the establishment through the back door while the police broke into the front door," she bragged. "You should have heard the screaming and cursing. Of course, the bartender had broken the booze bottles before the police could confiscate the evidence."

"How did he do that?" She had my wholehearted attention.

"Well . . ." she hunched over and whispered, "they say that he had a brass lever beneath the bar. And when the cops broke in, he pulled it and all the booze crashed down onto a bed of cobblestones beneath the building.

"Where are these bar owners getting the stuff?" I asked innocently. "It's not available any longer."

"You are joking, aren't you? It comes in from all over—Canada, the Caribbean, the South, Kentucky. It's everywhere. Little Appalachian grandmas cook up the stuff in the mountains behind their shacks, for pity's sake."

"Really?"

"Everyone's making big money with booze, except my parents." Her lower lip protruded into a pout. "My father says it's blood money, and he won't touch it. Uncle Cyrus says the same thing. Can you imagine such a thing? It's liquid gold."

I frowned. "Perhaps you should be proud of your family for living according to their principles. That takes courage."

"Yeah, and what good do principles do you when buying your next Packard?"

I laughed aloud. "Packard? The average American can barely afford to buy a Model T."

"Average? I never said I was average."

The *Tribune* reported on the booze-smuggling operations. I was pleased to add my little bit to the uncovering of the criminal underworld that was mushrooming in the city. In my father's letters, he told of "whiskey runners" on their way to New York City from Kentucky being picked up by the Shinglehouse police. I laughed. I couldn't feature the bucktoothed and bowlegged Benjy, the police chief, as a big-time crime fighter.

I was always on the lookout for a hot story or a news tip that would lead to a good article, or series of articles, for D. M. Spencer to write. But on one particular day in early summer, I set out for the Bowery to fulfill a promise to a ten-year-old boy. I'd promised Bobby that I'd take him to the docks the first day after school let out for the summer. I promised Molly that we'd do something special together a week or two later.

With the birth of Megan, Rosealie O'Reilly had arranged to stay home with her children by doing piecework for one of the shirt factories. Her job was to finish off collars and cuffs for men's shirts. While she worked at this job twelve to fifteen hours a day, at least she could care for her growing baby.

Bobby and I had become great pals in the two years I'd known him. He tagged along with me as I buzzed about the neighborhood. I was convinced that he'd follow me home if I let him. He introduced me to interesting people that I could use for my articles. Occasionally, he found great story leads as well. Like the rest of my world, he knew I had connections with the paper, but he didn't know I did the actual writing.

Located on the lower east side of Manhattan, the Bowery district ran alongside the East River. The O'Reillys wisely restricted Bobby from wandering down by the docks. Not only was it a dangerous area for a young boy to play, but the characters who hung out there were less than desirable influences for a child.

Bobby met me at the subway station. His eyes danced with excitement. "Are you ready, Miss Dorothy?"

"Absolutely. I even packed a picnic lunch."

His eyes widened. "Really?"

"Yes, sandwiches, fruit, and . . . chocolate cupcakes with chocolate frosting."

I'd said the magic word in *chocolate*. Bobby loved chocolate. Whenever I could, I'd bring chocolate bars for him and his sister, Molly.

"I'll carry that basket for you," he volunteered.

"It's pretty heavy."

"I can do it." He took the basket and strode ahead of me down the street. After two blocks, I spelled him off by carrying the basket.

"On the way back home," he reminded me, "it will be a lot easier to carry." His eyes twinkled with delight. "The chocolate cupcakes will be gone."

Growing up in his tough little neighborhood, Bobby knew

more about the seedier side of life than I did at twenty-three. Yet in other ways, his innocent trust, his witty sense of humor, and his eagerness to please reminded me of my brother, Amby. Maybe that's why I enjoyed his company so much.

We walked along the docks until we found longshoremen unloading a freighter from the Middle East. Choosing a spot to sit well out of the way of the action, Bobby and I ate our lunch and watched.

"When I grow up," Bobby volunteered, "I want to be a longshoreman."

I laughed. On past excursions around the city, Bobby had, at one time or another, declared that when he grew up he'd become a firefighter, a police officer, a librarian, an artist, a subway engineer, and a ship's captain. I wondered what his reaction would be after a visit to Papa's farm.

As we ate our sandwiches, we shared the crumbs with a flock of warring pigeons and sea gulls. Bobby enjoyed the antics of one particular pigeon who wouldn't let the larger birds intimidate him into abandoning his dinner. I'd just removed the cupcakes from the basket when a sleek black-and-silver Packard drove up behind us. The rear door swung open and a voice called, "Hey! What are you doing here, Dorothy?"

I leapt to my feet and stared into the automobile. "Mr. Claiborne, what are *you* doing here?"

"I asked you first. I certainly didn't expect to find you on the lower east side, especially here at the docks."

"My friend Bobby and I are having a picnic and watching the ships. Here," I offered, "please have a cupcake."

"I don't mind if I do." The man stepped out of his automobile and took the dessert from my hand.

"Bobby, this is my friend Mr. Claiborne. Remember, I told you about my friend Georgie? This is Goergie's father." George extended his free hand toward the young boy. "Nice to meet you, son."

Bobby shot a glance at the remaining cupcake then scowled at

197

the gruff-sounding man. "Good afternoon, sir."

"So, Mr. Claiborne, what are you doing down here?"

"Business, just had some business to conduct." He stuffed half the cupcake into his mouth. Bobby did the same with his dessert. Both ended up with chocolate frosting rimming their mouths, which was more a problem for George than for Bobby, since George had both a mustache and a beard. As I knelt to retrieve a cloth napkin from the picnic basket, a Ford flivver drove up and stopped on the opposite side of George's Packard.

"Mr. C." a familiar voice shouted from the second car. "I got good news for you."

My eyes widened in surprise. What was Vinnie Rullo doing here? And how did he know oil magnate George Claiborne?

"Vincent, good to see you again." George's voice sounded a trifle too jovial.

I grimaced. Seeing Vinnie Rullo could hardly be considered good, at least by me. Before I could decide what to do, Vinnie Rullo and his brother walked right up. I caught the startled looks on the two brothers' faces.

"Vinnie, let me introduce you to one of the sharpest and most beautiful women I know." George urged me forward. "Vincent, meet my friend, Dorothy Spencer. Dorothy? This is Vincent Rullo and his brother Joseph, associates of mine."

With the grace of a wooden soldier, I extended my hand toward Vinnie. He did the same toward me. The second he clasped my hand, I remembered the last time we'd met. Pasting a gracious smile on my face, I gripped his hand with all my strength. He winced. "Good to meet you, Mr. Rullo."

As I intensified the pressure on his fingers, he sent me a withered smile. "Nice to meet you, too, Miss Spencer."

I continued shaking his hand and squeezing his fingers with my "country girl" grip developed from summers of bailing hay. "Mr. Claiborne, did you know that Mr. Rullo and I have met before?"

Now, it was time for George's eyes to bulge in surprise. "You?"

"Why, yes, through mutual friends." I stared at Vinnie, daring him to complain about my handshake. "How long have you and my friend, Mr. Claiborne, known each other?" I squeezed his hand tighter. He tried to pull away, but I held fast.

"Forgive me for not asking sooner, but how is the extortion business coming, anyway?" Both George and Vinnie gulped in surprise. I saw Joey's hand slip under his suit jacket to what I suspected was a holstered gun. A warning look from Vinnie, and Joey relaxed. Giving Vinnie's hand one last hard squeeze, I let go. "I believe it's called a shakedown, isn't that correct, Mr. Rullo?"

Vinnie glared at me as he nursed his hand. I curled one corner of my mouth into a sneer then waved the folded napkin in front of my face. "Mr. Claiborne, I was wondering if you could give Bobby and me a lift back to his house. It was a longer walk down here than I realized, and it is becoming so warm." I simpered in the tone of a fragile gentlewoman. "And it was so nice seeing both of you again, Mr. Rullo, and you too." I nodded toward Joey.

Relieved and eager to leave as soon as possible, George helped Bobby gather up our picnic fixings. "Oh yes, of course, my dear, we need to get you out of the sun. And you without a parasol. Shame! Shame! My Katherine never leaves the house without her parasol on sunny days like this." George asked his chauffeur to put my basket in the car and to help Bobby and me in as well. "You make yourselves comfortable now, while I conduct a little business with Mr. Rullo; then we'll be on our way."

Vinnie cast me a hateful look before swaggering around to the rear of the Packard with George. Bobby's eyes remained round and frightened as he sat beside me in the back seat of the automobile. I patted the rich black leather upholstery. "Isn't this a beautiful car?" I knew he had never ridden in such a luxurious automobile. Perhaps he'd never ridden in a car of any kind.

"You shouldn't have done that, Miss Dorothy," he whispered. "Mr. Rullo's a big man, even in my neighborhood. He's mean."

"Yes, he is, Bobby. A very mean man, definitely someone you should avoid."

"But you insulted him, didn't you?"

I splayed my gloved fingers across my throat. "Did I? My, my. I was just trying to make polite conversation."

Bobby clicked his tongue. "Miss Dorothy, why are you playing games with such a person?"

I glanced out the window. The two men were still talking. Joey stood to one side watching Bobby and me. "Believe me, I was not playing a game with Mr. Rullo. I believe that he needs to know that not everyone is intimidated by his bully tactics."

Bobby blew his breath out between his teeth. "I hope you know what you're doing."

I laughed. "I assure you, I don't. But bullies are bullies the world over. And I found they cower when confronted with the truth."

Bobby shot a warning look toward Joey. "But these guys— Here comes Mr. Claiborne!"

My smile widened as George and his chauffeur climbed into the car. "Well, did you get your little business venture settled? I'd be very careful about doing business with the likes of Mr. Rullo, Mr. Claiborne. He's not a principled man, you know."

George cast me a sick smile. "Thank you for being concerned, Miss Spencer, but I'm accustomed to dealing with all kinds of individuals."

"The latest gossip on the street is that Vinnie Rullo is dealing in bathtub gin, as well as rum being smuggled in from the Bahamas," I confided.

George broke into a spasm of coughing. The chauffeur cast a worried glance back at us. I patted George on the back until he stopped coughing and cleared his throat. "Miss Dorothy, I would be very careful about saying that to too many people."

I widened my eyes, looking quite innocent. "Oh, I am. I haven't told anyone except you, Bobby here, and, of course, Matthew."

George broke into another spasm of uncontrollable coughing. "You told this to Matthew? Matthew Collingsworth? The newspaperman?"

"That's right," I said, as naive to the situation as possible. "Matthew's looking into the problem right now. It seems bootleggers are smuggling shiploads of booze into the United States from Canada and from the Caribbean. You might not believe it, but much of the illegal contraband is entering through the port of New York."

George asked me where we could drop off Bobby. I told him. Then George fell silent. When we reached the O'Reilly's house, I started to get out of the car with Bobby. George placed his hand on my arm. "No, we'll take you all the way home."

"Are you sure? I can take the subway."

"I wouldn't think of it, Miss Dorothy. Katherine would never forgive me if I didn't deliver you safe and sound to your doorstep. New York can be a dangerous city, you know."

Out of the corner of my eye, I could see the tight grimace filling George's face. "Was that warning general or personal, Mr. Claiborne?"

The worry lines on his face softened. He took one of my gloved hands in his and lifted it to his lips. "I would hate to see anything untoward happen to you, Miss Dorothy. You are a very special friend to my wife, and, of course, to my departed son."

"That's very nice of you, Mr. Claiborne. I truly appreciate your concern. But I'm hardly the kind of woman to sit at home and knit, you know."

"I wish you were," he growled. "I don't know what you're doing to my wife, but she's becoming a much more forceful person. Did you know she's volunteering her time at a women's clinic of some kind?"

"She is?" I clapped my hands with glee. "Wonderful. She told me she was thinking of it."

He scowled at me. A smile teased at the corners of his lips. "You are a bad influence on Katherine, Miss Spencer."

"Dear friend, do you truly mean that?"

He shook his head. "On the contrary, I like the changes I see in Katherine since she met you. She's a more interesting person and definitely more outgoing. What's in that tea you serve, anyway?"

I laughed. "Just mint leaves, I assure you."

The chauffeur stopped the Packard in front of my boardinghouse. He hopped out of the car and came around to open the back door. George climbed out and assisted me. "Should I walk you to the door?"

I chuckled at the thought. "No, thank you. I'll be fine from here. Thank you again for the lift home."

"Well, I had to, after eating your chocolate cupcake the way I did." George nodded and climbed into the car. The chauffeur closed the door and rounded the car to the driver's seat. Within seconds the car eased into the afternoon traffic and was out of sight.

I pondered the strange encounter throughout the rest of the afternoon. Why was George, an oil magnate, making deals with the likes of Vinnie? Was Vinnie shaking down George's incoming ships? If so, what incoming ships would be docking on the East River? Wouldn't George's oil tankers dock on the New Jersey side of the Hudson River, especially since most of the oil comes from Pennsylvania?

With unexpected time to spare, I took my time dressing for a dinner party at Chloe Mae's place that evening. After a quick bath, I sat down to the dressing table, undid the braid wound around my head, and brushed the snarls from my hair. Pulling my hair away from my face, I wondered what I would look like with a bob. I examined the contours of my face from one angle then another. I'd been going through the same routine for months. Hair as thick and as heavy as mine often led to severe headaches. The cooler, more relaxed hairdos filtering into the states from Europe were attractive and comfortable. "*Hmm*, not bad." If I'd had scissors handy, I think I would have done it right then. I thought of my father and giggled. "He'd be scandalized!" Then I wondered what Matt would think.

I styled my hair so as to give the illusion of a bob, swooping it down over the ears then back in a roll away from the face. Once I'd pinned it securely in place, I slipped around my forehead a wide velvet ribbon that matched my gown.

Eagerly, I removed the muted sea green chiffon confection of a gown from the armoire. Cool and light, the dress dropped straight from my shoulders, flaring at the hips down to midcalf. Matching fabric swooshed across my hips and gathered in a dyed-to-match fabric rose on my left hip. I adjusted the shoulders of the dress to lift the dress's V-neckline a couple of inches then turned to examine the drape neckline down my back. I smiled to myself. If only Matt could see me tonight, I mused. Unfortunately, I'll probably be stuck laughing at the jokes of some dyspeptic old man or a pimple-faced student from Princeton.

When the car that Cy sent for me arrived, I swung a matching chiffon shawl about my shoulders and hurried down the stairs. My landlady met me at the base of the stairs. "Will you be getting in a little late tonight, Miss Dorothy? I can wait up for you, if you like."

"That's very sweet of you, Mrs. Stahl, but I'm going to my sister's place for dinner. If the dinner party runs much past ten, I'll beg a bed off her for the night."

"Oh? Your sister Mrs. Chamberlain?"

"Yes."

"She's a dearie. Did you know that she brought by a flat of strawberries for me the other day? She is so thoughtful."

I smiled. "That's my sister Chloe."

"Have a good time, then. By the way, you do look lovely. Will Mr. Collingsworth be at the dinner?"

I shrugged. "I'm afraid I don't know my sister's guest list, Mrs. Stahl." I blew her a kiss and ran out the door and down the steps to the waiting automobile.

The dinner party went as expected. Mr. and Mrs. Carlin, business associates of Cy's, were visiting from Charlotte, North Carolina, with their adult son, Bertrum. Barely out of his teens and terribly ill at ease, Bertrum spent the evening telling me about his passion for breeding and racing horses. I smiled and nodded at what I hoped were the appropriate moments and swallowed my urge to yawn throughout the evening.

The Carlins and Chloe's other guests departed after ten. Before Bertrum joined his parents in the waiting cab, he grasped my hands in his. "I have had a delightful evening, Miss Spencer. Do you think it might be possible for you to take me on a tour of the city, you being an experienced woman and all?" He winked suggestively.

Horrified, I snatched my hands out of his. "I am sorry, Mr. Carlin, but my datebook is filled. If you need a guide, one can be hired downtown. Thank you, Goodnight."

Bertrum looked at me bewildered and mumbled his Goodbyes to me and to his hosts. The door closed behind him.

" 'Experienced woman of the city!' " I huffed. "Of all the insults! Chloe Mae, as much as I love you, don't match me up with the likes of Bertrum Carlin ever again!" I stormed past her into the parlor. "It's getting late. Could you please call your driver?"

"Wait!" Cy strode into the parlor. "I need to talk with you, Dolly."

I blinked in surprise. "Of course, about what?"

Chloe followed him in, closing the parlor doors behind her. I hadn't noticed when CeeCee and Rusty disappeared from the group. "I think it will be best if you stay here for the night, Dolly. Please sit down."

I looked questioningly at her. "What is this all about?"

With her eyes, Chloe deferred to her husband. I perched myself on the edge of her damask sofa, my hands folded tightly in my lap.

Cy cleared his throat. "I've been told, Dolly, you visited the East River docks today."

I bristled at his authoritative tone. "Yes, I took my friend Bobby there to watch the big ships. We had a picnic, in fact."

Chloe sat down beside me. "Dolly, the docks are not a safe place for a young woman to be right now."

My mouth dropped open in surprise. *What a time to be getting protective of me,* I thought. *I've toured this city from one end to the other in search of articles, and now she's protective?* "Chloe Mae, how can you say I shouldn't be in that part of town? Aren't you the one who scoured the worst sections of San Francisco for prostitutes you could help?"

Chloe reddened. "Er, yes, but that was different."

"What is so different about it?" I challenged her.

She gave me a sheepish grin. "You're my little sister. I need to protect you."

"Oh, I see. You can wander about in unsafe neighborhoods, but I can't because I'm your little sister?"

"It's not only that." Cy cleared his throat a second time. "Some rather nefarious individuals work out of the dock area."

"Oh, you mean dirty, rotten scoundrels like Vinnie and Joey Rullo?"

"You know these men by name?" It was Cy's turn to drop his jaw in amazement.

I laughed. "I've run into the likes of them all over the city. Those two miscreants have fingers in several illegal protections schemes. For that matter, Matthew Collingsworth was the one who first introduced me to them. He's known them a long time." I frowned. "How do you know all this? It just happened a few hours ago."

Cy shot a glance at Chloe then back at me. "It doesn't matter how I know. Trust me on this. Please don't go alone to the docks. Promise me, Dolly."

Baffled and frustrated, I shook my head. "I love and respect you both, but I can't make such a promise. I have to go where my story leads."

"Honey, forgive me for being a hypocrite here, but this situation is very different from mine. It could be very dangerous for you if you stumbled into the wrong area." Chloe placed her hand on my shoulder.

"Like George Claiborne meeting the Rullos? I wondered about that. Was it rum running?"

"Dorothy!" He turned to Chloe. "Talk to her, Chloe. She doesn't have any idea what danger she could be in right now."

I lifted my hand toward Cy. "I don't know how or why you've been given this information. But I do know that you love me and are just trying to protect me. I promise to avoid picnicking at the docks again."

"That's not good enough. You have already seen more than you should." Cy balled and unballed his fists.

"I don't know what to say. I can't out-and-out promise never to go down to the river, but I promise that if I do go, it will be for a very good reason." I glanced at my sister. "Is that good enough?"

"Oh, honey, I'm so afraid for you, and I feel I must protect you. You're my little sister, you know." Her eyes flooded with tears. "You don't know how cruel these people can be."

"I know. And I love you for being worried about me. But tell me, how did you folks find out about my visit to the docks this afternoon? Who told you?"

Cy's jaw tightened. "I can't divulge my sources."

Chloe slid closer to me and put her arm around my shoulder. "Just remember, Cyrus works for the federal government."

"Chloe Mae!" he interrupted.

Chloe glanced defiantly at her husband. "She needs to know how serious this situation is."

"You're right, of course—" The ringing doorbell interrupted his reply. Cy growled and walked from the room.

"I wonder who that could be at this hour of the evening?" Chloe stood and started toward the hallway when Matt suddenly burst through the double doors and into the parlor.

"Dolly! You're here!" He ran to me and grabbed both of my upper arms. "You're safe."

I looked up at him in surprise. "Of course, I'm here. Of course, I'm safe. What did you think?"

Matt stared down at his hands still clutching my arms. "I-I-I didn't know. I went to your boardinghouse, and your landlady said you were spending the night at your sister's. I'm so glad you're safe."

I pulled away from his grasp. "Whatever is going on here? First Cy and Chloe warn me from visiting the docks, and then you burst in here like a wildman concerned for my safety."

Matt crushed me against his chest and buried his face in my neck. "I'm so thankful you are safe. I prayed all the way over here that you'd be all right."

Uncertain how to react, I slowly wrapped my arms about him while Cy and Chloe stood watching in stunned silence. "Matt, I'm glad you care, but why shouldn't I be all right? What is going on?"

He straightened. His hands dropped to his sides as if he suddenly realized what he'd done. Stammering over his words, he said, "I heard about your encounter with Vinnie and Joey today. What did you think you were doing?"

I bristled. "Why are you using that tone with me? Why is everyone treating me like an errant eight-year-old?"

"Because we love you, you foolish girl!" Matt blurted without thinking of the consequences.

I took a step back. "I beg your pardon?"

Matt glanced at the surprised faces of my sister and brother-in-law then back at me. "We care about you."

I pursed my lips. "Which is it? Care or love?"

Matt reddened. "Both. Like Cy and Chloe, I love you like a sister."

"Oh." That was the same thing I'd said to Franklin the last time I saw him. Matt turned and walked to the mantle and stared into the unlighted fireplace. He whirled about.

"Forget it. Now that I know you're safe, I can go home."

"Yes, I guess you can. Thank you for being concerned over my welfare."

"Excuse me?" Chloe touched my arm. "It's late. Cyrus and I have a busy day tomorrow. May we leave the two of you alone to discuss your problem?"

Cyrus wrapped an arm around my sister's waist and yawned broadly. "Your sister's right. The two of you take some time and hash out your differences in private."

I felt ambushed. How a simple little picnic could turn into such a fuss, I didn't know. "Fine. I'll see you both in the morning. Am I sleeping in the yellow guest room?" I asked as they turned to leave.

"If that's all right with you, sweetheart," Chloe called as she closed the parlor doors behind them.

"Now, what's this all about, Mr. Collingsworth?"

He cast me a sheepish look. "Let's drop the Mr. Collingsworth. After all that's happened, it hardly seems appropriate."

"Forgive me, but I don't understand anything that has happened." I knew that I looked as bewildered as I felt. "How in the world did you hear about Bobby's and my little picnic?"

His voice rose. "How did I find out? I saw you there. And I saw Mr. Claiborne with Vinnie too."

"I don't understand."

"A couple of reporter friends have been following Vinnie for the last few weeks. We think he's involved with the off-shore rum smuggling."

I chuckled. "I knew that. And I suspect George Claiborne is somehow involved as well. Perhaps he's backing Vinnie with the cash he needed to get started."

Matt rolled his eyes toward the ceiling. "That is yet to be proven. But you're right, you walked right into the middle of a liquor deal being made." He wiped sweat from his brow. "You scared the daylights out of me, woman."

"So tell me, did George come back to the docks to finish the deal?"

Matt nodded. "Within the hour. Maybe George is just an innocent buyer?"

"Innocent buyer? Isn't that an oxymoron?" I grinned and arched one saucy eyebrow. Matt took my hand and led me to the sofa.

"You laugh, but men have been killed for less. You've read about the bodies found floating facedown in the East River? Even my father is running scared. He's asked me to back off on my reporting on the rum running. Of course, I won't do that."

We sat down beside one another on the sofa. He continued holding my hand. Turning it over, he traced over the lines in the palm of my hand. "Please promise me that you'll stay away from the likes of Vinnie and Joey."

"I don't go looking for them, if that's what you mean." I told him about the encounter we had at the tailor's shop. Matt leaned back against the sofa and closed his eyes.

"Why didn't you tell me this sooner? What else should I know about your adventures into the sewers of New York City?"

As I told him about Vinnie and my battle of hand crunching, he leaned forward, studying my face intently.

"I could thumb wrestle my brothers to the table," I bragged. "Vinnie was nothing by comparison. He went home with a sore hand, I can tell you that much."

He heaved a sigh and shook his head. "What am I going to do with you, Dolly Spencer? You may have won a battle, but sooner or later, I hate to think what will happen."

I tilted my head and arched my brow. "What would you do with any other of your many good friends, under the circumstances?"

"I beg your pardon?"

"You asked what you should do with me, and I asked you in reply what you would do if I were any of your other friends."

CHAPTER THIRTEEN

Surprises and More Surprises

Dressed in a red bolero jacket and cocky theater cap, the furry brown monkey danced in circles while the organ grinder cranked out a tune on his hurdy-gurdy. At the end of the tune, the animal picked up his small brass cup and held it out to me. I squatted down and petted the creature on his head. "Just a minute. I have something in here for you." I opened my purse and drew out a coin—Georgie's silver coin. "Oh no, I can't give you that one. Here's another." I dropped a penny into the cup, and the monkey moved on to other members of his street audience.

I gazed at Georgie's coin in my hands, realizing I'd almost lost it. And it wasn't the first time. I'd have to come up with a better way to carry it than loose in my purse. Spotting a jewelry store across the street, I made my way through the midday traffic and entered the shop. A short, rounded, white-haired gentleman, with a matching mustache and carefully groomed beard, stood up from behind a high display case. "May I help you?"

"I hope so." I held out my coin for the jeweler to see. "This is a special coin to me. It was given to me by a friend before the war.

I want to carry it with me, but I'm afraid I might lose it."

"Would you like to put it on a chain around your neck?"

I shook my head. "I don't think so." I thought of the brass ring that held my room key. The ring was big enough to slip over my wrist should I choose to do so. "Could you put a hole in the coin and attach it to my key ring? I never go anywhere without my room key."

He studied the coin while I found the ring. He held both up for inspection. "That would work. It will cost you two cents though."

"Fine." I gazed at the interesting pieces of jewelry in his display case while he carried out my request. The coin sparkled in my hand as I stepped out into the sunlight. *Oh, Georgie,* I thought, *I do hope your father isn't involved in something illegal.* I dropped the ring into my purse, pulled the strings, and looped it over my wrist.

By the slant of the late afternoon sun, I knew I should hurry home and change for the youth meeting, especially since I'd coerced Ashley into attending with me. I wasn't sure how things would be between Matthew and me after the other night. Ashley's presence would ease the tension between us.

Ashley kept her word. But after she scanned the group, she whispered, "The only decent eligible man in this place is your Mr. Collingsworth."

My lower jaw dropped in surprise. "My Mr. Collingsworth?"

"Please, do I look blind?"

I coughed and glanced toward the evening speaker, a returned missionary from South Africa. He was telling about the living conditions for the people after the Great War. I thought about Chloe Mae's thwarted desire to serve God in China, and I felt guilty. *Why don't I feel such a burden, Lord? Am I too crass? Too self-absorbed, like Ashley?*

During closing prayer, I asked the Lord to search my heart. "If there's anything holding me back from completely abandoning myself to You, please show me what it is. And make my heart willing to give it to You."

Matt met me in the back of the auditorium and asked to drive me home. "And Ashley too," he added.

"Why, that would be nice."

"Perhaps we can stop for English shortbread cookies and a hot cocoa."

"You can be very persuasive, Mr. Collingsworth."

He smiled, and without moving his lips, added, "Stop calling me Mr. Collingsworth, or I'll call you Dolly right here in front of everyone."

"You wouldn't dare."

"Oh? Wouldn't I?" A devilish grin spread across his face.

Ashley walked up behind me and tapped me on the shoulder. "Are you ready to go home? I am."

"Matthew has offered to buy us cookies and hot cocoa." I smiled sweetly at Matt.

"Hot cocoa? In the middle of the summer? Make it a lemonade, and I'm yours."

Matt placed his arm around my shoulder. "Good idea, Miss Ashley. Lemonade it is."

Once the Pierce-Arrow was in motion, Ashley leaned past me. "Mr. Collingsworth, would you please take me directly home." She waved the back of her hand lightly across her brow. "I do believe I am feeling lightheaded."

We turned to look at her. Instantly I understood the game she was playing. I wasn't certain Matt did, however.

"Will you be all right? Perhaps I should take you directly to a hospital. There's one on—"

"Oh no," Ashley interrupted. "Home is where I need to be."

"Ashley, it's out of Matthew's way to take you home first," I reminded her.

She glanced at me out of the corner of her eye and swooned back against the seat. "I'm sorry, but I must get home. Only Mummy can make me feel better."

The car leapt forward, barely missing a pedestrian stepping off the curb at the corner. I held my breath as Matt zigzagged through the maze of streets. *Fortunately, the evening traffic is light,* I thought. This dizzy gal will get us killed.

We skidded to a halt in front of the McCall's townhouse. Matt hopped out of the car and ran around to open the door for Ashley. He helped her from the vehicle. I started to get out as well, but he assured me he could handle everything from there.

Ashley leaned on his shoulder as they made their way up the marble steps to the front door. The butler anticipated their arrival. It was only a moment before Matt reappeared. Drucilla stood in the doorway and waved at me. I returned her wave.

I noticed a lightness in Matt's step when he returned to the car.

"How's she doing?" I asked.

"Just fine, er, I mean, she'll be doing fine now that she has her mother to look after her." He eased the automobile out into the light evening traffic. "Are you hungry? Suddenly I'm starved."

I eyed him skeptically. Why did I have the feeling I was being hoodwinked? Did those two weasels contrive this whole act?

We spoke little as we rode a scant mile to where he pulled over in front of a tiny delicatessen. He turned off the engine and leaned toward me. "Could you eat a sandwich?"

"I suppose so." I nodded my head cautiously.

"Great. These folks make the best sandwiches. They make great potato salad as well—German style. Have you ever had it?" He hopped out of the car and ran to open my door.

"At this hour? It's past eight o'clock."

"Refined dining . . ." As he helped me from the automobile, I squinted up into his eyes. "Do you know every immigrant restaurant owner in Manhattan?"

He laughed. "What do you mean 'Manhattan?' Make that the entire five boroughs." He took my hand and placed it on his arm.

"My, my, you are certainly in fine fettle tonight. You haven't stopped grinning since you walked into the meeting tonight."

"You think so? Maybe I'm just a happy person."

I met his friends Heinrich and Mette Swartz. They stuffed me full of potato salad, homemade apple cider, a pastry called strudel, then insisted I take some cinnamon doughnuts home with me.

By the time we arrived back at my boardinghouse, it was close to nine. Mrs. Stahl would be peering out from between the lace parlor curtains, watching for me. Matt walked me up the wooden steps to the porch. A porch swing hung still in the quiet summer night. "Dolly, there's something I've wanted to talk about with you."

I glanced at the closed door. "But Mrs. Stahl . . ."

He looked at me then at the closed door. Suddenly the front door opened, and Mrs. Stahl appeared on the other side of the doorjamb.

"Well, good evening, Miss Dorothy and Mr. Collingsworth. A lovely evening tonight, isn't it?"

"Yes, it is." Matt stepped closer to my landlady. "Ma'am, I realize what I'm about to ask is an imposition on you, having to stay up late and all, but Miss Dorothy and I have some serious business to discuss. Would it be proper for us to talk a while longer out here on the porch?"

The woman's face beamed in delight. I frowned in disbelief. This is the woman who scolded Mr. Wallace in 2B for coming in fifteen minutes late one Saturday night. "Mr. Collingsworth, of course, it would be quite proper. And I don't mind at all if Miss Dorothy comes in a little late this evening." She patted my cheek lovingly. "Just lock the door behind you, sweetie." With a cheery goodnight, she stepped back and closed the door behind her.

Bewildered, I allowed Matt to lead me to the porch swing where we sat down together. I placed my box of doughnuts on the swing bench between us.

Matt picked up the doughnuts and set them on the floor, moved closer to me, then set the swing in motion. A soft warm breeze ruffled the tendrils of curls slipping from beneath my straw sailor hat. A full moon floated over the trees and buildings on the other side of the silent street.

From an open window across the street, someone played the

old Sigfield Follies tune "Let Me Call You Sweetheart" on a player piano.

"It's beautiful out here tonight, isn't it?" I glanced at Matt out of the corner of my eye. He stared straight ahead, his forehead knitted and his eyes narrowed. I doubted he'd heard me. "Matt?"

"Hmm? Oh yes, it is a beautiful night tonight."

The music from across the street stopped. I peered up in his face. "Matt?"

"Hmm? Yes, what is it?"

"You said we had something important to discuss tonight?"

"Oh, I'm so sorry. Of course I did. I'm just not sure this is the right time to . . ."

"To what? You're not going to keep me out here until all hours and not tell me what you're thinking, are you?"

He grinned and laughed. "Nothing would drive you crazier, would it?"

"No! Now, tell me."

The player piano from across the street began a new roll of songs. Matt heard the first notes of "You Made Me Love You," and he blushed furiously, like a schoolboy.

"Dolly, remember when I told you I'd never marry again?"

My heart stopped for an instant. "Yes?"

"I really meant it. I didn't plan to fall in love. I'd never been in love, so I had no idea how powerful an emotion it could be."

I nibbled on my lower lip but said nothing.

"It struck me when I was at my parents' home in Long Island." He stopped to exhale. "My folks threw a dinner party and, of course, matched me up with one of the local beauties."

Without warning, my stomach knotted. I felt nauseated and dizzy. I swallowed hard. It was like I was hearing Bud Ames' declaration of love for his fiancée all over again. *Oh, dear Lord,* I prayed, *am I doomed to being a "good buddy" for the rest of my life?* I thought of Franklin. No, I knew it was best that I remain alone rather than marry a man I didn't love. And I had never come to love him, not the way I knew I loved Matthew.

"Anyway, during the evening, Maude and I talked—"

Maude? I blinked in surprise. You love a woman named Maude?

"She told me that she lost her fiancé in Belgium during the war. And I told her about Lyssa and never wanting to marry again."

I gulped several times. The familiar love song mingling with his words ripped at my heart. Tears welled up in my eyes.

"Anyway, Maude is a straightforward person, a lot like you." When he looked at me, I turned my face away from him.

"What's the matter? Dolly, you're crying."

I tore off one glove and swiped at my tears with it. My hand shook in time with my lower lip. I couldn't stop either from their revealing dance of despair.

"Dolly, what's wrong?" He lifted my quivering chin toward him. Rather than look into his eyes, I closed mine. "Tell me, what did I say?"

"Matthew, sometimes you are so intelligent it scares me. Other times, you can be a complete dolt."

He released my chin and leaned back against the back of the swing. "Somewhere in this conversation, I took a wrong turn. I'm totally lost. What are we talking about?"

"You were telling me about this marvelous woman you met and fell in love with at your parents' place, remember?"

"Fell in love with? What are you talking about? I don't love Maude. I love you!"

"Me? But you said—"

"She made me see that I would be a fool to lose you because of a bad first marriage."

"She did?" I looked up and turned to him in surprise.

"Yes. I was trying to tell you that I love you and that I fully intend to make you fall in love with me as well."

I giggled once, then twice, then broke into uncontrollable giggles. My laughter filled the night air. A second floor window in the house next door opened, and a neighbor yelled, "Shut up, woman!"

217

I tried to stop. However, my laughter refused to be curtailed before its time. I buried my face in Matthew's jacket lapel hoping to smother my giggles. My straw hat slipped to one side of my face. I pulled it off and let it fall to the floor. When I did, the pins holding my hair in place came with it. My hair tumbled down around my shoulders.

I heard Matt's breath catch in his chest. Suddenly, I froze. My laughter dissipated. He lifted one of the heavy curls from the side of my face and smoothed it down my back. He did the same with a second large curl. "Do you know how beautiful you are?"

Feeling foolish, buried in his shoulder, I tried to straighten. He held me fast.

"Matt, I . . ." My voice sounded as weak as a kitten's. I lifted my gaze to meet his. "I am far from beautiful."

"Oh, Dolly, you are so wrong. You're like . . . This isn't going to sound very romantic, but you're like an onion, each layer I discover, I find more to love beneath it."

I laughed nervously. "Maybe, like an onion, there won't be anything left when you get to the center."

He shook his head several times. "No, like all good analogies, mine falls apart when taken too far. I remember the day you first walked into my office, confident, cocky, and ready for bear."

I ran a hand over his jacket lapel. "Actually, I was so frightened, I was afraid you'd be able to hear my knees knocking."

He lifted my chin until our eyes met. "That's when I began to love you, when my brother accused you of extortion."

I laughed nervously as he held my face between his two hands. "So, tell me, do I have a chance of winning your love?"

Nervously I licked my lips and swallowed hard. My eyes revealed what was in my heart. He took me by the shoulders and drew me close to him. For an instant we stared into each other's eyes, then his attention shifted to my lips.

When I was in high school, my friend Annie and I joked about how she always knew her boyfriend, Billy, was getting up the nerve to kiss her. He'd study her lips for an instant before kissing her.

My heart stopped. I knew Matt was about to kiss me. I'd never been kissed before. Franklin had kissed my cheek and my hands but never my lips. For a second I felt foolish. I didn't know what to do. The moment his lips touched mine, my fears of inadequacy dissolved into the warmth of his touch. I closed my eyes, and he drew me into his arms.

When the kiss ended, I struggled to catch my breath. He gathered me close and whispered into my ear, "Oh, Dolly, I've wanted to do that for so long."

I opened my eyes and saw the curtain in the window behind us move. Mrs. Stahl! "I think we're being watched, Matthew," I whispered.

"Your landlady?"

I nodded. "Perhaps I should go on in."

"May I see you tomorrow night? We've lots to discuss. I want you to meet my parents, and I can hardly wait to meet yours—"

"Wait!" I put my fingers up to his lips. He nibbled on my fingertips while I tried to speak. "I can hardly think straight, let alone imagine meeting your parents for the first time. Everything's moving too fast. I need to catch my breath."

"You're right. First things first." He stood and drew me to him. "Will you marry me?"

My mouth fell open. My eyes widened in surprise. "Uh? I beg your pardon?"

He curled one of my stray curls around his finger then traced his finger around my left ear. "When I make up my mind I want something, I go for it. I did want to wait until I was certain you wanted the same thing, however. You do, don't you?"

I pulled out of his arms. "Matthew, for two or three years you do nothing, no indication whatsoever, and suddenly you propose marriage?"

"Well, you do, don't you? Want to marry me, that is?"

"Yes, of course, but—"

"But what? I love you. You love me. What else is there?"

I took several breaths. "Our families, for one thing."

"I agree. OK, I won't ask you to marry me until both families agree to the proposal. Will that make you happy?"

I wasn't sure from what Giles had said about Matt's stuffy "upper crust" parents.

"Matt, you're right. I want our parents' blessings before I marry, but even more important is God's blessing. You may know what you want, but God and I haven't had time to talk about this yet."

His eyes softened. "That's another reason I love you, Dolly. You take your relationship with God seriously. And you're right. I believe God brought us together, but you need to be convinced of that as well." He kissed the tip of my nose then placed a gentle kiss on my lips as well. "Take all the time you need deciding, my sweet. And I will respect your decision, whatever it is."

He caressed my upper arms for a moment then kissed me again. When he pulled away, I knew I'd been soundly kissed. My fingers flew to my lips.

"There, that's for you to remember while you discuss our love with God."

Whistling a few bars of "Let Me Call You Sweetheart," he bounded down the porch steps and hopped into his car. And with a wave, he was gone.

Reluctantly, I opened the front door and stepped into the silent, dark house. I tiptoed across the entry and up the stairs. I rounded the staircase on the second floor when someone whispered in the darkness. "So, did you say Yes?"

I jumped and gave a startled yip.

"*Sh, sh*, you'll awaken the borders. So, are you going to marry that nice young man?" my landlady asked again.

"I-I-I'm not sure right now," I stammered.

"Oh, bosh! You love him. What else do you need to know?"

I grimaced at the thought of her eavesdropping on Matt and my conversation on the porch. "I'm sorry, Mrs. Stahl, I am so sleepy I can hardly think straight. Please excuse me."

I stepped inside my room and closed the door behind me. Pressing my back against the door, I remembered the surprised gasp my landlady gave then the abrupt "Good night." *I'll have to apologize tomorrow morning,* I told myself.

Slipping into my nightclothes, I curled up on the carpet in front of the window and, hugging my favorite bed pillow, I watched the moon climb into the night sky. "Heavenly Father, I am so excited. *Matt loves me!* Imagine that? He loves me. You and I've talked about this for so long. And now that it's happened, I am afraid." I hugged my pillow closer to me. "I'm afraid our relationship might be more my will than Your will. I would never want to go my own way unless I am in complete agreement with Your plan for me. Let me know if it is Your will for Matt and me to marry."

The last word came out in a whisper, as if saying it aloud would doom my dreams to failure. "I love You more than life itself, Father. And if I wasn't certain Matt loved You as well, I wouldn't consider his proposal . . ." My thoughts tumbled over one another like leaves caught by the wind.

After a while, I gave up and went to bed. I put in a restless night, awakening several times and finding my bedding wrapped around my legs and body. Just before dawn, someone banging on a door awakened me. I snapped awake when I realized they were pounding on the front door of the boardinghouse. I heard the front door open, followed by Mrs. Stahl's irate voice and the anxious tones of a child. I recognized the voice. *Bobby!* It was Bobby's voice. *What is he doing here at this hour?* I wondered as I untangled myself from my bedding, threw on a robe, and dashed to the top of the stairwell.

"I'm sorry, but I can't awaken Miss Dorothy. You'll have to come back—"

"I gotta see her," the boy demanded, pushing his way into the foyer. "Where is she?"

"Listen here, young man—"

"It's all right, Mrs. Stahl, I'm awake now. I'll come down." I tightened the belt of my robe and hurried down the stairs. I couldn't help but hear the grumbling of the other borders.

"What is it, Bobby? What are you doing here?" I took him by

the shoulder and marched him into the dimly lighted parlor.

Behind me, Mrs. Stahl sputtered, "This is highly irregular, Miss Dorothy. We will discuss it tomorrow morning, er, this morning." She marched up the stairs to her bedroom.

I looked in Bobby's round, frightened eyes. "What is wrong?"

Tears welled up in his eyes. "I was hanging around The Fox's Den tonight—"

"What were you doing in a place like that?"

"I was making a little extra money protecting the patrons' cars, when there was a police raid. About half an hour after the raid, two men took a blond lady from the place. She didn't want to go with them. I could tell." He paused to catch his breath.

"And?"

"One of the men saw me. It was that Vinnie fellow we met down by the docks. He grabbed me by the arm. I thought he was going to make me go with him." Bobby's voice shook with fear. "But he didn't. He shoved me and told me to find you and tell you they had Ashley."

"Ashley? This doesn't make sense. What would they ever want with Ashley?" I shook my head, trying to remove the cobwebs of sleep from my brain. "Do your parents know where you are?"

He hung his head. "No."

"How did you get out without them knowing?"

Bobby gave me a pitiful hound-dog look. "I waited until they were asleep then sneaked out as if I were going down the hall to the bathroom."

"How did you find me? You're a long way from the Bowery."

Bobby brightened. "I remembered hearing you give directions to that Mr. Claiborne's driver. So I walked here."

"You walked? All the way?"

"*Um-hm.*" He nodded proudly. "What are we going to do now?"

"Well, the first thing that's going to happen is I'm calling Ashley's mother then I'm taking you home. Did Vinnie say where he was taking Ashley?"

"No. He said you'd know."

"Well, I don't." I stepped out into the hall and wound the crank on the wall phone at the foot of the stairs. The bells on the phone sounded much louder in the darkness than they did in the daylight. A sleepy butler answered the telephone at the McCalls. I explained that I had to speak with Mr. McCall immediately.

"I'm sorry, mum, but do you know what time it is?" he huffed.

"No, I don't. But this is Miss Dorothy calling. It is an emergency. I must speak with Mr. McCall."

"Very well. Hold on." The man's voice drifted off. I could picture him hurrying up the carpeted stairs to the master suite. Finally, Ian's groggy voice came onto the line.

"Dolly, what's wrong? Why are you calling at this hour?"

I took a deep breath. "Maybe nothing. But do you know if Ashley is home?"

I could hear Drucilla asking who was on the line. Then I heard Ian ask about Ashley and Drucilla's offer to go check her room. "No, she's not," I heard Drucilla shriek.

"Dolly," Ian shouted into the phone, "she's not here. Where is she?"

"I'm not certain. But I've been told by a reliable source that she's been abducted by two ruffians from the docks. Docks! That's it. They're holding her at the docks!" I slammed the receiver onto the hook and dashed up the stairs two at a time. "Just sit down on the bottom step until I can put on some clothes, do you hear, Bobby?"

"Yes, ma'am. You should put on a pair of pants, if you want my advice." Bobby plunked himself down on the bottom stair.

"Pants?"

"Yeah, ladies' skirts will get in your way."

"Of all the . . ."

One of the borders yelled, "Be quiet out there!"

I tiptoed down the hall to my room and dressed hurriedly in a loose-fitting jersey blouse and a cotton skirt that flared at the hips and ended midcalf. "This will have to do, since I don't own a pair

223

of ladies' trousers." I put on some sturdy Oxford shoes. Shoving a dark cloche hat over my hair and grabbing a jacket from the armoire, I stuffed my key ring in my pocket and hurried back down the stairs.

Frightening shadows lurked in the corners of the tiled subway tunnel as we waited on the platform for the next train downtown. I fluctuated between scolding Bobby for his foolish actions and hugging him for telling me about my stepniece. Finally, the train screamed into the station. We climbed aboard for the short ride to the Bowery. As the train winded its way along the bowels of the city, I prayed as I'd never prayed before.

"Father," I whispered, "Your Son said 'Ask, and it shall be given you; seek, and ye shall find; knock, and it shall be opened unto you.' Well, I'm asking for Your protection over my foolish stepniece. And I claim Your promise in Luke 11:9, 10 to answer my prayer. Thank You for being faithful. Give me wisdom in what I am about to do."

Sunlight burst over the East River as we emerged from the subway tunnel several minutes later. I'd decided what I would do. Once I had Bobby safely in his own home, I'd head down to the docks. Surely, at such an early hour, there would be several stevedores already unloading the ships that had docked during the night. But when I turned to speak with Bobby, he'd run into an alley somewhere. I ran up the street toward his home, calling, but no one answered.

Frustrated, I pounded my fist against the metal pole of a streetlight. "Now what, Father?"

CHAPTER FOURTEEN

Comes Around

The docks and warehouses on the Lower East Side throbbed with life as the early morning shift got underway. Not wishing to be seen by the longshoremen or the ships' crew, I made my way between massive crates filled with who knows what.

Stepping around or over pools of stagnant water, I scurried along the corrugated walls of the warehouses, hoping the shadows would hide me from curious eyes.

Hearing the sound of male voices behind me, I darted around an open door and slipped inside the yawning chasm. I pressed myself against the corrugated wall behind the door and waited. A pale wash of early morning light filtered through cobwebbed transom windows above my head.

I waited until the men's voices faded into the distance. "What do I do next, Lord?" I breathed. The shell of a warehouse, silent and deserted, slumbered around me, ignoring my intrusion. *I can't stand frozen here forever*, I thought. Somewhere in this maze of buildings, Ashley is being held captive, and I don't know which way to go to start looking.

8—S.D.D.S.

Creeping out of my hidingplace, I peered around the edge of the doorjamb. "Go to your left, Miss Dorothy."

I jumped and whirled about in terror. "Bobby! What are you doing here?"

"Waiting for you. I knew you'd come here."

I shook my finger in his face. "I am very upset with you, running off like you did."

"You were going to make me go home." His lower lip extended into a pout.

"That's where you should be right now."

He shrugged. "You need me."

"Bobby, there are some things that are better left to adults. Please go home."

He shook his head. "You can send me away, but you can't make me go home."

I heaved a frustrated sigh. "All right, you can stay. At least if I keep you with me, I'll know where you are."

A big grin spread across his face.

I wagged my finger in his face. "But later, you're in big trouble, do you understand?"

He faked a look of contrition to go with his solemn nod.

"So, why do you think we should go to the left?"

"Because I've seen Vinnie and Joey going in and out of a warehouse three docks north of here."

"Tonight?"

"No, other times."

So our little excursion to the docks was only one of many regardless of his parents' restrictions, I realized. "You little scamp," I mumbled under my breath. Like it or not, and I didn't, he knew his way around these ghostlike buildings better than I. I needed his help to find Ashley. *When you find her, what do you intend to do?* The wisp of a thought flitted through my mind, but I brushed it aside. *One step at a time, Dorothy,* I told myself. I reached in my jacket pocket and removed the key ring holding Georgie's souvenir coin. I pressed the coin into the child's hand.

"I need you to do something for me, Bobby. This is very important. Do you remember the man I introduced you to last week?"

"Of course, Mr. Clairborne."

"I need to get a message to him. He lives at—"

"1142 Central Park West."

I stared in surprise. "How did you know that?"

"It was on the top of the papers sitting on the car seat, remember?"

"No."

"Oh yeah, he had a stack of papers sitting next to him in the car last week. And I read the top sheet."

"And you remembered the address?"

"Of course. I remember everything I read. Mama says I started reading at three years old and have never stopped wanting to read more. I read her set of Rudyard Kipling novels when I was five years old. Then I would recite them to my little sister to get her to go to sleep."

"I don't believe this. You have a photographic memory?"

"That's what people say. Anyway, you want me to tell Mr. Claiborne that you need him?"

"Yes, that's the plan. He'll know what to do. Maybe you should tell the police as well."

Bobby shook his head. "No, Miss Dorothy. Too many are getting a piece of the action here on the docks."

"All right. Be careful."

"You got it." Bobby dashed around the edge of the door and around the corner of the building.

I heaved a relieved sigh to have him gone. Whatever I had to do, I felt safer doing it without having to worry about a ten-year-old child in the process. I peered out the doors, looking both ways. No one was in the area. Gathering my skirts in my hands, I darted across the alleyway between warehouses and slipped inside the first open door I found.

I waited in the shadows for several seconds then peered outside once more. As I did, a heavy hand covered my mouth. An arm wrapped around my waist and dragged me into the shadows. I kicked and pummeled the unseen body manhandling me. A husky voice whispered in my ear. If I remove my hand, will you promise not to scream?"

I nodded. As the hand came off my lips, I bit down on the man's fingers. Then scooping my skirts into my hands, I broke into a run. The man yelped in pain and tore after me.

I knew my assailant was close behind, but I didn't waste energy looking to see how close. All those races against my brother had taught me that much. I zigzagged around heavy wooden crates and large pieces of machinery. My assailant didn't lose me until I skidded to a stop and climbed inside a massive crate half filled with packing straw. Quickly, I hauled the side panel of the crate closed behind me and prayed he wouldn't find me.

From my hiding place, I could see the form of the man pacing back and forth, searching the area for me. I was doing fine until the dust I'd stirred up inside the box filled my nostrils. I pinched my nose to keep from sneezing. I held my breath. I swallowed one sneeze, but another grew to take its place. I buried my face in my lap. In spite of my perilous position, a tiny "ka-choo" escaped.

"There you are!" The side of the box flew off, and sunlight poured in. A giant shadow of a man filled the box opening. "What are you doing here?"

I gasped in surprise. "Matt! What are *you* doing here?"

"I asked you that question first. Of all the foolish ideas." He reached down to help me to my feet.

Irked at his scolding, I refused his help and scrambled to my feet. "I happen to be here by request. What's your excuse?"

"I'm on the job."

"What job?"

"I've been following Vinnie and Joey. What request?"

"Did you leave me off last night and come down here right away?"

Matt frowned. "No, I got a call from Gabe at three this morning that something big was coming down here at the docks this morning. That's why I'm here."

"Who's Gabe?"

"A junior reporter at the paper. Now, what invitation?"

"It's a long story." I took a deep breath.

"Give me a summary." He glared down at me.

"Vinnie sent Bobby to tell me that his goons were holding Ashley."

"Ashley? Why?"

"I have no idea."

"Why didn't you call me for help?"

"I knew you'd make me stay away, and they asked specifically for me."

"I don't believe this." Matt glanced in all directions. "We've got to get you out of here."

I crossed my arms defiantly. "I'm not going anywhere."

"Oh yes, you are! It's not safe for you around here."

"You got that right, Mr. Collingsworth. You're both going with *me*." We whirled about to see Joey Rullo's handgun aimed straight at us. "Glad to see you could make it, Miss Spencer." He snickered. "Pretty little Ashley is waiting for you."

At the mention of my niece, I started. "You'd better not have hurt even one hair on her head."

He grinned devilishly. "Don't worry. Except for her mouth, she's one classy lady."

"Her mouth? What did you do to her?" Matt glared.

"Nothin'." Joey waved off Matt's question as he would a pesky fly. "She just never stops talking."

I laughed in spite of the situation. "At least we know they kidnapped the right woman."

"That's not funny," Matt growled.

"Kidnap? Who said anything about a kidnapping?" Joey looked bewildered. "We're just detaining her for a little while, that's all."

Matt glared at Joey and his gun. "Is that what Vinnie told you? Detaining? The law won't look at what you did that way. Kidnapping is a serious offense."

Joey frowned then prodded us with his gun. "Come on, get moving. I'm taking you to Vinnie—both of you."

With our hands in the air, Matt and I walked to the next building, a gray corrugated warehouse like all the others on the waterfront. Joey ordered Matt to open the warehouse door. "Get in there. Hurry it up." He glanced around nervously.

We stepped inside the building out of the sunlight. Joey used the gun to prod me along. I lurched forward into the semidarkness, my eyes straining to see what lay before me. In the middle of dozens of heavy-looking boxes, an area had been cleared. High above our heads hung a serpentine catwalk.

Sunlight from the high transom windows fell on a table where five men sat playing cards. A sixth stood in the shadows beside a straight-back wooden chair where Ashley sat, her hands and feet tied. Another checked us out as we entered the area.

Vinnie looked up from his cards and smiled. "Well, well, if it isn't D. M. Spencer. Nice of you to drop by."

"Dolly!" Ashley screamed. "These baboons tricked me into telling, honest."

"Tell what?" Bewildered, I shot a glare at Vinnie. "What is this all about? Why did you want me down here at this unearthly hour?"

"Tell them who you were—you know, the news reporter for the *Tribune*. Ashley reddened. "I'm terribly sorry. Now I understand why you and my folks didn't tell me about it."

"It's all right, Ashley. Actually, I told these thugs who I was the last time we met, if you remember right, Mr. Rullo."

Vinnie glared.

"Well, didn't I? You asked me about D. M. Spencer, and I told you it was me." I arched a defiant eyebrow.

From the shadows, Ashley added, "I can't believe you didn't guess Dorothy's identity a whole lot sooner. I mean, D. M. Spencer, same first initial, same last name? Talk about slow-witted. And then she says she told you to your face she was D. M. Spencer—that's the cat's pajamas, if you ask me."

"She did, Vinnie, I remember," Joey volunteered. "I heard Miss Spencer say—"

"Shut up! Who would have thought the *Tribune* editor would have gone addle-brained and hired a woman as a reporter?" He eyed Matt. "Speaking of which, thank you for dropping by this morning, Mr. Collingsworth. This way we can kill two birds with one stone."

"You didn't say anything about killing," Joey hissed.

Vinnie glared. "It's a figure of speech."

"A what?" Joey questioned. "I don't know what you said."

"Don't worry about it, Joey. Everything's fine. You did good bringing these two here."

Joey preened upon receiving his brother's compliment.

Vinnie laid his cards face down on the table and rose to his feet. "Look"—His gaze swept the faces of the other men in the room—"we're reasonable men. All I really want is for D. M. Spencer and the *Tribune* to get off my back, to stop writing about the rum-running. When I realized who Miss Ashley was—by the way, her compliments for you, Miss Spencer, were effusive—and that her claims regarding you were true, I realized I had a perfect solution to my problem." Vinnie rubbed one hand with the other. "And you have been a problem."

I grinned. "Oh, you liked my piece on shipping whiskey in from Canada? What about the article about the local bribing of police and judges? Did you like that one too?"

"Miss Dorothy, you are not in a position to irritate me right now. All I want is your word not to write about my business any longer, and the secret of your identity will remain a secret." Vinnie almost seemed to be begging for my cooperation. "I'm not in the habit of shooting ladies. If you were a man, I'd break your knee-caps and dump you in the East River, but you're not."

"Our ma taught us to respect women, Miss Dorothy," Joey added.

"Shut up!" Vinnie shouted. "You don't need to give them our life histories."

"Sorry, Vinnie," Joey muttered.

"However, we don't have such a compunction regarding men." Vinnie adjusted his suspenders then shot a grin toward Matthew. "A promise from the editor of the paper would be even better than one from you, Miss Spencer."

Matthew shook his head. "I only print the truth, Vinnie, as I see it."

A familiar voice called, "Then I suggest you buy yourself a pair of spectacles, Matthew, 'cause you aren't seeing things too clearly now."

"Mr. Clairborne? Is that you?" I peered into the darkness behind where Ashley sat tied to the chair. "What in the world are you doing here? Please don't tell me you're involved with scoundrels like these."

"Sorry to disappoint you, Miss Dorothy." George stepped out of the shadows. A second man dressed in an expensive silk suit and bowler hat followed him. "Meet my associate, Mr. B. Mr. B. is in the import-export business."

"Mr. Clairborne, why?" I asked. "You have more money than King Solomon. Why would you get involved with these people?"

George chuckled. "For the adventure and for a good bottle of port."

The man at George's side swaggered forward. "I don't like the looks of this. Too many people know too much. You can't just let everyone go." Mr. B. eyed each one of us. "You have a serious problem, Mr. Rullo. What are you going to do about it?"

"Well, I, uh, wanted to put a little scare into a couple of busy-body women. That's all. I didn't plan on—"

"If you want to play with the big boys, ya' gotta' have the guts to clean up your mistakes." With a nail on a finger of his left hand, Mr. B. cleaned under his right pinkie nail. "And these people are definitely mistakes in the making."

George strode to the far side of the circle of light. "These people are social acquaintances. This isn't Chicago, you know."

"No, if it were, they'd be floating facedown in Lake Michigan by now," Mr. B. said.

A female scream came from the doorway behind where Matt and I stood. We whirled about to see Katherine Clairborne standing there, her hand clapped over her mouth. When she realized what she'd done, she rushed forward into her startled husband's arms.

"Katherine, what are you doing here?"

"What are *you* doing here?" she replied, clutching the coin of my key ring in her left hand.

"How in the world did you get here?"

"I took the subway."

"B-b-b-but—"

Katherine grabbed his lapels and shook her nonplused husband. "You can't let them hurt Dolly, for Georgie's sake."

"Katherine, you can't stay here. You don't belong here." An edge of fear entered George's voice. "Trust me. I know what I'm doing."

"For money? Is that it? You'd betray the memory of your son for money? Or is it, like you said, for a good glass of port?" She pushed him away. "You disgust me."

"Katherine . . ." George's face fell. He reached for her, but she stepped farther away.

"I don't like this. I don't like this at all." Mr. B. shifted his weight from one foot to the other. "Vinnie, give me my money. I want out of here. Clean up your mess, or my men will do it for you."

Vinnie shot a nervous glance at Mr. B. then at George. George heaved an exaggerated sigh. "Do what ya' gotta' do."

"George!" Katherine whirled about and stared at her husband. "You are going to let them—"

"Hey, what can I do?" He shrugged. "I didn't tell you to come down here snooping around, did I? You should have tended to your knitting, woman!"

"George?" Katherine whimpered then rushed to my side. I held her in my arms as if I could do anything to protect her from these ruffians. I stared in disbelief at George, the man I thought I knew.

Beside me, Matt clenched and unclenched his fists, barely containing his frustration.

"Hey, what about me?" Ashley interrupted. "All I did was get into an argument with Ralph, my date, about the ability of women to do the same work as men. I used my aunt as an example. That's all." She squirmed in the chair. "My wrists are hurting! All I want to do is go home and take a hot bubble bath. Can't you untie me? I won't remember a thing by this evening, honest."

"Untie her." Vinnie nodded at one of his men. "We can't get rid of them here at the warehouse—too many people outside."

A female voice shouted from the catwalk above our heads. "Wherever you take my daughter, I'll follow!"

"Mama!" Ashley cried. "Oh, Mama, you won't believe what happened."

I looked up at the determined face of Drucilla. "What are you doing here?"

"What did you expect I'd do after you called?"

Now it was my turn to be confounded. "I-I-I thought you might send Ian or something."

"Ian! I'm not leaving the welfare of my daughter to Ian or anyone else," Drucilla said.

"And I feel the same way about my sister." Chloe Mae stepped out from behind a piece of machinery abandoned near the catwalk.

"Me too!" Bobby darted out from behind a smaller box and ran straight to me, standing between me and Joey's gun.

Mr. B. stared in horrid fascination at the two newest arrivals. "What is this? A family reunion?"

"You could say that." Cyrus's voice came from behind the boxes to the side of me.

"What's the—" Vinnie shot a look of terror at Mr. B. Joey aimed his gun first one way then another, uncertain as to who was the greatest threat. The men at the table leapt to their feet and reached for their handguns as well.

"Stay where you are, gentlemen." Cyrus emerged from his hiding place and strode over to the circle of light. I stared at the rifle in his hands. "Take your guns from your holsters and toss them toward me. We have you surrounded. Vinnie, Joey, yours too. Come on out, fellas."

Suddenly, armed men, federal agents, popped out from behind boxes everywhere. Several stood on the catwalk, aiming their rifles in our direction. Mr. B. sprang toward the door, only to run into a barricade of blue, five local police officers. I recognized one of them from Bobby's neighborhood. He smiled. "Not all of us are crooks, Miss Spencer."

I grinned. "Praise God," I croaked, my voice heavy with emotion.

While the authorities rounded up and handcuffed Vinnie and the other criminals, Ian strolled into the warehouse. "What are you doing here?" I asked.

"Who do you think brought the local police?" His face beamed.

Ashley ran to her father's arms. "Oh, Daddy, I knew you'd come to my rescue."

Mr. B., handcuffed to one of the federal agents, shook his head. "Will someone tell me what is going on here? Who are all these people?"

Matt laughed and wrapped his arm about my waist. "You said it—family."

"I don't understand. The feds, the locals, the newspaper, these ladies, and a kid?" Mr. B. shook his head again.

"You, my dear sir," Cyrus began, "walked into a fiasco of a sting. George, here, has been working for my team of investigators for months now. We've been following the Rullos. Matthew, here, was working independently for the newspaper, also watching the Rullo brothers. As to Dorothy? She just reported the news."

"What about those two busybodies?" Vinnie pointed to Drucilla and Chloe Mae.

Cyrus waved to the women to come down off the catwalk. "One of those two busybodies is my wife and the other is Ian's, here." Ian strode over to Cyrus. The federal agents gathered their prisoners together. The one handcuffed to Mr. B. started toward the door.

"Wait! Stop! I gotta know the whole story. What about the kid?" Mr. B. pointed to Bobby.

"He's a good friend of Dorothy's." And he's the one who brought you fellows down. He spread the word that Dorothy and Matthew were in trouble. And you know the rest."

Bobby and I exchanged grins.

Splashed across the front of the evening edition of the *Tribune* was the headline, "Bootlegging Bust in the Bowery." Matt brought a special copy over to the boardinghouse for me to see. Mrs. Stahl proudly told the story to the other boarders at dinner. As Matt and I sat on the porch swing, I studied the photograph of the Rullo brothers and Mr. B. being taken into custody. Of course, Matthew had made sure a *Tribune* reporter and photographer were present for the arrest.

I laughed. "Great photo. I spent the afternoon at the police station trying to explain my part in the entire episode. I almost didn't get my exclusive written in time."

Matt put his arm around my shoulders and drew me closer to him. "Well, we did it—together. Though I must confess, I hope we'll never repeat the morning's event."

"Do you think the Rullo boys would have killed us?"

"I don't know. I do know that murder is a part of the mobster's lifestyle. Whether or not Vinnie is corrupted enough yet to take another's life, God only knows." He gave me a hug. "I shudder every time I think of how close I came to losing you. Don't ever do anything like that again."

"And you? You were equally in danger."

"I love you so much. It scares me to think of losing you."

I leaned my head back against Matt's shoulder. "Do you think they'll be convicted?"

"Oh yeah. Cyrus's team of investigators are very thorough, though we almost messed up their entire operation." He kissed the side of my forehead. "I never would have guessed Cyrus to be a federal investigator."

"I wondered how he learned of my picnic with Bobby so fast, but I never imagined he—"

"Yeah, let's forget it for a few minutes and talk about us. So, when can we go to Shinglehouse to meet your father and all those tough brothers of yours?"

"Tough? They're not so tough." I poked him in the side. He doubled over. "Ticklish? Ah, I've found your weakness."

He trapped my hand in his, kissing my fingers as he spoke. "Dolly dearest, you are my weakness."

"And what about your parents? When will I meet them?"

Matt chuckled. "Oh, I think it will be sooner than either of us imagine. Giles contacted my father after the raid this morning. He was furious."

"Who? Giles?"

"My father. I'll guess he'll be down here before sundown to-morrow night."

Matt's prediction proved accurate. He called me around four in the afternoon, saying his folks were in the city and wanted to meet me. I gathered from the tone in his voice things hadn't been going too well between Matt and his parents. Before saying Goodbye, Matt confided in me. "My father has decided to make Giles editor-in-chief."

"What?" I gasped.

"It's true. He says I'm too much of a cowboy, too hard-hitting. He says it's for my own good."

"Oh, Matt, I'm so sorry. What will you do?"

"Dad says he'll make me associate editor-in-chief. *Hmmph!*" A moment of silence followed. "I must go. I'll be there for you at seven."

Troubled by Matt's problems with his father, I prayed for him as I went up to my room. Although I felt proud of him, I knew he must was hurting very deeply. I planned to do my best to support him. After talking to God about it, I felt that my faith had been renewed. I trusted in God to lead, and I'm sure Matt felt the same.

Wanting to make a good impression on Matt's parents, I turned my thoughts to the upcoming evening.

"What shall I wear?" I stared at the disheveled woman in the mirror. "Something conservative." I laughed. All my clothes were conservative. "Something more conservative, then." I held up my light green dress—no, too low in the back. I checked out a light blue chiffon—no, shows too much arm. A pink? Absolutely not. *How about the lavender silk,* I thought. *Matt loves the lavender one.* I discarded one dress after another onto the bed.

"What am I going to do?" I noticed a dark blue silk-and-chiffon dress, which had slipped off its hanger. I held it up in front of me. The dyed-to-match crocheted-lace sailor collar gracefully draped over the sleeveless top. The fabric hung from the shoulders to the hips. Cut on the bias, the sweeping chiffon skirt softly flared from a matching wide satin band. *Yes, this is the one,* I thought.

I'd barely had time to bathe and style my hair when I realized it was almost seven o'clock. After slipping into my silk underdress and chiffon overdress, I checked to be certain the dark blue satin ribbon I'd tied around my head was firmly in place, along with a matching ostrich feather and brooch.

At seven sharp, Matt's Pierce-Arrow glided to a stop in front of the boardinghouse. Grabbing a pair of midnight-blue crocheted wrist gloves from my bureau drawer, I ran down the stairs to meet Matt. Mrs. Stahl and the other boarders stared out the windows as Matt escorted me to the waiting vehicle.

I looked at the empty automobile in surprise. "Where are your parents?"

"They decided to eat in tonight. They decided to entertain their future daughter-in-law at their townhouse." He closed the door, rounded the car, and got into the driver's seat.

It was a short drive up Fifth Avenue to the Collingsworth's townhouse. Like most New York townhouses, the outside of the building gave no clue to the luxury inside.

As Mrs. Collingsworth greeted me and led me through the parlor to the massive rosewood-paneled dining room, I couldn't believe what I saw—crystal chandeliers big enough to light a Broadway stage, intricately carved furniture imported from France and Italy, heavy draperies from Spain, and carpets from the Orient. And I thought the McCalls were wealthy!

Mrs. Collingsworth noted my fascination. "Oh, don't let this fool you. It was my parents' place. When they died, they left this mausoleum to me to maintain. My brother got the rest of the assets."

I nodded like a toy on a spring. The surroundings left me speechless.

"Matthew, go tell your father that our dinner guest is here," his mother commanded. "He's in the library, talking newspaper business with your brother."

"Of course." The clipped tone in Matt's voice warned of trouble.

"Now, Matthew—"she patted his hand gently—"you promised."

Matt mumbled something and left the room.

"He's a good boy, you know." She smiled lovingly at me. "You're the first woman he's looked at since his poor wife passed away. I'd given up hope."

She put her arm around me and led me down the marble-tiled foyer to the dining room where Mr. Collingsworth, Giles, his wife, Gloria, and Matt waited. The elder Matthew strode quickly to me, clasping my hand in his. "So this is the remarkable D. M. Spencer? I love your column. You have such a pithy style."

I smiled, in spite of my preconceived opinions about the man. He led me to the seat to his right at the head of the table. "And you're fired."

I coughed. "I beg your pardon?"

"You're fired. I don't want a daughter-in-law of mine tramping around with the riffraff of the city. You're fired." He glanced toward the butler standing beside the door that I assumed led to the kitchen. "Now, can we get some food here? I'm starved."

I shot a look of despair at Matt. "Is he serious?"

Matt nodded, his lips tightened into a grimace. "Afraid so."

"B-b-b-but, I don't understand," I sputtered.

"Matthew Brewster Collingsworth! This is neither the time nor the place for such announcements." Mrs. Collingsworth glared at her husband from the far end of the extended mahogany table. "Your announcement could have waited until later!"

"Mildred! This is business, and not yours, I may add."

"It's my business if it is conducted at my dinner party!" The woman glared across the glimmering candle flames.

The dinner party never improved from that moment on, no matter how hard Mildred Collingsworth tried to retrieve it. As we were leaving at the end of the evening, she drew me aside. "Please know that I think you're perfect for my son. I feel like I know so much about you from your articles. Please, my husband can be a bull in a china closet, if you know what I mean. He's not as bad as he may seem."

I smiled uncertainly.

"Give him a chance, for Matt's sake. Give us a chance." Her eyes pleaded for my understanding. She grabbed Matt's arm. "If you let this one go, you'll be making the biggest mistake of your life. She's a keeper."

We made our farewells with promises of seeing them again soon. Climbing into the car, I asked, "A keeper? What's a keeper?"

Matt laughed; his face reddened. "Dad used to take me fishing when I was a boy. Some fish we caught were too small or too whatever and had to be thrown back in the pond. A keeper is—"

"I got it." I shook my head in wonder. "A fish! You realize that without employment, I will have to move back to Pennsylvania. I don't want to sponge off Chloe Mae and Cyrus's generosity. Besides, I'm too accustomed to making it on my own. I suppose I could go back to school in Boston."

"To that Bowles fellow?" Matt grimaced. "Don't pack your bags yet."

I laughed. "I won't until God makes it clear that's what He wants me to do."

Matt guided the automobile into Central Park and eased to a stop beside the narrow park lane. He leaned back, his hands firmly planted on the wheel. "Do you realize that we've known each other for at least three years now? We've attended church together twice a week most of that time, and we've never prayed together."

I frowned. "You're right. We haven't."

He gathered my hand into his and looked into my eyes. "There couldn't be a better time to do so—since neither of our futures is very certain."

"I've been praying for us both for some time now."

"So have I."

I laughed. "Really? You too?"

"Absolutely. It's only by trusting God to lead us that we will find true happiness together." His eyes sparkled as he continued studying my face.

We prayed, not in stilted church language, but as friends, three friends discussing the future. When we finished, I felt the heavy weight I'd lugged with me from the Collingsworth's home fall from my shoulders. I could see the same peace in Matt's eyes. He leaned across the car seat and kissed me tenderly on the lips. "And now, I need to get you home."

I nodded, biting my lower lip. The confusing rush of feelings I felt for him warned me that sitting together in the car at the edge of Central Park in the darkness was dangerous indeed, perhaps more dangerous than all the encounters with the Rullo brothers ever could be.

CHAPTER FIFTEEN

A New Day

"You what?" Chloe Mae's voice raised an octave. "You've been out of work for a month, and you didn't tell any of us? What do you think families are for? I would have thought you'd have figured that out by now." She turned toward Cyrus. "Did you know about this?"

He shrugged behind his evening newspaper. "I did notice that the paper no longer carried her column."

"*Hmmph!*" Chloe Mae sputtered. "What kind of investigator are you?"

He peered over the top of the paper. "The kind who doesn't investigate his own sister-in-law."

"Well, there's only one solution. You need to move back in here with us until you decide what you want to do next."

"Chloe, you're overreacting." I glanced toward Cyrus for help, but he burrowed deeper behind the *Tribune.* "I do have a little money that I saved out of my weekly pay envelope. I'm not completely destitute." Even as I protested, I knew she was right. My little nest egg wouldn't last forever.

"Why are you so reluctant?" The hurt tone in her voice softened my heart.

"I'm sorry. I'm being selfish. I've enjoyed my independence so much I hate giving it up. But you're right, and I do thank you for opening your home to me once again." I strode to my sister and gave her a hug. "Just until the trial, then I'll need to make some hard decisions about my future."

"I thought you and Matthew were planning to marry."

"Perhaps." A sudden shyness enveloped me. I stepped back from my sister. "I want Papa to meet him before I give my word."

"Then I'd say that as soon as this legal mess is settled, you and Matthew need to make a trip to Pennsylvania." She twirled about; her dressing gown whirled about her ankles. "Just imagine! A wedding in the family!"

I made the move with Matt's help. Saying Goodbye to my comfortable little room and to Mrs. Stahl broke my heart. After Matt carried the last box down the stairs to his car, I walked through the room one last time, touching the bed, the sofa, and the mantelpiece. I sighed and walked down the stairs and out to the waiting automobile.

During the weeks that followed, Matt came to call almost every evening. Sometimes he'd spend the evening chatting with Cyrus and the family. Other times, I'd have him all to myself. We spent some evenings with the Collingsworths, getting better acquainted.

When we were alone, I voiced my discontent at having nothing to occupy my days, and he let it be known that he wasn't happy with his working conditions.

"Giles has given me mundane administrative duties. I hate it. I want to be where the action is."

Each evening before he left, we would stroll out onto the front steps and, hand-in-hand, pray together about our future and our present situations.

Matt and I agreed to witness for the prosecution in the Rullo brothers' trial. We knew that by doing so we could be putting ourselves in danger, but we couldn't bring ourselves to let them go free.

The two brothers were convicted of smuggling liquor into the country and given a five-year term at Sing-Sing prison.

The kidnapping charge was dropped in order to keep Ashley's identity hidden. As to Mr. B., his lawyers managed to get him off before the case saw the inside of a courtroom. We never did learn his real name.

Immediately after the trial, Cyrus and Mr. Dugan, from the prosecutor's office, asked to meet with Matt and me. By the somber expressions on their faces, I knew that what they had to say couldn't be good.

"Mr. Dugan and I've been talking about the two of you. You realize the danger you might still be in, what with Mr. B. at large." Cyrus began. "We think you should get out of town for a few weeks, until everything cools down."

Mr. Dugan tapped a pencil on his scarred desktop. "I don't know where this underground crime movement is going, but its tentacles seem to be spreading into all levels of society. It's bad, much worse than any of us could have predicted a year ago."

Matt leaned forward in the straight-back office chair. "So, you're saying that while Vinnie and Joey might be behind bars, the big shots aren't?"

"That's right."

"Fine. We'll leave town." Matt turned to me. "It's a perfect time to visit your family in Pennsylvania, don't you think?"

I smiled and took his hand in mine. "The leaves are beautiful around Shinglehouse this time of year."

Papa met us at the train station the next afternoon. I ran into his arms and kissed him on the cheek. "Hi, Papa, I missed you."

"I missed you too." He kissed the top of my head. "Been worried about you, messed up with those crooks."

"How did you—"

Papa chuckled and gave me an extra squeeze. "I keep in touch with things concerning my children."

A wave of shyness came over me as I turned to introduce

Matthew to my father. Under my breath, I begged, "Like him, Papa. Please, for me? Like him?" Yet I had no reason to worry. From the moment they shook hands, I could tell the two men admired each other.

Since Christmas, my father had purchased a used Model T, and he was still learning how to handle his "bucking bronco." On the way home, he drove us through the town, pointing out the sights of interest, including the *Shinglehouse Sentinel* offices. As I gazed at the red brick building, I remembered Bud Ames with fondness. I cast a furtive glance at Matt, admiring his strong, serious profile and smiled to myself. I realized for the first time that the "little girl" crush I'd felt for my former employer had since been replaced by the real thing. The words to the familiar text, Romans 8:28, flashed in my mind. "All things work together . . ." I squeezed Matt's hand. He looked at me and winked.

Matt appeared interested in everything. My father kept him craning his neck first one direction then the other, as if Shinglehouse had that many sights to see. As for me, I was so thankful to be home. I hadn't felt safe since long before the trial. And after Cyrus's warning, I felt even less secure, knowing I could be putting Chloe Mae and her family in danger as well.

Papa waved to pedestrians and other drivers as he drove past. I waved as well, for I knew the name of each one of them. Mrs. Carter called Hello as she dead-headed her late-blooming roses. Mr. Humphreys smiled and called out, "Welcome home, Dolly," as we passed his tiny cottage on the edge of town.

When we pulled into the yard, the front door burst open. Out tumbled my nieces and nephews, followed by my sisters and brothers, and I was engulfed in hugs and kisses. At one point I searched for Matt, only to find him surrounded by my family.

That night, after everyone returned to their own homes and Papa and the younger kids had gone to bed, Matt and I sat out on the porch steps watching the myriad of stars studding the sky. "How did you bring yourself to leave this place?" Matt stared at the bright show over our heads. He looked so relaxed.

"I've been asking myself the same thing ever since I got off the train today." I linked my fingers with his. "I believe God led me to Boston and then to New York City, but I do miss it here more than I realized."

The next morning, I didn't awaken Matt. After fixing breakfast, I saw the children off. Before my father left for work, he gave me a hug and thanked me for making breakfast. "Just like old times," he said. "I like your man. He's got character."

I grinned at him in surprise. He kissed me Goodbye, grabbed his red-and-white woolen jacket and lunch pail, and headed down the road toward town the way I'd seen him do so many times during my life. Filled with happiness, I tackled the dishes, singing as I scrubbed the maple syrup off the plates. I'd finished washing the griddle when Matt came out into the kitchen. "Good morning, sleepy-head." I placed a dollop of soap bubbles on the end of his nose then returned to my dishpan. "How did you sleep?"

"Beautifully." He placed his arm around my waist and held me close. "I stayed outside on the steps for some time after you went up to bed."

"I know." I leaned my head back against his chest. "I saw you from the window. I wanted to come down to you, but I didn't think it would be proper."

He turned me around by the shoulders and lifted my chin with his hand. "I'm looking forward to the day when such an action will be most proper."

"Me too." I smiled and let him kiss me.

He continued to hold me in his arms. "Do you think your father approves?"

"I guess you'll have to find that out for yourself when you ask for my hand," I teased.

"Your hand? Woman, I won't settle for only your hand. I love all of you."

Hearing my brother's footstep on the back porch, I returned to my dishwashing. "Did you see those incredible apples on the back porch? I have the worst urge to make cinnamon-apple bread for supper. Would you mind?"

"Mind? Sounds delicious."

I laughed and dried my hand on a dishtowel. "Don't be too sure about that. I'm not known in these parts for my baking expertise."

"I'll take my chances."

"What will you do with yourself if I do?" I dried the oatmeal pan and placed it on the shelf where it belonged. "Papa has quite a library of books along the wall in his bedroom. I'm sure he won't mind if you help yourself."

"Maybe later. I might take a walk into town this morning."

I brightened. "That sounds like a good idea." As much as I loved him, baking would be much easier without him watching me stumble through the process.

Matt left soon after. By midafternoon when the children arrived home from school, he hadn't returned to the farm. When my father arrived home from work, Matt still hadn't appeared.

"Where could he possibly go?" I asked my father. "The town isn't big enough to get lost in."

My father looked up from the evening paper. "He's an intelligent young man. I'm sure he's fine. If he doesn't arrive by supper, I'll go looking."

I kissed the bald spot on the top of his head and returned to the cookstove where I had a large kettle of lentil stew simmering on the burner. Cooling on the warming pan were two picture-perfect loaves of apple-cinnamon bread.

I removed a stack of plates from the cupboard and began setting the table.

"Where are the kids? They should be doing that," my father said.

"I gave them the night off, a special treat from me to them. They did their farm chores, though, before you got home." I placed a soup bowl on each plate then opened the silverware drawer when the front door burst open.

"Matt! Where have you been?" I ran to him. "Did you get lost?"

He laughed. "Hardly. Getting lost in Shinglehouse would take some doing."

My father glanced up from his paper. "I tried to tell her that, but you know women. Or, at least, you will, by the looks of things." He returned to his paper.

Both Matt's and my face reddened. When he'd recovered from the awkward moment, Matt cupped my hands with his. "I have so much to tell you, I can hardly wait."

"So tell me."

He glanced toward my father. "Not here. Not now."

My father closed the paper and strode to the base of the stairs. "Hey, kids, it's time for supper!" Then he said to me, "He's saying he'll tell you later, when the two of you are alone."

I blushed again. Releasing Matt's hands, I served up the stew. After finishing a second slice of my apple-cinnamon bread for dessert, Matt rose to his feet. "I was wondering, sir" —he turned to my father—"if you're up to a walk after Dolly's delicious supper?"

Nervously I twisted the cotton napkin in my lap and held my breath. A slight grin teased the corners of my father's mouth. "I don't mind if I do. You kids help Dolly by doing the supper dishes, ya' hear?"

They nodded and began clearing the table as the two men left the house. I ran to the window and watched as they sauntered down the road. "Oh, dear God," I prayed, yet I was unable to continue my prayer. After all, what could I say? All that needed to be said I'd prayed many times before. I'd asked that God's will be done in Matt's and my relationship. Now it was time to apply my faith.

I took a deep breath, marched into the parlor, and sat down to my mother's upright piano to do what she always did whenever she was worried or nervous. I opened the family hymnal to "Standing on the Promises," the only song I'd learned as a child to play with any skill at all.

"Standing on the promises," I began to sing. The words took control of my thoughts, and I forgot about the drama unfolding outside the house. When I finished singing all the verses, I sang them again and again and again, until my brother poked his head into the parlor and said Goodnight and would I stop playing that song?

I obliged by wandering out to the kitchen and sitting in Ma's rocker by the hearth. They were gone an hour before I heard Matt's footsteps on the front porch. I ran to meet him at the door. With great solemnity, he led me to the parlor and insisted I sit down on the sofa.

"Dolly, I promised I would talk with your father before I formally asked for your hand in marriage. I've done as you requested. Your father asked some pretty tough questions of me. And I feel I need to ask them of you."

I nodded slowly.

"You know I've not been happy with my job lately." He waited for me to nod again. "Today I did something very foolish, as your father pointed out to me. I went to town to meet with the managing editor of the *Sentinel*." He took my hand and nervously traced my knuckles. "I quit my job at the *Tribune*, and I bought the paper."

"You did what?"

I know I should have talked it over with you, but everything happened so fast. I called my father. He's furious with me, I'm afraid. Now, I suppose you are, as well?"

My breath came in short, angry gasps. "I can't believe you would do something like this without mentioning it to me. It does affect me as well, you know."

Matt nodded. "Your father pointed that out to me too. I guess I'll have to get used to having a wife. Or will I? While I'm a rich man's son, I'm not a rich man. I used all my savings to buy the paper today. If I sell my Pierce-Arrow and get a cheaper car to drive, and if I get a good price for my brownstone in the city, we should have enough to buy a small place here in town."

"I don't believe you."

"If you wanted to marry a rich man, I'll understand. But regardless of your decision, I will stay here. I know this is the place for me. I knew it the minute I got off the train yesterday."

I couldn't think of what to say. It had all hit me so fast. Yes, I loved Pennsylvania's rolling hills and gentler lifestyle, but I enjoyed city life as well, at least I did until the trial. I gazed into his eyes. "Are you doing this to run away from the likes of Mr. B.?"

"Oh no. I've been restless at the *Trib* for a long time now. My father replacing me with Giles as the editor and the prosecuting attorney's warning only added two more good reasons to my already restless spirit."

"I don't know what to say. I'm still overwhelmed by it all."

"Dorothy Mae Spencer," Matt said, slipping to his knees and gathering my hands in his, "will you marry me? Just as I am. No money. No glamorous New York City parties. No hobnobbing with the governor's wife. Just me and a newspaper with a printing press older than my grandfather."

Tears welled up in my eyes. "Matthew, I would love you if you hadn't a penny to your name. As to the press, I know a few tricks to making it cooperate." I lifted his hands to my lips. "Yes, I will marry you, with my father's blessing, of course. Where did he go? What did he say?"

Matt frowned. "I don't really know. He seemed accepting of our engagement. But when I came back to the house, he headed toward the barn. He said he needed to retrieve a twenty-dollar gold piece. Does that make sense to you?"

I burst into laughter.

"What? What's so funny?"

I grabbed Matt's face between my two hands and kissed him soundly in the lips. "He said Yes, Matthew. Papa said Yes." I kissed him again. "Yes, I will marry you. I love you so much. Do you know how much I love you?" I giggled at the confused look on Matt's face. "I don't want your money or your father's, for that matter. I want you! Only you. All of you."

"Then you forgive me for rushing ahead with buying the paper?"

"Only if you vow never to do something so rash again without talking it over," I warned him.

"Absolutely. Your father made that quite clear to me. You are so beautiful. I can't believe you've agreed to become my wife." This time he kissed me, then held me in his arms for several seconds. "When did you know you loved me?"

"The night of the snowball fight."

"Really? I would have thought—"

"That I would have known sooner?" I smoothed an imaginary wrinkle out of his collar. "I'd never been in love before. I'd had crushes, but I've never known the real thing. I had to be sure of myself, and of you."

"I am still terribly confused about one thing."

"About what?" I nuzzled his neck with my lips.

"How do you know your father agreed to our marriage?"

"The gold piece in the barn." I looked at him as if he should know the entire tale. He looked more bewildered than ever.

I snuggled up to him again. "It's a long story."

He brushed a stray tendril of a curl from my face. "Well, Mrs. Matthew Collingsworth-to-be, you have a lifetime to tell it to me."

I sighed with delight at the thought of a lifetime together. "I do, don't I?"

He kissed the tip of my nose. "Yes, you do, though, I warn you. My curiosity won't be contained much beyond tomorrow."

The series that started it all

The Chloe Mae Chronicles
by Kay D. Rizzo

Never before have you shared the power of a dream and the emotions of young love as you will in this memorable early-pioneer series. As Chloe Mae flees from her father's iron rule, she starts down a path of experience she never bargained for. Silence turns to love, and tragedy turns to forgiveness as Chloe Mae lifts her heart to God for strength to face whatever life brings.

This inspiring drama is captured in four books: *Flee My Father's House*, *Silence of My Love*, *Claims Upon My Heart*, and *Still My Aching Heart*.

Paper. (4-volume set) ISBN 0-8163-1132-3.
US$29.99, Can$43.49

Flee My Father's House ISBN 0-8163-1154-4
Silence of My Love ISBN 0-8163-1135-8
Claims Upon My Heart ISBN 0-8163-1133-1
Still My Aching Heart ISBN 0-8163-1136-6
Individual Prices US$9.99, Can$14.49

Available at your local Adventist Book Center.
Call 1-800-765-6955 to order.
www.adventistbookcenter.com

The saga continues

The Chloe Celeste Chronicles
by Kay D. Rizzo

A magnificent saga of love continues as Chloe Celeste, gifted daughter of Chloe Mae, struggles to forge her unique destiny during a time of war and change. This extraordinary series is captured in four books: *Love's Tender Prelude, Winter's Silent Song, Sweet Strings of Love,* and *Love's Cherished Refrain.*

Love's Tender Prelude 0-8163-1219-2
Winter's Silent Song 0-8163-1220-6
Sweet Strings of Love 0-8163-1221-4
Love's Cherished Refrain 0-8163-1222-2
US$9.99, Can$14.49

Available at your local Adventist Book Center.
Call 1-800-765-6955 to order.
www.adventistbookcenter.com